On the
Rocks

On the Rocks

A TURTLE ISLAND NOVEL

Kim Law

Montlake Romance

Published by Montlake Romance, Seattle

www.apub.com

Amazon, the Amazon logo, and Montlake Romance are trademarks of Amazon.com, Inc., or its affiliates.

ISBN-13: 9781503950719
ISBN-10: 1503950719

Cover design by Laura Klynstra

Printed in the United States of America

*To my readers. Thank you for allowing me
to have the best job I could ever imagine.*

CHAPTER ONE

"With this ring, I thee wed."

Ginger Atkinson sniffed, managing to hold back her tears, but she couldn't contain the sigh. She loved weddings. "It's so beautiful," she whispered.

Sean Cagle, her date for the Labor Day weekend wedding, murmured in agreement at her side.

No doubt Sean assumed she meant the bride's dress, or the couple as a whole. Or maybe he thought she was swooning over the entire setup on the bow of the ship. Sprays of gardenias and lilies were mixed in with little white party lights and hanging crystal accents, all surrounded by a backdrop of sparkling ocean and clear blue sky. The ceremony was breathtaking. A vision created by Kayla Morgan, the event director for Seaglass Celebrations.

But none of *that* was what Ginger was talking about.

What she found so beautiful . . . what she couldn't force herself to avert her gaze from, even for a second . . . was the sheer love shining between the two people standing in front of them. A love that—if she were to be honest—had become as tiresome to see as it was romantic.

Over the last eighteen months, Ginger had watched both of her best friends get married—*and* move away from Turtle Island—as well as witnessed numerous other nuptials, either on one of her ships or on the island itself. Though Ginger didn't personally know everyone whose maritime wedding she attended, she tried to be on board during the festivities as often as possible. As owner of the boating company, she felt it an important personal touch to be in attendance.

Today's lucky bride was Angie Townsend, who'd come to the small Georgia town for a one-month contract earlier in the year to teach ballroom dancing at the senior center. It hadn't taken her long to fall in love, though. Both with the island and the bartender at Gin's.

She and her new husband would make their home on the island, and Ginger was happy for her. Love was a very special thing.

Even when it seemed that every person in the world could find it but her.

"I now pronounce you husband and wife." The minister turned to the groom. "Kevin, you may kiss your bride."

The tears did well up then, and Ginger didn't try to hide them.

As the small crowd stood and clapped, the newly married Kevin cupped his bride's face as if she were the only important thing in his life. It was honest and heartfelt. It was *beautiful*.

And it made Ginger's tears trickle faster.

She'd turned thirty this year. *She* had wanted to be married by now, too. It had been the plan. Love, marriage, dream home, kids. Happily ever after. Only, the right man had yet to show up. And she was now building her dream home by herself.

She kept a smile on her face through her depressing thoughts, and tucked her hand inside Sean's elbow as he led them from their seats. Maybe Sean would be the one. She had high hopes.

They followed the happy couple inside to the main cabin, where Kayla already had the champagne flowing and the DJ warmed up. It had been a beautiful wedding, and the reception was the icing on the cake. All that was left to do now was dance. And thanks to the seniors allowing Ginger to intrude on their spring classes with Angie, she could finally do just that.

She turned to Sean, determined to show him what a great catch she was, and gave him the best smile she owned. The lace edging of the azure-blue dress she'd borrowed from her mother itched at the base of her throat, but she refrained from tugging at it. She had a man to win over. And her much more feminine mother had proven time and again that cute dresses provided a leg up in that department.

"Please tell me you're a dancer?" she asked, adding a hint of sauciness to her voice.

It wasn't the ideal first date—a wedding—but when Sean had asked her out last weekend, she'd jumped at the chance not to show up alone.

"I can hold my own," he answered. He held out a hand, added in a hot smile, and Ginger's heart knocked hard against her ribs. He really was cute. And totally her type. Dark hair and a great disposition, he was perfectly nice and gentlemanly. No bad habits that she'd picked up on, nice to people and children, and he even had a good job as head of the island's tourism department.

And his voice was like heated body oil spreading slowly over her limbs.

Or maybe you're just hard up since you haven't been naked with a man in over two years.

She ignored the taunting in her head, and with firm determination to make this date turn into a second one, she closed her hand over his . . . and silently groaned at the quick look of repulsion that crossed his face.

His gaze had landed on her fingernails.

Dang. She'd forgotten to clean up her nails after working on the engine of one of her boats that morning. She had a small sunrise cruise scheduled for first thing tomorrow morning, and her mechanic had been called away for a family emergency. And, of *course*, today was the day the boat had given them problems.

She'd fixed it. Then she'd made it home in time to shower and change for the wedding. She'd just overlooked cleaning the grease from the cuticles of her nails.

Unable to do anything about it now, she did her best to shield the sight from Sean's eyes, and laughed and flirted as he twirled her around the floor. At the first opportunity, she excused herself and hurried from the room.

As soon as she was out of sight, she dashed to the lower level to rummage through the compact office. There had to be something there she could use. Hand sanitizer, maybe.

She took a peek at her fingernails and groaned out loud. It wasn't only that they were dirty, but two on her right hand had the appearance of being chewed on by a ravenous mouse. She needed an emery board. Badly.

"What are you doing down here?"

Ginger looked up from her frantic search to find Kayla standing in the doorway of the confined space. Her eyes darted to the drawer Ginger was rummaging through before coming back. Worry tightened the skin around her mouth.

"I saw you run out as if there was a problem," Kayla said. "Is something wr—"

"My fingernails," Ginger interrupted. "I had to work on an engine this morning."

That sent Kayla into action. "Your purse?" she asked, moving into the small room and grasping Ginger's hands in hers.

"No purse," Ginger admitted. She rarely carried one.

Kayla shot her a look. "You're on a date, Ginger Atkinson. What about lipstick? A mirror? Money in case your date forgets his wallet. Mace in case your date isn't very nice."

"I forgot," Ginger whispered frantically. "I have one, I swear. But I was running late."

Kayla clucked and disappeared from the room. Like a true event director, or maybe a Boy Scout, she was back within seconds, carrying an unrivaled assortment of items—hand cleaner, tissues, a four-sided nail file, a cuticle stick, and even clear polish. Within minutes, Ginger's nails were cleaned and buffed, and Kayla had the bottle of polish open.

"No time for that." Ginger curled her fingers inward. "I need to get back to my date."

"But it'll help."

"You've already performed magic." Ginger shook her head. "This will do. Thank you." And hopefully, it wasn't already too late. The island was lacking in the available-young-men department, and every single female in the area knew it. Some of those females were on that very boat today. It wouldn't do to spend too much time away from her date.

Kayla's mouth pinched as she looked at Ginger. Kayla was only a year older, but her frequent state of agitation aged her. "Next time, carry a purse," she instructed.

Ginger took a moment, forcing a deep breath and a smile. "A purse. Got it. With Mace."

"*Yes.* You never know what—"

"With Mace," Ginger repeated gently. "I promise." As far as she knew, there had been no reported needs for Mace on the island in at least the last decade, but that didn't mean it couldn't happen. Or so Kayla would inform her if asked.

She blew Kayla a kiss and hurried back up the stairs, glancing at herself in the mirrored backsplash of the bar as she passed, hopeful she hadn't managed to mess up anything else about herself. She tried, really she did. She dressed in cute clothes when she went out on dates, and she took the time to curl her hair and paid special attention to her makeup. And her body was popping, even if she did say so herself. Larger-than-average breasts, curvy behind. She could attract a man. But regardless, on the inside she remained her father's daughter.

The man had died while she was in her sophomore year of college, which had brought her home to take over the business. Staying hadn't been the plan—she was supposed to be a kindergarten teacher by now. But what she'd discovered was that she was adaptable. And that she had a real knack for running the company.

Since taking over, she'd grown the business from ferries only to dinner cruises, dolphin and nature tours, and fishing expeditions. Basically, if it could be done on the waters off the coast of Georgia— and there were people willing to pay for the adventure—Ginger made it happen.

She was happy, her mother was doing great, and business was thriving. Her dad would be proud.

But she was lonely.

She sucked at dating, at being a girly-girl specifically, and that interfered with the one thing she wanted the most. To be a wife and mom.

Pulling up short as she made her way through the crowd, her gaze landed on Sean dancing with a blonde. Her heart sank. Was that what he preferred? Ginger had recently gone back to her natural copper red after being blonde for the last several years. She supposed she could—

She cut her thoughts off midstream. No. She wouldn't dye her hair. Not to win a man.

And Sean shouldn't have asked her out if he preferred blondes.

Of course, it might not be the hair color that had attracted him to the other woman. Ginger eased to the side of the crowd and watched the two of them dance. Sean seemed to have forgotten that he'd come to the wedding with someone else.

The blonde was the complete opposite of Ginger. She had a total Southern-belle type of charm going for her with her flirty off-the-shoulder dress and the bold orange necklace dipping to her breasts. The sleeves of her dress ballooned just above the wrists, ending in lace—giving it a vintage look—and the overall image was one of a sorority girl. The type of person everyone loved and whom Daddy bought a convertible for just because she was so darned perfect.

Her hair was slick and shiny, her makeup only enhanced her beauty, and her fingernails were polished and long. She even looked like she was comfortable in the heels she wore.

Exhaustion suddenly pulled at Ginger. She was so tired of trying to date "right." Of laughing and flirting, and wearing the appropriate clothes. And all for what? More often than not it didn't go the way she'd hoped. Either the guy lost interest, *she* had no interest, or the occasional relationship that went longer than a couple of weeks quickly sank.

Sean's hand slipped lower on the blonde, continuing its path until it landed on her butt, and Ginger closed her eyes. Clearly, the date was over. At least it was for her.

She returned to the office below. There was always paperwork to be done. The computer on the lower level was hooked into the server at her office, so she might as well take care of some business until they returned to port.

~

"Hey, Mom. You home?" Ginger called out later that night as she entered the midcentury, Tudor-style home she shared with her mother.

"In the kitchen."

Ginger kicked off the heels she'd worn to the wedding, wiggled her toes in freedom, and headed to the oversized kitchen. Her mom had remodeled the room a couple of years ago, and since then, if she wasn't at work at the bank or out on a date of her own, she could often be found whipping up something sinful.

"What are you doing home so early?" Pam Atkinson asked as Ginger entered the room. Her mother had her arms elbows deep in dough and her platinum hair pulled out of her face with a hand-painted silk scarf. And she looked as vibrant and dainty as always. Even with the smudge of flour outlining one cheekbone.

Her mother, without a doubt, *had* that girly-girl trait that Ginger was lacking.

"Sean had other plans for the evening," Ginger explained. She wasn't in the mood to provide details, nor to share that the man hadn't so much as sought her out before leaving the ship. She'd already moved past it.

She leaned in and kissed her mom's unfloured cheek, and ignored the fat orange tabby at her feet who was actively ignoring her. The cat was the only feline Ginger had ever known who would tolerate wearing accessories, and currently sported a purple daisy-shaped bow at the back of her neck. It made a statement against the orange fur.

"Thought maybe you and I could hang out tonight," Ginger said. "I'll help with dinner."

Her mother's hands slowed.

"What?" Ginger popped a waiting blueberry into her mouth.

"Clint's back in town." Clint was her mom's boyfriend.

Unlike Ginger, her mother never had trouble keeping a man, and in fact, had been known to have more than one calling on her at the same time. She and Clint were monogamous, though, and had been for over five months. It was as serious as her mother got.

After being devastated over the loss of her husband, Pam had finally turned the corner a few years back, working hard to drag herself out of the hole of depression. Since then, she'd learned to enjoy herself. She'd especially mastered reveling in the attention she received from men. And, from Ginger's point of view, tended to be a little naughty at times. But, good for her. Everyone should have fun in their lives.

"I'll cancel," her mom added. "Clint and I can see each other tomorrow."

"Absolutely not." Ginger swiped a muffin off the cooling rack, ignored the woe-is-me attempt at self-pity vying for attention in her head, and grabbed a beer from the fridge. "You have a hot date with a man who adores you. Whom you haven't seen in a week. I won't get in the way of that."

"We're just having dinner in. You could join us?"

Ginger chuckled drily. "No." Playing third wheel had never been fun. "But thanks."

She'd change and head to the bar . . .

She quickly retracted the thought. She wasn't in the mood for any more of the opposite sex tonight, and being a holiday weekend, the bar would be hopping. Grabbing an apple to round out her dinner, she shifted to plan B. "I'll check on Julie, then head over to the house."

"The house" being the one she'd begun building shortly after her birthday four months before. It was an impressive two-and-a-half story with a 180-degree view of the ocean from the top deck. Only, it wasn't finished. Work on the inside had stalled—the delays, hers. She wanted everything to be just right, but she'd begun to question what exactly "right" even meant. She hadn't even been able to pick out a countertop for the kitchen.

The stall had gone on for so long that the construction crew had been forced to move on to other projects, but that didn't mean *she* stayed away. There was a pier at the north end of her property, and she had a stash of fishing rods tucked away in her basement. She'd fish off the pier until late tonight. That would give her mom and Clint plenty of time to catch up without Ginger having to hear evidence of it through the too-thin walls of the house.

"Tell Julie I said hi," her mother called out as Ginger exited the room. "I'll take a casserole to her tomorrow. And invite her over for a cookout on Monday night, will you?" With Labor Day being Monday, Clint would be at the house, and the grill would be fired.

Ginger mumbled an acknowledgment around the bite of apple in her mouth, and headed up the stairs to her bedroom. Julie Ridley was a twenty-two-year-old recent college graduate who'd moved back home over the summer to manage the new art gallery in the small community. She'd also shown up pregnant with no sign of the baby's father.

Julie's parents still owned the house next door, but they'd barely been home the past four years. They'd been traveling the world and were currently on a mission trip, not scheduled to return until closer to the baby's due date. Since Julie was alone, Ginger and her mother had taken it upon themselves to occasionally check in on her. See if she needed help with anything.

Ginger glanced out the window as she entered her room, taking in the closed curtains of the bedroom across from hers, and couldn't help but wonder what Carter was up to these days. Did he know that his baby sister was pregnant and alone?

Similar to his parents, her childhood friend didn't frequent Turtle Island, either. He'd gone away to college, married a law student, and according to Mr. and Mrs. Ridley, had settled somewhere in the New England area. Ginger couldn't recall which state.

Wherever it was, she hoped he was happy.

But she couldn't help but be a little disappointed that he hadn't once come home to check on his sister. There was a time when he'd been the epitome of the overprotective brother.

CHAPTER TWO

The mid-September fog lying low over the water didn't surprise Carter as he stood, arms crossed, at the railing of the ferry and watched the morning crowd milling inside. The day matched his mood. In fact, it would have surprised him to have anything *but* a dark cloud hovering nearby. The gray mist was on par with everything about his life these days, but good had actually come from it today. The heavy dampness in the air had allowed him to have the uncovered deck to himself. He needed a few minutes before driving off the ferry and back into his past. He was on Turtle Island again. Or he soon would be. And he didn't want to be.

How long had it been? Six years? Eight?

Too long, probably. But at the same time, not long enough. If things hadn't changed . . .

He didn't want to be here, it was that simple. And it was all he'd let himself focus on. He wanted to be back in Rhode Island in his own house. He wanted to be at his desk. Writing the next great American novel.

Or the next great horror novel. Which, in his mind, was the same thing.

Not that he'd be writing, even if he were at home. With his big breakthrough and a major contract had also come his first bout of writer's block. Along with so many other things he hadn't expected.

He ground his teeth together as he forced those other things from his mind. He was back on Turtle Island for at least the next few days, but he refused to stay the three weeks his mother had asked of him. It wasn't his job to watch over a sister who should have had enough sense not to get knocked up. Add to that, Carter wouldn't even get the pleasure of beating the guilty party to a pulp. The man wasn't on the island, not that Carter knew of. Not that he knew *who* the father was.

With Julie seven months pregnant and his parents on the other side of the world, Carter's mother had pleaded with him to come home and keep an eye on his sister. She'd insisted for the last week that Julie wasn't feeling well. Said she could tell by their phone conversations.

But Carter wasn't an idiot. Julie was fine. He'd talked to her himself. It was *he* his mother was worried about. His parents had made a quick trip to the States last month, and had stopped by his place on their way back out of the country. And in a moment of great weakness, he'd shared things he'd had no intention of sharing. His mother had not let up on him since. She thought his coming here would "fix" him.

But he had news for her. He didn't need fixing. He wouldn't *be* fixed. He liked who he was these days, and no amount of coaxing from his well-meaning mother would change that.

But he would come home and check on his sister. Just in case.

He'd visited her in college in North Carolina occasionally, had been at her graduation ceremony in May, and she'd even spent part of last summer with him. But he hadn't been the brother he could have been over the years. If he had, maybe Julie wouldn't have ended up pregnant and alone.

So, he would check on her. But he wouldn't stay long.

The horn sounded on the ferry, and Carter pulled a pack of cigarettes from the pocket of his black peacoat as he watched the small island come into view. The fog fuzzed the lights glowing through the thick morning, making him think of a particularly horrific scene from one of his earlier novels. It had been a good book, but he hadn't gotten paid big money for it. Not like the one due to his editor at the end of next month. The one he had yet to start.

He lit a cigarette and held it in front of him, studying the burning tip and thinking about his life. His mother hoped this trip would fix this, too—his latest bad habit. Probably she thought he drank too much as well. And for a second, he wanted to have the kind of hope that she did. He wanted to be fixed.

But none of it was as simple as a trip home. Shit happened, then you had to live with it.

He brought the cigarette to his mouth and drew deep, closing his eyes with the sting of the nicotine. He'd never smoked before this year, but he liked it. He liked the wrongness of it.

Opening his eyes, he exhaled, and through the smoke he watched a woman exit the side entrance on the far end of the ferry. She headed away from him, her red hair swishing at her shoulders as she moved in quick, sure strides up the back staircase. She had on a clear raincoat, but hadn't bothered with the hood. Her lack of concern for the wet day made him suddenly think of the girl who'd lived next door when he'd been a kid. Ginger had been like that, only the girl he'd known probably wouldn't have bothered with the coat at all. She would have simply stood out in the rain, not caring if she ended up drenched. And she would have laughed while doing it. She'd had the brightest outlook of anyone he'd ever met.

He hadn't thought about Ginger in years, but memories suddenly filled him. Being in the same class and living next door to each other, their friendship had been a given. They'd played in their yards together as children, had explored the island side by side once they got bikes . . . then they'd slowly found their own paths after starting high school.

Their friendship had remained intact, though. In their own way. Though their time together during their teen years had been less, the friendship was something he'd cherished.

He wondered if she still lived on the island. Her dad had died while they were in college—he remembered his parents telling him about it. She'd come home to be with her mom then, but had she stayed? Had she ever gone back to finish school?

He looked up the back stairwell again, but the woman was no longer visible, and then anger hit when he realized the reason she'd grabbed his attention to begin with. Her hair. The way she carried herself.

She reminded him of his ex-wife.

He took one last hard drag on the cigarette before tossing it over the railing and pulling the keys to his rental from his pocket. The last thing he wanted to think about was his ex. She'd occupied far too many hours of his time over the past months as it was. But he couldn't seem to keep her away.

Love sucked. That's the lesson that had come from marriage. Do everything right, and it didn't matter. Some heartless person would still trample on your heart as if it was as cold and lifeless as hers.

So no—dear, good-intentioned mother of his—sending him back to Turtle Island would not "fix" him. There was no fixing to be done. This *was* the new him.

The stench of fish guts clung to Ginger's clothes as she entered the combination mud and laundry room that midmonth afternoon. After a too-long fishing trip and an even longer workday, she closed the door, leaned into it, and pressed her forehead to the cool wood. And sighed. She was exhausted. And in a foul mood. And the last thing she wanted to do was come home and face reality.

Her eyes suddenly burned with threatening tears, but she held them at bay. She'd have a good cry later tonight while soaking in the tub. Maybe she'd even take a bottle of beer in with her. Or six. Because every once in a while a girl deserved a night, just her and her favorite six-pack of IPAs. But right now she had to get out of her stinky clothes.

She undressed, underwear and all, and started the washer without adding any other clothes to the pile. She noted the fact that they were almost out of washing liquid, mentally added it to the grocery list, then stooped to scoop out the litter box.

Mz. Lizzie was nowhere to be found, of course. Because Ginger wasn't her mother. The blasted cat only came out when the older Atkinson was home, but Ginger's mom was with Clint right now. They'd taken the day off together.

When Ginger stood, she sniffed the air and frowned. She still smelled like fish. It was in her hair, and probably ground into her skin. That bath might come sooner than she'd planned.

Though the day had started in the thick fog of the early morning ferry, she'd later been pulled into a last-minute charter. Which had turned into a hugely productive trip for the customers. As part of the cost of expeditions, guests' fish were cleaned and gutted—if they wanted them to be. And today, everyone had wanted them to be. Which normally would have been fine. It was part of the experience, and Ginger saw it as a small price to pay for the benefit of having a job where she got time on the water whenever she wanted it.

Except today's group had been all men, and too much beer had been consumed. The alcohol encouraged three of them to declare that a female fishing captain was their ideal woman. Then they'd gotten grabby—while she'd had a knife in her hands.

She'd had to set them straight, which had only turned them on more.

Sigh.

It had been a frustrating day for so many reasons, but the sad reality was that the jerk men hadn't even been the worst of it. She stepped through the door into the kitchen, and turned her gaze to the small blue box sitting in the middle of the quartz-topped island.

That was the worst of it.

Her mother and Clint's six-month dating anniversary had arrived the day before, and they'd gotten engaged. *To be married!*

An engagement had been the last thing Ginger had expected to learn about when she'd come down to catch the sunrise that morning. As well as seeing her mom's smiling face before dawn. Yet there she'd been. Beaming. And holding out her left ring finger.

The engagement made no sense. Her mother was a compulsive dater. She didn't get engaged.

Only, she had.

And she was floating in the clouds over it.

After telling Ginger all about the special evening Clint had planned the night before—and waving that chunk of a rock under Ginger's nose—her mother had posted a picture of it to Facebook.

Ginger wanted to be happy for her. Really, she did. Her mother deserved love and a happily ever after. She'd been destroyed when Ginger's dad had died from an unexpected heart attack. He'd been the love of her life. So yes, her mother should be first in line for a second chance at forever. And Ginger *was* happy for her.

Only, she couldn't help the thought that had echoed in her head all day.

It's not fair.

It wasn't fair that everyone could find the man of her dreams except her. It wasn't fair that, try as she might, all dates tended to backfire. In one way or another. And it wasn't fair that she could no longer hide from life by living in her mother's house, pretending it was okay that she was single.

Her world was moving in a new direction, and Ginger either had to get on board and go along with it, or she would be left watching by the sidelines. Her mother *was* getting married, Clint *would* be moving in, and *she* would be underfoot.

And unless something changed, that marriage would be taking place in a short six weeks.

She ignored the robin's-egg–blue box, and grabbed her phone. She needed to talk to her friends.

Andie Kavanaugh and Roni Alexander had been her best friends since the age of seven. The other two hadn't grown up on the island, but Andie's aunt lived there, and Roni's mother was a die-hard fan of the beach, so they'd visited every summer. A few years ago all three of them had seen the pact they'd made as kids come true when Andie and Roni had both moved to the island full-time.

Only, they'd subsequently fallen in love with men whose lives were *not* on the island.

That wasn't to say they didn't come back when they could. Roni, her husband, Lucas, and her stepdaughter, Gracie, had been there in June. Gracie had turned five, and she'd wanted a birthday party on the beach. Since Roni still owned her house here—and Lucas could telecommute from anywhere—they'd stayed for the month before Lucas and Gracie had returned to Dallas, and Roni had headed off for her first concert tour in years. She was a concert pianist. And she was amazing.

Roni had managed a day away from the tour after Andie and Mark's first child had been born in July, and both she and Ginger had flown to Boston to see the young man just a few days after he'd entered the world. Theodore Wayne Kavanaugh had been born with a head full of dark hair and the kind of blue eyes that would some-day turn many a girl's head. Ginger had lost her heart to the little guy immediately. As well as promised countless hours of babysitting anytime they came for a visit.

Then Roni had confessed that she'd also be joining the ranks of motherhood. And Ginger had smiled through her envy.

Unwelcome jealousy or not, they were her girls, and she needed them now.

After running upstairs and tugging on a pair of shorts and a T-shirt, both of which had seen better days, she went to the front porch to make her call. She tried Roni first, but there was no answer. Her tour would be finishing in a couple of weeks. Probably she was in the middle of prepping for tonight's show.

Andie *did* answer her phone. With the sound of crying not far away.

"Hey, hon," Andie said. She sounded completely exhausted, and not a little frazzled. "Can I call you back in just a bit? I'm sorry, I'm—"

"Yes," Ginger interjected. "Call me later. Whenever. Take care of that cutie of yours. He sounds hungry."

Andie laughed tiredly. "He's always hungry."

"Then feed the little guy. Don't worry about me."

The sounds of suckling suddenly came through the phone, and a pang tugged at Ginger's heart. She wanted that, too.

"I'll talk to you later," Ginger whispered, ready to hang up.

"Wait," Andie shot out. "You said worry. Don't worry about you. What's wrong?"

Ginger leaned her head against the back of the glider and closed her eyes. Moisture pushed at the seams. She missed having her friends close. "I didn't mean *worry*," she said. "I just meant . . ." She pictured her mother's ring. Then she pictured little Teddy at his mother's breast. "It's nothing. We can talk anytime. You sound like you could use some sleep after you get Teddy down."

"I can always use sleep." A yawn followed the words, right on cue.

"Then feed that baby, close your eyes while he's eating, and doze for a few minutes. We can talk later. Give him a hug for me, will you? And tell Mark I said hi."

"Will do." Andie yawned again. "You sure it's nothing important?"

"Just checking on you."

"'K." She yawned for a third time, sounding half asleep already, and they said their good-byes. Then Ginger stilled the seat and sat staring at nothing. Her life was changing. Her life had already changed. She had to get moving on that house.

She pulled her mother's Facebook page up on her phone and loaded the picture of the ring. It really was stunning. Two carats of diamonds in a unique flower pattern that surrounded a center stone. There was even a row of smaller diamonds circling the band. It was a little much for Ginger's taste, but she recognized the fact that it was perfect for her mother. Very romantic. Very girly. Clint had done well.

Studying the ring made Ginger wonder if she'd seen this coming all along. Was that why she'd started the house to begin with? Her mother had never suggested Ginger should live anywhere but here— thus the reason she'd been in no hurry to finish. But had Ginger somehow known this was on the horizon?

Or had her mother only become open to the idea *after* Ginger started the house?

Had *she* subconsciously told her mother it was okay to move on?

And did it even matter why it was happening? The fact was, her mother was in love and getting married. And Ginger had a house to complete.

She went inside for her notepad and the paint cards she'd collected two months ago, and began to jot down her thoughts. The house was complete on the outside, but there was practically nothing done internally. Studs framed the rooms and the subfloors were down, but that was it. No walls, no cabinetry, no fixtures. No personality. She'd been frozen at the thought of making final choices.

Somehow, the design for the structure had been in her head, but nothing else would come.

Her phone rang, and with a little squeeze of her heart, she reached for it, hoping it was Andie. Instead, it was her mom.

"Hey, Mom."

"Hi, baby. Are you free tonight?"

"Sure." She looked up from her notes and noticed a strange car in the Ridleys' driveway.

"Good. Clint and I wanted to invite you to dinner. We're having a celebratory evening out with some friends."

Ginger pushed the notepad off her lap and rose, moving to the other side of the uncovered porch so she could see their neighbors' house better. The blinds were closed.

Julie wouldn't be home from work yet, but she usually opened the blinds before leaving.

"Tonight?" she asked absently as she stood on tiptoes, trying to see over the shrubbery.

"Yes. We've got a reservation at the hotel." The best restaurant on the island was at the historic Turtle Island Hotel. "And Clint invited this nice young man that he works with," her mother added. "Clint thinks he might be perfect for you."

Clint was a real-estate agent who covered both the island and surrounding communities. And now he was fixing her up? She held in the sigh. The last thing she wanted to do tonight was get dressed up and pretend to be interested in someone she didn't know. There was a bubble bath and a good dousing of beer waiting for her.

"What's he like?" she asked, trying to be a good sport.

"Clint says he has a great personality and he's really nice. He still lives with his mother, but given that you live with me, you might have something in common."

Ginger stared at the phone. A great personality? And he lived with his mother. She did not have a good feeling about this. She pulled the ends of her hair to her nose and sniffed, wondering if this nice-personalitied mama's boy liked the smell of fish. She couldn't muster any enthusiasm for even trying.

"I don't know, Mom. I was going to—" A light came on in the house next door. "Someone's at the Ridley house."

"What?"

"A car that isn't Julie's. Did you see it before you left?"

"No. What's it look like?"

"Black. Expensive-looking, huge. Like a town car."

"Maybe she has a new boyfriend?" her mom suggested.

Ginger knitted her brows. "She's seven months pregnant. What would she want with a man?"

"It could be the father," her mother said after a pause. They both went quiet. They'd worried about Julie and whoever the father might be, but given the age difference between her and Carter's sister—making them little more than neighborly toward each other—Ginger hadn't felt she had the right to ask.

"All the blinds are closed," she said. She had a bad feeling about this. "That *is* odd."

She nodded, her mind made up. "I'm going over."

"Be careful. Text me and let me know everything's okay." After Ginger agreed, her mother added, "Then you can tell me all about it tonight at dinner."

Ginger felt her left eyelid twitch. She wanted a bubble bath, not a blind date.

"You can wear that green dress of mine that you like so much."

"Fine." She didn't know why she agreed, but she vowed not to give up the alcohol, too. "But you're driving me home. And buying me expensive wine. I've had a long day." If she had to drink wine instead of beer, it had to be pricey enough to compensate.

Her mother's laugh was light and airy. "Clint will be happy to buy the wine, baby. But maybe your date will take you home."

Ginger just shook her head at her mother's suggestion. The sad thing was, she thought her mother wanted to see her married off as badly as *she* wanted to be. But no amount of setting her up, or letting her borrow cute clothes, or reminding her to talk about something other than the job seemed to do the trick.

All of it was enough to edge Ginger toward considering that maybe love, marriage, and babies wasn't the dream after all. She had her friends' babies she could play with. That could be enough. And that wouldn't impact the other things she liked to do. Like spending hours floating in the middle of the ocean.

And enjoying bubble baths while drinking beer.

Heck, maybe the dream was *only* the house and not the man. If so, she was on the right track.

But she wasn't quite ready to surrender. "I'll see you tonight, Mom."

She disconnected and took Kayla's advice before heading next door, returning to the house to dig through the drawers of the front entry table until she found the can of Mace she'd gotten for her birthday. Then she headed out the front door and slipped through the shrubbery separating the two houses.

CHAPTER THREE

D amn it," Carter growled when a shot of grease launched itself out of the cast-iron skillet and landed on his wrist. He shoved the pan full of chicken from the hot burner and thrust his hand under running water. Then he stood, teeth gritted, and thought about the cluster fuck that had been the entire day.

After getting off the ferry, he'd stopped by Julie's gallery to clear his conscience. To ensure she was fine. But when he'd seen her, his conscience had been anything but cleared. She was too small to be that late in her pregnancy—at least, in his limited experience she seemed to be. And although Julie had pretended joy at seeing him, there had been something else lurking behind her eyes.

Exhaustion had come to mind first. Weren't pregnant women tired all the time?

But that was before he'd caught her in the back room, leaning against the wall, her arms wrapped around her tiny stomach. She'd been so hunched over that she'd looked like a preteen girl.

She'd straightened when he'd said her name, but had refused to admit there was a problem. He hadn't been able to get the hollow look of her out of his head all afternoon. The look encompassed both her eyes and her entire body. So after she'd kicked him out of the gallery for hovering, he'd made a trip to the grocery store and had come home to cook what had once been her favorite meal. Fried chicken, mashed potatoes, and gravy. With banana pudding for dessert.

It wasn't the healthiest of foods, but from what he could tell, she could use some fattening up. And honestly, he'd thought he would enjoy an afternoon spent in the kitchen. It had been a while.

But instead, he'd reeled from the sight of the house upon entering. What in the hell had Julie done? And why? The wallpaper in the kitchen was half down, the other half either glued fast to the walls or hanging in shreds, and every last item that belonged in the cabinets and drawers had been moved to somewhere *other* than the cabinets and drawers. Two cabinet doors had even been taken down, and from the dings on the hinges, it looked as if she'd removed them with force.

And now he had a blister the size of a nickel on his wrist.

He turned off the water, and cursed again when he went to get a dish towel, only to remember too late that the drawer was empty. *And* that he'd left it open. His hip slammed into the wood, emitting a cracking sound that he presumed meant the integrity of the frame had been compromised. The damned room was too small.

He'd always thought so, but it had never seemed to bother his parents. With his dad traveling 75 percent of the time for his job— and his dad being the only parent who'd actually liked to cook—the kitchen had been relegated to low priority. Extra money had instead been put into trips taken together as a family.

A home is only where you lay your head at night.

That had been both of his parents' view when it came to upgrading the house that had been in the family for three generations, but Carter had never agreed. A home was where you made your life.

Or so he'd once believed.

Then he'd built his and Lisa's dream house, only to find out that she wanted to make her life somewhere else. She *had been* making her life somewhere else.

Sonofabitch.

He continued to grumble as he returned to cooking. Straight out of college he'd been hired as a civil engineer, same as his father, and had proceeded to travel wherever the jobs took him. Lisa had gone on to law school, before the two of them had eventually settled just outside of Providence. She'd wanted to live in Manhattan, but that large of a city hadn't appealed to Carter, so they'd compromised with Rhode Island.

Their apartment hadn't been on the coast, but with a short drive he could get there.

Lisa had commuted to New York City weekly, at least in the beginning. It had worked for them. He'd grown up in a similar fashion—his dad always traveling—so it had made sense.

Only—

A knock sounded at the door, cutting off his thoughts. Which was fine. Those thoughts never ended well. Except, he didn't want company, either.

He stood by the stove and listened, being completely silent. The chicken even seemed to pick up on the need for silence, and the frying became a slight sizzle instead of the popping bonanza that had been going on only seconds before. He would ignore whoever was at the door. It would be either a solicitor or someone looking for Julie.

The knock sounded again. Harder this time.

He grunted and reached out to slap at the light switch, turning off the overhead light. He shouldn't have turned it on, but after closing the blinds when he'd come in, it had been too dark to cook in the cramped space. Maybe whoever it was would get the hint and leave.

Nope. The knock this time was an obtrusive thump.

With a quick flick of the wrist, he turned the stove burner off and stomped through the house. The damned chicken wouldn't be edible if it sat in the oil for very long.

Grabbing the knob, he yanked open the door.

"Stop right there!"

He immediately took a step back, hands in the air at the weapon raised toward him.

Then he squinted, his heart pounding wildly inside his chest, as he forced himself to fully take in the situation. It wasn't a gun, as he'd first thought, but what looked to be a can of pepper spray.

Not that he wanted *that* in his face, either.

He took another step back, then sniffed. Good god, whoever it was reeked of fish.

Then a memory came to him. Of a certain redhead who'd lived next door with whom he used to go fishing. And the trim waist and those bare legs showing beneath the tiny pair of white shorts *did* imply this was a woman.

"Ginger?" he questioned cautiously. The arm in front of him stiffened. "Is that you?" he added.

Seconds later, the can lowered an inch and red hair and clear green eyes peeked out above the tightly clenched fist. The arm lowered another inch, and Ginger Atkinson looked him up and down. "Carter?"

He almost smiled.

Except, he didn't smile these days. And he wasn't about to break his streak now. "Why in the hell are you pointing pepper spray at me?" he grumbled. "Put that thing away."

The can didn't disappear. "Is that really you?" She squinted at him.

Carter pushed her hand down, putting himself out of harm's way, and crossed his arms over his chest. "It's me. Now tell me why you're over here trying to blind me?"

Or worse, double him over and make him cry like a baby. He'd been sprayed once, as research for a book, and though he might not have cried exactly like an infant, tears had for sure made an appearance. It had been embarrassing. And painful. And he did not want to repeat the experience.

"I didn't know you who were." She pursed her lips, still seeming to size him up.

She finally put the can out of sight, tucking it into the back pocket of her shorts, and Carter's gaze involuntarily followed the move. The cotton across her chest pulled tight, outlining her curves, and the shorts were short. The sight of her forced his brain to acknowledge the feminine picture she made. While at the same time his nose pointed out the smell.

"You stink, Red."

She made a face. "Nice to see you, too. What are you doing here?"

"Came for a visit." He said the words as if visits for him were common. As if he'd been home more than twice since he'd graduated from college.

The expression on her face said that she was aware of the facts.

"Mom wanted me to check on Julie," he added grudgingly.

She nodded like she approved of his words. "And how long are you here for?"

As few days as possible.

He shrugged, then eased his stance and glanced back toward the kitchen, remembering how Julie had ripped the room apart. "I don't know," he said. Long enough to find out what was going on with his sister. He'd discovered several gouges dug into the walls as if she'd been as intent on taking out personal frustrations as she was on taking down the wallpaper.

Why she'd been doing either, he intended to find out.

Ginger crossed her own arms over her chest then, and poked out a hip, and damned if his pulse didn't pick up at the pose.

Seriously? He was attracted to his childhood friend?

Well, at least he felt something for someone. It had been too long since anything had so much as stirred down there. Feeling disgust toward the opposite sex did that for a person. Stewing in his own anger did, too.

Maybe his mom had a point in dragging him out of his house.

He couldn't help it then. He looked Ginger over from head to toe. Even with the stench, she was darn cute. No shoes, her clothes looking like something she'd probably owned for ten years, and her hair pulled back into a ponytail, with flying strands floating around her face. She didn't seem to have on a speck of makeup, and her skin had a few more freckles than he remembered. He found the sight of her incredibly refreshing. And though she very much looked the same as she always had, there was also something different about her. He just couldn't put his finger on what it was. Of course, it *had* been a long time since he'd seen her.

"Good to see you, Red," he finally admitted. It was a small concession to his bad mood, but it was true. They'd been close for years. It *was* good to see her.

She smiled at him, and his pulse raced once more. "I haven't been called Red in years."

"No?" He glanced toward the kitchen again, thinking about the chicken sitting in the grease, and when he turned back, Ginger had the tip end of her ponytail twisted in front of her face, staring at it.

She frowned. "Could be because I was blonde until recently."

"Blonde?" he asked, unable to picture it. "No." He shook his head. "You should never be blonde." He reached for the edge of the door, ready to close it and return to his chicken. "Julie isn't home."

But she didn't take the hint. Instead, she wedged herself into the limited space between them, her bare feet almost touching his loafers, while he eyed her movements.

"I assumed you just came over to shoot me with Mace," he pointed out.

"I did." She peeked around him. "And to see why all the blinds are closed."

"I like the blinds closed." It was none of her business that he preferred sitting in the dark these days. Ignoring things like fucking happy blue skies.

She inched farther into the room, her neck craning to check out the darkened space, and he merely stared at her. He was not in the mood for her at the moment. Her innate cheeriness irritated him, and try as he knew she was, her antics were not humoring him.

Good to know she hadn't changed, though.

"I'm busy," he told her.

"In the dark?"

Annoyance had him reaching out and flipping the light switch by the front door. He could see she didn't plan on leaving easily. "Happy?" He shot her a smirk.

"Getting there. Why'd you close the blinds?" She brought her eyes back to him. They were so light in color that they could almost be classified as mint. "You're not doing anything untoward in here, are you?"

Carter just stared at her.

"What?" She blinked innocently. "I haven't seen you in years. I don't know anything about you these days. Maybe you kidnapped your sister and have her tied up in here. Do you plan to cut her up into pieces?" She sniffed, her nose turned up in the air, then regarded him suspiciously. "Is that what I smell cooking?"

What in the hell was wrong with her? Could she not see he wasn't in the mood for jokes?

"Close the door when you leave, will you?" He pivoted and headed to the kitchen, leaving her just inside the front door. His chicken was probably ruined, and he didn't have time to stand around listening to her foolishness.

But when she went quiet behind him, he looked back, seeing that she'd moved to the bookcase in the living room. An entire set of his books lined one shelf, and he wondered if Julie or his parents had ever mentioned that those books were his. He'd used a pen name from day one—mostly because he'd still been working in a different career at the time—but he'd found that he preferred his anonymity.

However, he *was* intrigued with the idea of Ginger knowing. What would she think?

Had she read his novels? He had once told her that he wanted to write for a living.

She ran a finger over the spine of his latest book—making his chest clench at the action—before lowering her hand and heading for the kitchen. Then she stopped. She slowly took in the room, and if the lines marring her brow were any indication, the look of the place surprised her.

"So this is new?" he asked. He waved a pair of tongs toward the wall.

"You mean, you didn't do this?"

He raised his brows. "Why would I do this?"

"I don't know. Why would Julie?"

That was the twenty-thousand-dollar question. He'd called his sister the minute he'd seen the room, but she'd claimed to be too busy to talk.

"I was just over here last week," Ginger said, her tone soft as she took in everything once again. "It was fine then." Her words stopped as she nudged at the corner of the single picture hanging on the wall and exposed the hole behind it. It looked like the head of a hammer had been pounded through the once-smooth surface. She shook her head, but didn't say anything else.

"What's wrong with her?" he asked.

Luminous eyes turned to him. "I didn't know anything was. Mom and I check on her once in a while, but we thought she was fine."

"She's too small." He moved the chicken pieces to napkins to blot out the excess oil. "I went by the gallery to see her before coming here, but other than admitting she could gain a few pounds, she swore everything was fine."

"I have no idea," Ginger said. The words sounded more like an afterthought, as she once again surveyed the room. "I do think she's lonely. I've never heard her mention the baby's . . ." Her words trailed off and she shot him a grimace, but he knew what she meant. Julie didn't talk about the baby's father. The only thing Carter or his parents knew was that she'd gotten pregnant before graduating college. She'd also never said if the father intended to be a part of hers and the baby's lives or not.

"I'm worried about her," he admitted. He hadn't spoken to Ginger in years, yet it was easy to share his thoughts.

At least, thoughts about his sister. Everything else he'd keep to himself.

"I am, too, now." She went to the windows and opened the blinds, letting in the late-afternoon light. It was hard to stew appropriately with sunlight streaming in, but Carter didn't point that out.

A car pulled up outside, and they both looked toward the front of the house.

"I should go," Ginger said. She glanced at the picture hiding the hole in the wall. "Let you and Julie catch up."

She was at the front door before he could say anything to stop her, but then, he didn't want to stop her. He needed to have a talk with his sister, then he needed to figure out what to do about this room. Hopefully those two things would take only a couple of days, and he could be back on a plane, heading north, by the weekend.

The ringing of his phone prohibited anything else he might have said, and Ginger tossed him a wave and slipped out the door. Carter brought his phone to his ear as he moved to open the blinds at the front of the house. He watched Ginger stop to speak to Julie in the driveway.

"Hello, Mother," he said into the microphone. The attitude he'd perfected due to her recent daily calls was evident in the two words.

"Did you get there?" his mom asked.

"Came across on the ferry this morning."

"Why didn't you call and tell me?"

He kept an eye on Ginger as she crossed the grass and ducked through the row of arborvitae that separated their yards, his gaze lingering on her white shorts for a little too long. "Because I'm a grown-up," he finally answered. "And because I haven't updated you on my whereabouts for years."

"I'm worried about your sister, Carter," she said primly. "Now I can rest easier knowing she's not alone."

"I'm not staying," he warned. "I told you that." Julie came in the door, and the first thing she did was fire a look toward the kitchen. The distress that washed over her face made him silently amend his words. He would stay as long as he needed to make sure his sister was okay.

"I'm here, and she's fine," he said a little more softly into the phone. When Julie hesitantly looked his way, he added, "I won't let her lift a finger."

That won him a scathing smirk. His little sister headed for the stairs then, her normal little-sister-to-big-brother swagger in her step and her dark hair swinging at her shoulders, and for the first time that day, she *did* seem okay. Maybe his worry was for nothing. Could be she'd just had a bad day when she'd decided to strip the kitchen of its contents. He certainly understood bad days.

He'd fix it back up, slap up some new wallpaper, and be gone.

"Thank you," his mom said in his ear. "We'll be back in three weeks. Surely you can stay that long?"

"I can't."

"Oh?" She let the word hang before adding, "Does that mean you're writing again?"

His mother could make a point with few words. She knew he wasn't writing. And she knew why.

He didn't reply.

"Maybe stay even a few days after we get back?" she tacked on. "Your father and I will be celebrating thirty-five years together next month, Carter. We've invited friends over. Stay and help us celebrate. Everyone would love to see you."

"Can't do it." The idea did have appeal—surprisingly—but he had more anger and staring at his blank walls to get back to. "I'll make sure Julie's okay, but then I'm going home."

His mother sighed dramatically, and Carter moved to the chicken and poked at it. Grease oozed out of a leg as if it had been purposefully injected into the meat.

"Will you at least try to enjoy yourself while you're there?" she asked. "You seem too—"

"No," he interrupted. He dumped the chicken in the trash—he'd take his sister out to dinner—and his mother sighed in his ear once again. "And don't call me every day," he added.

Though he hadn't seen his parents a lot over the years, they did talk on a regular basis. But since their visit last month, his mother had taken that up a notch.

"Fine, Carter." She used her annoyed-mother tone. "I'll just leave you alone. Quit worrying about you. Is that what you want to hear?"

"Do you promise?"

She growled at him, and for the first time in months, the anger he carried around so easily almost cracked. He didn't laugh, but he did take pleasure in irritating his mother. He missed her. He missed both of his parents. They'd visited a few times since he and Lisa had married, but not enough.

Of course, he'd often wished *he* were here.

After he hung up he heard Julie's phone ring upstairs. That would be their mother calling *Julie* to check on *him*. Which she would also do every day.

Instead of presuming he could change anything about his mother's meddling ways, he moved to the side windows and peered up to the second floor of the house next door. Ginger's curtains were closed in her room, but he could picture her there, framed by the yellow breezy fabric. As kids, they'd often waved to each other from across the short distance. Sometimes raising their windows and sharing the details of their days.

He wondered if she'd open her window tonight and talk to him if he opened his.

And then he called himself an idiot for the thought. He wasn't a kid anymore.

And he didn't want to sit in his window pretending the last few months of his life hadn't happened.

CHAPTER FOUR

"Do you own shrimp boats, too?"

Ginger paused at her date's question, a peel-and-eat shrimp halfway to her mouth, and caught her mother's downcast glance from the corner of her eye. Darn. She'd been shoveling shrimp into her mouth at a rate that had to appear gauche to everyone.

She hadn't meant to, but she was starving.

Lunch had been nothing more than a pack of cheese and crackers out on the boat, and since she'd had an errand to run before getting ready for the date, she hadn't had time to sneak in a snack before dinner.

She put the crustacean back on her plate, and ignoring the rest of the party of twelve sitting around the table, she went for "delicate flower" as she wiped her fingertips on her napkin and settled what her mother would call a winning smile onto her face. She also pulled her shoulders back, attempting to sit up straighter and look more feminine. She'd totally forgotten to work on being girly tonight.

"No shrimp boats," she told Patrick, the date her mother's fiancé had picked out for her. "We do fishing charters where guests can take home their catch if they'd like, but we're not in the business of providing seafood in mass quantities." She tried her best not to blush in abject humiliation, as she motioned toward her plate. "Doesn't keep me from enjoying them, though."

Patrick chuckled at that, a smooth tenor quality to his voice, and the tension eased from Ginger's shoulders.

So far, Patrick had been an ideal date. He was very pleasant and charming, and yes, he was her age and he did still live with his mother. But to hear him tell it, it was because he'd lost his father at a young age and he and his mother were close. Like her.

He also had his own side business selling wooden flutes that he made himself. Who made wooden flutes? And if his first two months on the job with Island Beach Real Estate were any indication, he would turn out to be a top-notch Realtor, as well. Clint had certainly bragged on the man's skills throughout the evening.

"Tell me about your flute business," Ginger asked. She eyed the scrumptious shrimp on her plate, and silently cursed her mother for pounding it into her head that a "lady" wouldn't be the first in a group to clear her plate. In fact, a lady probably shouldn't *clear* her plate at all.

But dang it, Ginger had a healthy appetite. She always had.

Her appetite had gotten her into trouble as a kid, but these days she worked hard enough to burn several thousand calories a day. If she wanted to clear her plate, she should be able to.

Instead of immediately answering her question, Patrick leaned in and whispered, "Eat your food. We can talk later."

And with those few words, she thought she might have fallen a little bit in love. She shot him a grateful smile, ignored her mother, and attacked her food. She loved shrimp. And she loved to eat.

She reached for her wineglass. And tonight she even loved wine.

As she finished her meal, she did talk with Patrick, but mostly she let him carry the conversation. While he chatted, she sipped her wine and studied him critically, looking at him with the eye of a potential mate. And she realized that there was something about him that reminded her of Carter. A similarity in the dark hair, maybe. Or their height. The tiny lines at the corners of his eyes?

Or it could be simply that she'd been thinking about Carter all afternoon, and he remained on her mind.

She'd been floored to find him on the other side of her can of Mace. For some reason, she'd assumed she'd never see him again. He hadn't disliked Turtle Island when they were kids. In fact, she'd always thought he loved it as much as she. But he certainly hadn't cared to come home over the years.

In her mind, he'd moved on. He was simply a part of her past. Yet there he'd been. Her teenage crush.

Of course, to him she'd never been anything more than a friend. The chubby friend. But she'd idolized that boy. She'd wanted him with the kind of desperation most teenage girls employed at one time or another. And now he was back, looking . . . *pretty good.* He actually was a little too thin. And cranky. The man had been in a seriously foul mood when she'd shown up at the house. But even thin and irritable, he painted a fine picture.

As far as Ginger knew, though, he was still married. Though she *hadn't* seen any sign of his wife, and he wasn't wearing a wedding ring.

"Don't you think, Ginger?"

Her mother had spoken to her.

Ginger blinked, having no clue what had been asked of her. Her mother knew it, too. She gave her the look. Geez, Ginger hated disappointing her mom. And she'd already gotten the look once tonight when she'd shown up in jeans instead of her mother's green dress. But in her defense, they were really nice jeans. And she'd worn her frilliest shirt. Even if she hadn't taken the time to do anything extra with her hair or makeup.

"The wedding," her mother prodded.

Again, Ginger blinked. She swallowed, feeling eleven pairs of eyes focused on her.

Patrick edged closer, his arm sliding around the back of her chair. "At the senior center," he whispered.

"The senior center?" Ginger parroted. She turned to the happy couple seated to her left. "You're not seniors." Her mother was only fifty-eight, and Clint couldn't be much older. Maybe sixty.

Her mother laughed lightly. "Not quite. But they have that large rec room that would be a great space for a reception, and the administrators have recently opened up the pergola-covered patio at the back of the property for rentals. It's not directly on the beach, but you do get the horizon in the distance. The nice blue of the ocean. Can't you picture it? All of us in the middle of those large live oaks?"

Ginger nodded. She *could* picture it. She'd certainly seen enough weddings over the last year and a half for the idea to form easily. "It sounds beautiful. Did you call Kayla about it yet?"

It was a given that Seaglass Celebrations would coordinate the wedding, since Andie was part owner of the company. Andie's mother owned the other half and ran the business with Kayla.

Excitement suddenly coursed through Ginger at the realization that Roni and Andie would both come in for the wedding. She would get to see her friends. The idea came like a cool breeze, and she slumped in her chair in relief, leaning into Patrick—who was still close at her side.

"Calling Kayla is on my list for tomorrow." Her mother smiled secretly at Clint. "Today was spent . . . celebrating."

Ginger gulped more wine. She didn't need to know about her mother's celebrating. She'd overheard too much of it during the last six months.

"So," her mother continued, turning to Ginger and reaching for her hand. Soft light from flickering candles throughout the dining room gave her mother's skin a warm glow, and Ginger couldn't help but think that being engaged made her look ten years younger. "Assuming we can get the senior center"—her mother paused dramatically—"will you be my maid of honor?"

Her mother looked so happy. And Ginger's heart pinched tight.

"Yes." She nodded enthusiastically. "Of course." She smiled so hard she just knew she'd get called out for being a fraud. Her envy shamed her.

Dinner finished with continued discussion about wedding plans, and Ginger found her wine topped off several additional times. She didn't protest. It wasn't every night she was treated to the best restaurant in town, with a good-looking man at her side.

"So, I'll see you in the morning," her mother said, and Ginger realized that everyone had stood from the table but her. Geez, maybe she'd had a little *too* much to drink.

She looked up at her mom.

"I'm staying over at Clint's," her mother explained. She stood, hand-in-hand with her fiancé, his size dwarfing her five-foot-two frame. Then she looked straight at Patrick—as if making sure he understood that Ginger would have the house to herself tonight—and Ginger did a full-body blush. "You'll see her home?" her mother asked.

"I—" Ginger tried to suggest a cab, but Patrick cut her off. "My pleasure, Ms. Atkinson."

Excitement warred with embarrassment as he held out a hand, and as Ginger rose, the room spun. Which was no good. She couldn't go home alone with Patrick if she was drunk. He was cute, charming, and he'd been nothing but a gentleman all night. He hit all her qualifications.

Except now she was too inebriated to think straight.

"Mom," she murmured, but her mother either didn't hear her, or chose not to.

"You ready?" Patrick asked.

Ginger gulped. "Yep."

All that kept running through her head was that it had been two years since she'd been with a man. Two years, and that length of time had not been *fully* due to lack of opportunity. She wasn't one to sleep around.

Yet in her current state, she feared she'd have her pants off and be entertaining offers in no time.

"Thanks again for dinner," Patrick said to her mom, then reached around her and shook Clint's hand. "And congratulations on the engagement. I look forward to attending the wedding."

A mixture of fear and anticipation coursed through Ginger as Patrick led her to his car, and five minutes later he was walking her to her front door. The night air had cleared her head, but only a little. She liked him. And she didn't want to sleep with him and not have him call her again. That had happened before.

"Patrick," she began as she turned to face him. They were at the base of the small set of steps leading to the porch, the light she'd left on shining down on them, and she was terrified to let him take one step closer to the house.

"I enjoyed tonight very much." He lifted her hand and pressed a kiss to her fingers. "But I'm going to leave you here." He inclined his head toward the front door. "I assume you can get yourself in?"

Oh. The air went out of her as the rejection set in. He was just being polite.

Here she'd been worried he'd make a pass and she'd have to choose between morals and physical need, and he'd just been making sure she got home safely. Probably to impress Clint. She nodded. "I can. Thanks for seeing me home."

She turned to go before she did something stupid like cry, but Patrick had other ideas.

He captured one hand and brought her back around to face him. "Hey," he said softly. "You do realize I'm leaving only because I don't want to take advantage of you, right?" He squeezed her fingers in his. "You look incredible, and I've had a good time tonight. I like you. But you've had a little too much to drink. If I come in, I might cross a line you wouldn't appreciate."

Dang. She hadn't seen that coming. She would definitely have to thank Clint for setting this up. What a gentleman.

"Maybe we could do this again?" Patrick suggested. "Only, without ten other people watching on the next time?"

Ginger smiled . . . just as a light in the house next door came on. Instead of answering, she glanced over and saw Carter's silhouette pass behind his bedroom window, and she instantly thought of years past. She'd sit near her window for hours in the evenings, just waiting for him to show up.

Of course, she'd always played it cool. Pretended she'd been there reading, maybe studying the stars in preparation for a college astronomy class she'd imagined. What a lame excuse.

But what she'd actually been doing, every time, was waiting to get a glimpse of Carter.

She wouldn't mind a glimpse now.

"Ginger?"

"Hmmm?"

Carter passed by the window again, and this time the curtains swished. She held her breath, but he didn't pull them back. He didn't look for her.

"Ginger?" Patrick spoke louder, jerking her attention from the Ridley house.

"Sorry," she mumbled. Mortification flooded her when Patrick turned to see what had captured her attention, and Carter chose that moment to open the curtains. He looked down on them, and Ginger felt every inch of her skin flame.

"Friend of yours?" Patrick asked. His tone was less than receptive.

"No." The word came out quick, and she took one more peek up at Carter's room. He was gone. She blew out a breath. "My neighbor's brother. He hasn't been home in years, and showed up today."

Her brain remained fuzzy, but she landed on an explanation for standing there gawking at one man through a window while another was trying to ask her out.

"Julie," she said, working overtime to think straight. "She's pregnant, and apparently Carter"—Ginger swatted a hand toward the now-dark window—"thinks something might be wrong. He came home to check on her."

Given that the excuse was accurate, and that Ginger had gotten a good look at their kitchen, she couldn't help but worry about the girl herself.

"So . . ." Patrick began. He looked at her again, still holding on to her hand, and she did everything she could to look cute. Her smile felt a little too sweet, and she knew her eyes were open too wide. "Do you want to . . ."

"Do it again?" she prodded. "Go out?" She would not let go of a second date easily. "I'd love to. How about Friday?"

Patrick didn't answer immediately, instead shooting another glance next door. "I have something going on Friday," he finally replied. He returned his gaze to hers. "Saturday? Seven?"

The smile on her face became real, and she nodded, grateful. "Yes. Seven."

Patrick left then—no kiss—and she hurried inside, leaning against the closed door and kicking herself for nearly blowing it. She needed classes on how to date a man, apparently.

In actuality, she hated dating. She just needed a man.

Which reminded her . . . she had one!

Her friend Cookie Phillips had called earlier in the day, letting her know that the latest Jules Bradley novel had come in to the bookstore, and Ginger had made a run to pick it up. Jules Bradley wrote the most god-awful horror stories, and she couldn't get enough. She'd actually started it before getting ready for tonight's dinner, which was why she hadn't put more time into her appearance.

Before taking another step into the house, she kicked off her heels and wiggled out of her jeans. Her shirt was long enough to cover her hips, and the night was still warm. She fluffed the tails of the silk from where they'd been tucked into her jeans, and grabbed the book. Then she headed to the back deck.

After lighting the tiki torches, she settled into her favorite Adirondack chair and opened to the last page she'd read. Any decent optometrist would chastise her for reading with such little light, but she loved getting lost in creepy stories in the dark of the night.

The only thing that would make it better was if she could hear the waves while reading, but that would be rectified as soon as she finished her house. She had a deck built there that not only overlooked the ocean, with nothing but grass and sand between, but she'd also planned muted underrailing lights for just this purpose.

The thought made her excited to get the house finished. She'd call the contractor first thing in the morning and see how soon she could get them back out there. The house probably still had a good month's worth of work to do to complete it, maybe more, and that left a little time before the wedding. Enough to pack her bags and move in.

She'd worry about making the call tomorrow, though. First things first. She leaned back, her legs stretched out in front of her, and disappeared in the words.

A few chapters later, she looked up from the book, her heart pounding. This one was his best one yet. She glanced toward the Ridley house, remembering that she'd seen the book on Julie's shelf when she'd been over a few weeks ago. She'd checked it out again that afternoon. How had Julie gotten a copy before it was released?

Whatever the source, Ginger wanted to be hooked up.

A funny thought hit her, and she rested her head against the back of the chair and smiled up at the dark sky. Maybe the father of Julie's baby was the author?

Laughter bubbled out of her, and at the sound of it in the quiet, still night, she let herself laugh more. The sound was freeing, and though others might think her somewhat nutty, she didn't care. Life didn't always go her way, but it could definitely be fun. At least people like Jules Bradley were around to entertain her on dark, lonely nights.

A movement caught her eye, and she shifted her gaze. It landed on Carter's window. The curtains were moving.

Had Carter been watching her?

Chapter Five

He hated wallpaper with the kind of passion that should be reserved for the bedroom.

Carter sprayed another patch of the wall with a mixture of water and fabric softener—a trick he'd learned years ago when working construction for summer jobs—and scraped at the stubborn spot. He'd been going at the walls most of the day, and still had two feet untouched.

The door in the other room opened, and he looked over, unable to see into the living room from where he was, but he knew it would be Julie. It was time for her to get off work. He'd spent the previous day at the art gallery with her, doing everything he could to help. Lifting boxes, dusting, sweeping. Whatever he'd seen her about to do, he'd jumped in and handled, thinking that if something were wrong with her or the baby, he was helping.

Of course, he'd only made her angry, and she'd banned him from the shop.

According to her, she didn't need her big brother's help. She also didn't need to tell him why she'd shredded the kitchen, apparently. All she'd said was that she felt like "doing some upgrades."

He'd been here for two days, and so far, Julie had refused to talk about anything of import. She'd gone to bed early both nights, had barely touched any of the food he'd cooked for her, and when he'd attempted to bring up the subject of the baby's father, she'd actually shoved earbuds in her ears.

When they *had* talked, it had devolved into arguments.

And she'd not caved an inch when he'd tried to find out if something was wrong with her. At least he was beginning to believe that whatever was going on, it didn't have to do with her health or the baby's. She seemed more despondent than in danger.

"I see you're still here," she said now. She stood at the entrance to the kitchen, a frown on her face as she took in his actions. "And you need to leave that alone. It's my project."

He looked at the wall and almost wished he *had* left it alone.

"Yeah?" Using the scraper, he poked at the picture still hanging behind the table, setting it to swinging until it fell to the floor. "That hole your project, too?"

"I messed up trying to get the paper down."

"You knocked a hole in the wall, Julie," he accused. "That wasn't an accident."

She crossed her arms over her chest, anger coloring her cheeks, and he noticed that she looked a lot like him. She also looked as unhappy as he was. That troubled him.

"What's wrong?" he asked, gentling his tone.

"Nothing."

"Bullshit." He got a corner of the paper loose and yanked. A strip about one foot by two inches was all that came down. "What's your plan once this is off, anyway? Paint?"

She mumbled under her breath, and he stopped what he was doing to look at her.

"What did you say?" he asked. He hoped he'd heard her wrong.

She stared, unblinking, looking like a mulish teen instead of a twenty-two-year-old adult, and after several seconds she finally replied. "I said I plan to redo the whole kitchen."

That's what he thought he'd heard. He sighed. "Why?"

Again, she didn't immediately answer, but when he refused to look away, she broke. "Because Mom and Dad are coming home to stay," she said. She jabbed her finger at her chest, her voice suddenly wobbling. "And they're coming home because *I'm* having a baby."

Then his sister burst into tears. That was the last thing Carter wanted.

"I'm forcing them to change their entire lives, and I didn't mean to," she blubbered.

Well, hell. He'd asked.

He groaned. "So this is about guilt?" It didn't pass his notice that he'd grown quite accustomed to not having to deal with female emotions. And that he'd liked it. "Do you seriously not realize how excited they are to be grandparents?" he asked.

"No, they're not."

He thought about the fact that he'd always imagined he'd be the one to give them their first grandchild, and he realized even *that* was bothering him. Terrific. He was jealous of his sister.

He tossed the scraper into the kitchen sink, and dragged Julie to a chair.

Sitting across from her, he propped his elbows on his knees and leaned forward. "Listen, moron. They're thrilled with the idea of a grandchild. And they're not upset about coming home for it, either. That's why they started traveling as soon as you went away to school. So they could be settled when grandkids did come. Dad worked hard when we were kids because they had the dream of traveling, of giving back to others on their trips. But they also want to be here for you now."

And for him. Which he knew was why his mom wanted him there. It was her way to help.

"Well, I still feel bad about it," Julie said. She hiccupped as she tried to get her tears under control. "And I hadn't planned on getting pregnant at this age. This is not how it was supposed to happen."

That was the first thing she'd said about the pregnancy, and Carter waited, holding his breath and hoping she'd say more. She didn't.

Instead, she added, "That's why I wanted to do this for them. Their anniversary is in a few weeks."

"You want to redo the kitchen as an anniversary present?"

She shrugged one tiny shoulder. "Yeah."

"And you intended to do it by yourself?" At her silence, he said, "You know they don't care about stuff like this?"

"I know." Her teeth appeared and nibbled on her bottom lip before she admitted softly, "But I want my daughter to be able to bake cookies with Dad. Or with Mom if Mom decides she wants to start cooking. And there's not enough room in here to do that."

Carter's chest clenched as he looked at his sister. "You're having a daughter?" He'd wondered, but until that moment he hadn't thought it mattered to him.

The slight smile on Julie's face beat at the hardened shell around his heart. "Yeah," she said. "The doctor says she's tiny, but she's healthy." She lifted her shoulder in another shrug. "I am, too. So you can quit worrying."

Carter reached for his sister then, and pulled her into his arms. Her tears cranked back up.

When he let her go, he shook his head at her. "You're an idiot, you know that, don't you? I *can't* quit worrying. You're my sister, you're alone, and you're pregnant. *And* you're trying to do a kitchen remodel by yourself." He dragged his hand over his face and eyed the sad state of the cabinets. "Please tell me that you've at least got someone lined up for the hard parts?"

Julie looked away from him then, and in that moment he knew

that he wouldn't be going home anytime soon. He had a kitchen to remodel.

His insides sagged. "What?" he asked tiredly.

"The store where I plan to order everything said they could install them."

"Julie." He scowled at her. "It needs more than some guys showing up and hanging a few new cabinets; surely you know that. Who's taking these down? What about countertops? Are you replacing them?"

More tears rolled over her cheeks.

"Can you even afford this?" he asked, frustration evident in his tone. He didn't know about her finances, but he remembered how difficult it could be to get started out of college.

Her silence was his answer.

"Got nothing to say?" he prodded.

"I got a loan."

He ground his teeth together. "You're having a baby, Julie. Your money needs to go to *her*."

"I know!" she burst out. "But I had to do something. I have to live here with them. At least for a while; I have no other choice. I couldn't *just* take advantage. I need to pay them back."

"You know you're behaving like you're sixteen, right? Not thinking things through."

"How would you know what I was like at sixteen? You weren't even around."

Her words knocked the air out of him. For siblings with eight years between them, they'd been close. But she was right, he could have been around more.

Only, Lisa had hated it here. He'd brought her home just once after they'd married. She'd made such a fuss anytime he'd suggested another trip that he'd finally quit bringing it up. Eventually he'd taken on more jobs that shipped him all over the country, and she'd begun staying longer with each trip to New York. He'd come home only one more time—for Julie's high school graduation—and that trip had been made alone.

Looking back, he couldn't believe he'd let his life be controlled like that. But he hadn't realized it was that bad. He'd been trying to make his wife happy. Only, she'd also hated the apartment they'd rented, the house he'd eventually built . . . and apparently him.

Geez, what a schmuck.

He rose to get Julie a box of tissues so she could dry her eyes, and on his way back from the bathroom, he caught sight of Ginger sitting on her deck. He paused, trying to see if she was wearing pants. He'd seen her out there the last two nights, both times reading a book by torchlight, and neither time with anything covering her from the hips down.

Or if she'd had something on, it had been as tiny as the pair of shorts she'd worn over here that first day. Who wandered around outside with no pants on?

"You should go over and talk to her," Julie sniffed. She took the box of tissues from him and shot him a haughty look. "Instead of just *staring* at her."

He eyed his sister. "I'm not *staring* at her."

But he took one more look, wishing he was upstairs where he could see more clearly, and Julie snickered. He speared her with a look.

"You're so obvious," she said. "She has great legs, doesn't she?"

She did have great legs. Carter said nothing.

"And I swear she doesn't even know it," Julie added. "Go on. You guys were good friends once. Go over. At least it'll get you out of my hair for a while."

He forced himself to look away. It had been a long time since he and Ginger had been friends. "Tough luck for you, kid. Because I plan to be in your hair every day. At least until you put some meat on your bones. My niece needs to be fed."

"Your niece is just fine."

"See that you keep it that way." He retrieved the scraper and went back to the wall. "This is *my* project now. You're on the sidelines."

She shot out of her chair. "You can't do that. This was my idea. I'm paying for it."

He guffawed. "Not anymore. And you're not lifting a finger, either. Your job is to eat and take care of yourself."

She snarled at him, and he could see her racking her brain for another angle to make her argument. But in the end she dropped back to her seat with a thump. "Big brothers can be such asses."

He pointed the scraper at her. "You got that right. Which brings me to my next issue. What's the deal with the father?"

She didn't miss a beat. "What's the deal with your wife?"

They stared at each other for several seconds, both refusing to cave. He'd spilled his guts to his mother in a weak moment, which also meant that his father knew, but he'd made them promise not to tell anyone. His stupidity was his alone. No one else needed to know about it.

"Had you already broken up when you came for my college graduation?" Julie asked. She sounded hurt. "Why didn't you tell me?"

"Because we were together then. I thought we were fine." Mostly.

He'd headed to New York right after leaving Chapel Hill, intending to read Lisa the riot act for not taking the time to be at his sister's graduation. At that point he hadn't even seen his wife in three months. He'd been finishing the house, working hard to get it done in time for their anniversary, and polishing the proposal for the new book.

Their marriage hadn't been without flaws, he'd known that. But the house was supposed to change that. She was going to cut back on her hours. They would live together for more than a night here and there for the first time in years.

They were going to have kids.

Only . . .

The hurt still ripped him in half. That was the worst part. He wasn't just mad, he was hurt. He'd put everything he had into their marriage.

Fuck irreconcilable differences. This one had been on her.

"The kitchen will be a present from both of us," he said, ignoring the fact that he knew Julie wanted to know more than that he and Lisa had split up. And maybe she deserved to know. But he wasn't ready to talk about it. "I'll call in a favor, get some help. If we're going to do this, we're doing it right."

"You're staying until Mom and Dad get home?"

Her question, and the timid way she asked it, made him realize that she wanted him here. That hadn't even occurred to him.

"Yeah." He nodded, not giving it another thought. "I'm staying."

Which meant that somehow in the middle of all of this he had to figure out how to write again. If he was about to sink tens of thousands into a remodel, he couldn't very well afford to return an advance.

But first, he had to know if there was a problem with his sister. She had to be honest about that. He gave her a penetrating look. "Are you really okay?"

She nodded, but her eyes told a different story.

"Sad?" he asked. "Hurt?" He recognized the look.

More tears slid from her lids. "Heartbroken," she whispered.

"And that's all?"

"That's all."

He studied her, thinking about the similarities between them. He didn't know the details of her relationship or lack thereof, but her pregnant-and-alone state said enough. "I'm here if you need anything," he told her.

She looked so small, but his words seemed to fortify her. Her shoulders straightened, and for a few brief seconds, she didn't look quite as miserable as *he* felt.

Then more tears fell, and he knew that they were quite the pair.

~

"One of your eyelashes is on crooked."

Ginger halted at the words—she was on her way out the front door—and faced her mom. "Which one?" She brought both hands to her eyes. She'd thought she had them on right.

Her mother put down the strands of ribbon she was working with—she was personalizing her wedding favors—and rose from her chair. She tilted Ginger's head back and Ginger closed her eyes in surrender, thankful someone was around who knew how to do this stuff.

It was Saturday night. Date two with Patrick. And she wanted everything to be right.

The other night she'd barely tried, and he'd really seemed to like her. Which made her almost giddy at the thought of the effort she'd put into her appearance tonight. She'd even gone by Samantha's and bought a new dress. Samantha's was the only boutique on the island, but that didn't mean the selection was limited. Samantha Greene, the owner, took regular trips to New York to stay abreast of the latest trends, as well as to secure pieces to sell in her store.

Tonight Ginger had on a design that had come in only last week. A cute little sleeveless frock with a sweetheart collar. The dark blue of the dress was covered with tiny butterflies.

It wasn't exactly her style, but it was lovely. And it made her feel very feminine.

She'd gone all out, too. Strappy silver heels, makeup, and her hair had never been so cute. Curls bounced at her shoulders. She'd even gotten a manicure that afternoon. Patrick didn't stand a chance.

"There you go." Her mother finished with the eye and patted Ginger on the cheek.

"Everything else look okay?" Ginger asked. Nerves had her suddenly wondering if she *shouldn't* have tried so hard. Was it too much?

She looked down at herself, hoping Patrick liked what he saw, and did a little spin for her mom.

"Perfect," her mother confirmed. She gave Ginger a soft smile, and Ginger expected wise words of wisdom to come from her. Instead, what she got was "Should I make myself scarce tonight? In case you two want to . . ."

"Mom!" Ginger's eyes went wide. "It's only the second date."

Which didn't mean she hadn't seriously considered bringing out the cute underwear.

But on the off chance that she was tempted to toss her morals out the window, she'd left the lace in her dresser drawer. She preferred cotton undies anyway. And with the nerves she had going on, she needed all the comfort she could get.

"Well, it's not like you're getting any younger," her mom pointed out. "And he did seem to really like you the other night." She cast a shrewd eye at Ginger. "You liked him, too, right?"

"I did." Ginger answered without thinking, but at the words she stopped and gave the question serious consideration.

Sure, she liked Patrick. He was nice and had good manners. And he was easy on the eyes. What wasn't to like? But it wasn't as if she'd been swept off her feet.

As her mom had just pointed out, though, she wasn't getting any younger. This fact, and the lack of *ever* being swept off her feet, had led her to wonder if that was purely an embellished teenage emotion. Was real life . . . *mature* love . . . calmer?

She hoped not. It was a sad thought.

"Yes," she reiterated, this time with a nod. "I liked him. He was great."

He was certainly better than any other option that had crossed her path lately.

"Then have fun," her mom said. "And don't worry so much." She kissed Ginger on the cheek, and Ginger pulled her in for a quick hug.

"Thanks, Mom." Stepping back, she picked up her purse and cell phone and nodded toward the door. "I need to make a call before he gets here. I'll do it outside."

It was after work hours, but she'd been trying to get her contractor to return her calls for three days. Before she completely shut down for the weekend, she intended to give it one more shot. She had to get things moving. She couldn't very well live in a house with no electricity or walls.

Stepping outside, she placed the call, and found herself heading to the side of the porch next to Carter's house while she waited. As the phone rang, she scanned the house, noting that unlike the last two days, the blinds were open. That must mean Julie was home.

"This is Darrin," a man's voice said in her ear.

Relief raced through her. "Darrin. I'm so glad I got you. This is Ginger Atkinson. The house on—"

"On Beachview," Darrin finished for her. "Yeah. What can I do for you?"

Unless the man never listened to his voice messages, that was a ridiculous question. She'd left three that week telling him what he could do for her.

"I need to get the house finished," she stated.

"Sure." She heard him flipping pages. "We've got a job to finish up first, but I could have a crew out there by the middle of November."

"November?" she screeched. She tossed her purse in a chair and paced the length of the porch. "But I need to move in in six weeks."

"Well, then . . . hmmm . . ."

More pages flipped.

"That seems to be a problem," he finally said.

"Two months before you can start is definitely a problem," Ginger grumbled. "My mother's new husband will be moving in *here* at the end of next month. I have to be out by then."

"I heard about your mother's engagement. Tell her congratulations for me, will you?"

She ground her teeth together and retraced her steps. "Tell her yourself. When you get back to work on my house."

"I'm sorry, Ginger, but that's just not possible right now. We had to move on."

Dang it. She knew she'd caused delays, but Darrin had known she would need it completed eventually. What good was an unfinished house?

"Should I put it on the calendar?" he asked.

Panic squeezed her chest. What else could she do? "Yes," she muttered.

They said their good-byes, and she palmed the phone. Maybe she could rent a place until it was done. Truth be told, she probably should have rented a place and moved out years ago.

The Ridley door opened, and she watched as Carter came out, said something to his sister, then stomped to the car. Frustration was evident on his face, but the thing that pulled Ginger's attention the most was that he looked . . . good.

Like . . . *good*. Had he looked like that the other day?

She remembered thinking he was too thin. And she'd been shocked to see him, so maybe she hadn't paid that much attention. And he'd smelled vaguely of cigarette smoke.

But dang, his jeans fit his body well tonight.

The sight reminded her of what he'd looked like as a teenager. When most of the other boys were just starting to fill out, he'd already had that part handled. And every girl in school had been aware of it.

She'd had his attention on occasion, only because they'd been friends for years, but she'd never had the kind of attention she'd wanted. She'd been so jealous of the girls he'd dated.

Carter looked up then, as if he could feel her watching him, and when his gaze landed on her, he did a double take. His eyes narrowed as he scrutinized her, and when she waved, he only frowned. Which made her smile.

When had the man become so grumpy?

And what had caused him to be that way?

The last question hit her more seriously. It had crossed her mind a few times over the past several days. He most certainly wasn't the same guy he'd been in high school. Back then, he'd been a joy to be around. And a gentleman to boot. Every girl he hung with would rave about how much fun he was. How considerate. How he rarely had a bad thing to say about anyone.

But it hadn't just been his fun factor, he'd truly been a happy person. He'd conquered optimism and held it by the reins.

He and Ginger used to meet up before daylight most mornings. They'd watch the sun rise together while doing nothing more than talking. Many mornings it would be about whatever had happened the night before, or the day before at school. She even heard about his dates. Although, never the naughty bits—which she'd been grateful for.

They'd talked about their hopes and dreams. They'd spent countless hours outlining the lives that lay before them. And they'd both known exactly what they'd wanted.

Hers hadn't turned out at all like she thought. She wondered if his had.

She also wondered if he still had a wife. There had been no sign of one. Was that the reason for his seemingly permanent snarl? Or was he simply unhappy with life in general these days? The thought saddened her. She may not have seen him in years, but that didn't keep her from caring about an old friend.

Patrick pulled up then, and she ignored Carter to focus on her date and his late-model BMW. She couldn't help but wonder if flute sales were good enough to support that vehicle, because it was one fine ride. Or if, instead, the car might belong to his mother.

When he stepped from the driver's-side door, she decided she didn't care. He was hot.

She remembered her purse at the last minute and snagged it off the porch chair, then tossed one more wave to Carter for good measure. Again, he only frowned.

When Patrick caught sight of her and did the same double take as Carter, she warmed.

That's right. I'm looking good tonight.

I've got this date in the bag.

CHAPTER SIX

She'd had nothing in the bag.

Frustration for the way the night before had ended once again burned through Ginger's body, bringing with it the sting of tears. She managed to hold them off, just barely, but it was only a matter of time.

What had she done wrong?

She brought her knees to her chest and wrapped her arms around her legs, ignoring the fact that the rock she sat on was damp from the dew that had collected overnight and that the dampness had seeped through her leggings.

The gray-blue of the presunrise morning sat before her, the waves rolling as the tide headed back out to sea, and Ginger gave in and let the tears fall. She'd come out to what she considered "her rock" this morning, needing to see the sun come up. She needed to know that the world was beautiful. That elsewhere, others were seeing the same start to the day. That—*hopefully*—at least one person watching this view didn't have as pathetic a life as hers.

Or maybe the entire world sucked for everyone.

Who needed a man, anyway? Especially a man who lived with his mother and made flutes?

For that matter, who needed a contractor?

Well, she did, she supposed.

Gravel crunched on the pull-off up the hill behind her, and as if the last ten-plus years hadn't passed, she instinctively knew who'd arrived. The knowledge soothed her in a way that surprised her. It would be Carter. Because this wasn't just her spot, it was theirs. It was where they'd watched sunrises together from a young age.

She wiped at her eyes, removing evidence of the tears.

"Ah, hell," Carter muttered behind her. She'd walked over instead of driving, so he wouldn't have had warning that he wasn't alone when he first pulled up. Both his tone and his words made her smile. Misery loves company and all that. And if ever there was a miserable person in this world, it seemed to be the man who'd just shown up.

She patted the spot beside her, not wasting the energy to look at him. "Don't even think about leaving," she said. "Come join me."

"I didn't figure you still came out here." His feet shuffled through the brush.

"And I didn't think you came out from behind those closed blinds," she replied when he stopped shy of the rock she sat on. She peeked over her shoulder, noticed that he still wore the jeans he'd had on the night before, and lifted a brow. From the rumpled condition of his clothes, he'd slept in them. And from his bloodshot eyes, he'd done a lot of drinking before that.

"Long night?" she asked.

"Long life," he countered.

He came closer, stopping beside her, but he still didn't sit. He held a plastic grocery bag in his hand, and she went back to staring at the horizon. She remained as silent as he. She wasn't in a good mood, and if he didn't want to talk, she certainly wouldn't encourage him to do so.

"Why are you here?" It surprised her when he spoke. "As dressed up as you were last night, I figured the date would still be going on."

"Yeah, well . . ." Her throat threatened to close. "As you can see, it's not."

And she had no idea where it had gone wrong.

The date had started off great. They'd been talking, she'd been looking good. She'd laughed in all the right places, and made sure she stroked his ego a time or two. She'd been at the top of her game. But halfway through dinner he'd seemed to lose interest. Just like that. Poof. He couldn't care less.

She'd continued to try, bringing up interesting topics and making sure she kept her attention focused on him. She'd even invited him in for a nightcap—though it would have stopped at that. But he hadn't been interested. Said he had to be somewhere early this morning. Then he'd given her a friendly hug . . . and he'd almost squealed tires getting out of there.

"So it didn't go well?" Carter tried again.

Ginger sighed. "What do you want, Carter? Why are you here?" She was not in the mood to talk about the sad state of her dating life.

He settled in beside her. "Came to watch the sunrise."

"Then watch it." *And leave me alone.*

They both grew silent, and as she stared out at the pale light spreading its reach over the horizon, Carter pulled a pack of cigarettes from his bag. He lit one, and she bit her lip to keep from calling him an idiot. Wasn't he aware that those things could kill him?

Not to mention they were just nasty. She wouldn't have thought he'd become a smoker.

"Maybe you should have played a little harder to get," he suggested.

She clenched her teeth to hold in the growl of frustration. What did he know about it? But she found herself turning to him anyway, curiosity winning out. If he had suggestions, maybe she should—

He blew out a stream of smoke as their gazes met.

"That's disgusting." She wrinkled her nose.

"That's what I hear."

His eyes were an intense mix of greens and browns, and with a thick frame of eyelashes and the way they sat deep in the sockets, they held an air of mystery. And a serious side of sexy.

Only, today they just looked angry.

He picked up his bag again, and rummaged inside it. What he pulled out that time was a beer and a bottle opener. He held the beer out in front of her. "Want to ream me about this bad habit, too?"

"Are you kidding me? The sun isn't even up yet."

"I know. Want one?"

She gawked at him.

He ignored her and popped the top, then took a long drink before putting the cigarette back to his lips. Her subconscious nagged at her to pay attention. To look beyond the obvious. This wasn't the Carter she'd once known. What was going on with him?

But she didn't care if he had bad habits or not. He could fill his lungs with cancer and drink his liver into rot. She was too busy feeling sorry for herself to waste time worrying about him.

"What did you mean?" she asked.

When he lifted a brow, she clarified, "What you said about me playing harder to get. I'm not *easy*. I didn't—"

"I didn't mean you were *easy*." He took another drag on his cigarette. "Not that I know about that one way or another."

"I'm not," she repeated.

She waited for him to say more, but instead, he took another drink. His stubbled jaw was set and hard, and her irritation increased the longer he remained silent. Was she really willing to take advice from a man she hadn't seen in years? One who looked to need more than a bit of advice himself?

Apparently so.

"*What* did you mean?" she asked again.

He blew out the smoke that had been swirling in his lungs, still taking his time, and when his gaze landed on her once again, he flicked a glance over her body before bringing it to her face. "I mean . . . do you really dress like that these days?"

She looked down at herself. "Like what?"

"Like you were last night. All dolled up, looking more plastic than real."

"I looked *good*!"

"You didn't look like you. I'll bet you even had a high-pitched giggle going, even if he wasn't funny."

Anger shoved its way to the head of the class. She had not giggled. Much.

And she'd worked darned hard fixing herself up. "I looked like me," she informed him. "It was just a better version of me." The version that didn't look like a fishing-boat captain. Guys wanted girls who smelled like flowers. Not fish.

Which reminded her, she needed to buy more perfume. She'd had to use her mom's last night, but it smelled too perfumey for her.

Was that what had turned Patrick off? He didn't like her smell?

Carter was still watching her, and she braced herself for a snide comment. He had the air of someone who was only capable of snide these days. Yet when he asked, "Are you sure?" in a brutally honest voice, it shredded her insides.

He didn't understand. This was what women did. They primped for dates. They put their best foot forward. They freaking giggled even when the jokes weren't funny.

"Forget it," she muttered. She'd been right the first time. She didn't want to talk about the sad state of her dating life.

He took another drink of beer and went back to the sunrise, and she once again hugged her knees tight. The sky was changing now, from all blues to showing some pinks. Clouds were also blossoming with pinks and oranges, and several paddleboarders could be spotted in the water.

There was something about this time of day. When everything was quiet and still. It made the world seem easier. It also made it less scary to voice things she wouldn't normally say.

"He just didn't like me," she said softly. She could feel Carter's gaze trained on her again, but she motioned toward the water. "You'll miss the sunrise."

He took the hint and looked away. "What didn't he like?"

"If I knew that, I'd fix it."

The top edge of the sun popped out from behind the ocean, and she held her breath. It was magnificent. Color filled the sky just above the water, and sprays of sunshine shot light through the clouds.

"He must have liked you if he asked you out," Carter pointed out.

That's what she'd thought, too. She didn't answer—she couldn't or she'd cry again.

The sun continued its climb, and as the bottom curve clung to the ocean for the last few seconds, she could feel her heart thudding. But the anticipation wasn't solely for the start of a new day. It was for this moment, with this man. She had her friend beside her again.

The two of them had watched many sunrises together in the past. From this very spot. Those mornings had been special, but she hadn't realized how much so until now. It was nice having someone experience the beginning of the day with you. Nice knowing you weren't alone.

Whatever had brought Carter out this morning, she could feel his need to experience the beauty before them. Just as he could certainly feel hers.

The fact that he would soon leave town as abruptly as he'd shown up tugged on the edges of her heart, bringing with it the urge to cling to this moment. To have her friend in her life—to have *someone* in her life—for more than the fifteen minutes of a sunrise.

The sun released its hold on the water and glided smoothly into the morning sky, and she turned to Carter. "Do you want to see my house?"

He didn't look at her. "You have a house?"

"I'm in the process of building it."

His jaw worked for several seconds while his gaze remained on the horizon, and when he spoke, the torment that came through in his tone was so pronounced that it transferred to her. "I just built one myself."

He turned to her then. There was much left unsaid in his words; she could tell. But she didn't ask.

"And, yes. I would love to see your house. We can take my car."

She gave him a comforting smile as they stood, and they began the trek up the hill. They moved beside each other—as if it were only yesterday that they'd taken this same path—and she soon bumped her shoulder into his. "I'm glad you're home, Carter."

He nodded, but didn't speak.

It was enough. He'd missed their sunrises, too, she could tell. He didn't have to voice it.

When they reached the pull-off, she looked at him full on for the first time that morning. The sun streaked across the land now, and his face was no longer in shadow. And she would swear that he was different than when he'd first driven up.

His eyes didn't look quite so forlorn. His shoulders not so weighted down.

A good sunrise had that kind of power over a person, she knew from years of experience. Sharing it with a friend only helped.

She held out her hand. "I may be glad to see you, but not enough to let you drive. You look like you haven't slept"—she nodded to his hand—"and you're halfway through a beer."

He chuckled then, one small vibrato without benefit of a smile, and the sound almost stopped her heart. It was dry and hoarse, as if his vocal cords had tried out the action after months of lying dormant. The effect was that she instinctively wanted to help. She wanted to give him a reason to smile. To laugh. Only, she had no idea what he needed. She didn't know what he'd been through.

He handed his keys over without question, and she rounded the hood. Before opening the door, she looked across the top of the car at him. He poured out his beer and snubbed out his cigarette on the gravel beneath his feet. Then he stood straight and faced her.

The two of them stared across the expanse, the black sedan sitting between them, each taking the other in. After a few seconds, Ginger spoke. "Are you okay?"

He didn't ask what she meant. His mental state? His personal well-being?

Would whatever he was going through suck him under, or would he be able to pull through?

"I'm better at this moment than I've been in four months," he finally replied.

The breath she'd been holding released, and as she slid into the car, the clench around her heart eased. It might not be a lot, but his answer had just gone a long way in making up for the very crappy ending to her night.

~

Carter lowered the passenger's window as they headed down the road. It was Sunday morning, and it felt as if the two of them had the entire island to themselves.

Had he been looking for this when he'd climbed into his car and driven over for the sunrise? Had he known Ginger would be there? Or had he just hoped?

He'd been home for only a couple of hours that morning, after spending the evening at a bar and the predawn hours sobering up with a long walk. But when he'd arrived at the house, he'd been unable to make himself go in. Instead, he'd sat on the front porch and thought about his life.

How had he gotten to this place?

That question had badgered him for months. Since the moment his wife had opened the door to her Manhattan apartment and he'd known instantly that their marriage was over.

He'd followed the rules. He'd played the game right.

Top-notch college, glowing reports from jobsites, plaques showcasing charitable donations. He'd been a kind and understanding husband. Lisa had gotten all the space she'd needed to work on her career, while he'd steadily built his name in the engineering field—remaining patient concerning his status as an author until their finances were secure. He'd made no missteps. Yet here he sat. Alone. Miserable.

And pissed.

And yeah, maybe his marriage hadn't been perfect, but whose was?

"There it is." Ginger lifted a hand and pointed off into the distance, and Carter pulled his head from the past. He saw the house then . . . and he was impressed.

"Nice location," he said. It was on a slight rise, overlooking the ocean.

"Right?" She glowed with pride. "My dad purchased the land years before he died. He'd planned to build a new house for him and Mom as the business grew, but he never got to do it."

She slowed and turned off the main road before picking her story back up.

"After he passed, Mom refused to think about taking the insurance money and building. She said she loved *their* house too much to do anything with this property. It's the home they'd always lived in together."

She glanced at him, and he remembered how much her parents had loved each other. They'd reminded him of his parents in that respect, but where his parents had two kids to devote their time and attention to, the Atkinsons had only Ginger. And she'd been a total daddy's girl.

"Do you still miss him?" he asked.

She nodded. Her smile grew tight, and her chest rose with a deep breath. "All the time."

They pulled into the driveway, and a few seconds later stopped beside the house. He whistled under his breath.

"It's not finished," she warned. "On the inside." She opened her door. "Mom deeded the property over to me on my twenty-first birthday. Which was also the same year I decided that running Daddy's business wouldn't be temporary."

They climbed from the car, and when her eyes landed on the pack of cigarettes in his hand, she gave him the same withering look that had crossed her face at the rock.

"No smoking in my house," she informed him.

He eyed the pack, unaware it had been in his hand, before tossing it back into the car. On their way up the sidewalk, he returned to talk of the house. "What made you build now? Was it simply a matter of having the money?"

That hadn't been it for him. It had been *time* to build. He'd reached all his other goals, and he'd been ready for kids.

Ginger didn't respond immediately, and when they reached the base of the steps, they turned as one to take in the view. It was breathtaking. Ocean as far as the eye could see, the beach spread out before them. And to the north, the outline of another barrier island.

Her house didn't sit too high above sea level—no land on the island did—but he could imagine the view from the top floor. That was what he'd wanted for his office.

Ginger put her back to the ocean and faced him, her chin tilting up. "I turned thirty this year," she explained. "And I decided that it was time to take my life into my own hands. To quit sitting around, waiting for things to happen."

Things to happen? He pictured the desolation that had surrounded her that morning. The BMW she'd gotten into last night. "Like a man?" He asked the question with uncertainty.

"A man"—she lifted her palms—"kids. There are no prospects on the horizon, and now even Mom is getting married." She glanced at the house. "And my house isn't finished," she mumbled. "It's my own fault. It would have been done last month if I hadn't dragged my feet."

She whirled around suddenly, apparently having said all she intended to on the matter, and marched up the waiting steps. Carter simply watched. When she reached the top, she unlocked the door, then looked back to where he remained.

So many things warred in his mind—why had she stalled on the house? Was she upset that her mother was getting married? And why would she ever sit around waiting on a husband?

He settled on asking about something else entirely. The subject that he found the most interesting at the moment. "Did you know your butt is wet?"

She reached behind her and swiped at her rear. "The rock was damp. Yours probably is, too."

"Maybe. But I'm not looking at *my* butt."

She made a face at him. "Well, quit looking at mine."

She stepped to the side, blocking her backside with the column of the porch. But he'd already made up his mind. He would *not* quit looking at her behind. Mostly because *it* was as nice as her legs.

He took the steps two at a time until they were eye level, and he zeroed in on her. "Nope," he said. Then he entered her house.

Ginger came in behind him. She shot him a quizzical look, but instead of responding to his comment, she fell into step beside him, and together they toured the structure. The studs were up, but no walls. He didn't know what final touches she might choose—the colors and trim—but he could "see" the house as clearly as if he'd drawn the blueprint for it himself. It was almost like walking through his own.

"The kitchen—"

"Will be in the back corner," he finished for her, moving in that direction without waiting. "With the eat-in area . . ." He saw it then, in the same spot as his. "Sitting in a bay window so you can have breakfast while watching the sun rise."

She had the view of the beach, while he had the city. But both houses faced east.

She stepped into the area with him, and pointed out the side door. "And if the weather is nice, all I have to do is take the steps down to the beach."

"Perfect," he murmured.

They finished the first floor before moving to the second, and everywhere he turned, Carter either fell in love with a feature she planned, or he suggested one she had yet to think of. When they entered the master bedroom, the closet plans he'd drawn up that morning came to mind. Since he and Julie were redoing the kitchen—a gift his dad would most enjoy—he'd decided to add in something for his mom, as well. A walk-in closet. The work would have minimal effect on the overall time line.

"Just so you know," he began, "and so you don't try to take me out with Mace again, I'll be staying in town longer than I'd originally planned. At least until Mom and Dad get home. Julie's kitchen remodel has to be completed, and I . . ." He paused as a bird swooped past the glass, grabbing his attention, and he ended up taking in the expanse of ocean out the wide back windows. There were shrimp boats on the horizon and a cruise ship even farther out. And the sun was so bright that the ocean glistened like rippled ice. He'd missed this, he realized.

His pulse kicked up. He'd missed the ocean. He'd missed being home.

He didn't want to admit that *he* wanted to stay, too. It felt weak after being gone for so long. But he did. He wanted to be right where he was for the next few weeks. Maybe longer. His house would still be waiting on him—*still empty*—when he returned. But right now he wanted to be here.

Bringing his gaze back inside the windows, he checked out the workmanship around them, and casually finished with "I think Julie might need me to be here for a while."

"And you might need to be here, too?" Ginger suggested quietly.

He shot her a quick look. Had he given that away on his face? "Julie needs me," he repeated. He wondered if Ginger would voice her suspicions again. It would be just like her. But instead she merely smiled.

And he decided that he'd missed her smiles, too.

"You should have been back before now," she told him. Her smile disappeared.

"I know."

She was right. He'd stayed away too long. He had little excuse.

"And I don't just mean to see your parents," she continued. "This summer, too. For Julie. She's been here all alone, Carter. And you're her big brother. You should have been here for her."

"I do have my own life," he pointed out.

"I know. Somewhere up north. You're a civil engineer, right?"

"Rhode Island." He ignored the question.

"Which isn't close, I get that. It's not easy to swing by and check on her, and I'm sure you've been busy. Vacation days have to be worked out and all that. But your parents are on the other side of the world."

"They were here last month," he told her. They'd stopped by before coming to see him.

"For one day."

He stared at her, unwilling to show guilt in either words or expression. Maybe he should have visited Julie over the summer, but the truth was, he hadn't given it that much thought. He'd assumed she was fine. And *he* hadn't been.

"You couldn't be bothered to check on her at least once?" Ginger pushed.

He let out a long sigh. "I'm here now, Red. Did you miss that? And I've talked to her on the phone plenty of times. She's fine. She's been fine."

Except she cries most nights.

Ginger nodded. "Okay."

He took her single-word answer to mean that she meant a hell of a lot more than *okay*. "She *is* an adult," he informed her. "And I'm not her keeper."

"I know that, too."

He growled. "And it's not like *I* had anything to do with her pregnancy."

She shot him a dry look. "You think? And I know, it's none of my business. Go ahead and say it. I shouldn't have brought it up. But I've been worried about her, Carter. And now . . . with the way the kitchen looked. It's just that she seems so young sometimes. So alone."

"She is young." *And alone.* "But it's not like I've been sitting in my shiny new house doing nothing."

Actually, it had been exactly like that. Heaviness pressed in on his chest, and with it came the urge to unload some of his burdens. Would doing so ease any of his pain? He couldn't see where it would.

"Can this conversation be over now?" he asked. "I'm here. I'm staying until Mom and Dad get home. And badgering me about the past few months is doing nothing but pissing me off."

"I suspect you've been pissed off for months," she grunted under her breath. But she shut up and turned away, and her words had the surprising effect of making him want to smile.

This was the Ginger he remembered. Not the one mooning over some man. His Ginger had always spoken her mind, had dressed for comfort, and hadn't cared one whit what anyone else thought of her. She'd been romantic, yes. And she'd wanted "the perfect boyfriend." He remembered conversations where she'd glaze over with talk of some imagined future man of her dreams. But he'd never thought she'd change herself to get him.

She'd been the type to laugh and enjoy every minute of every day, knowing that instead of forcing her plans, life would happen as it was supposed to.

He'd known that once, himself. So why had it turned out the way it had?

He'd never forced anything. He'd met Lisa in college, they'd fallen in love, and their lives had set up the way they were supposed to.

Only he was now divorced. And his wife wasn't.

He wanted to confirm Ginger's suspicions about his mood. That yes, he'd been pissed off for months. He wanted to tell her that life sometimes bit you in the ass when you least expected it, and that maybe she should be glad the BMW hadn't been interested. This way she could keep her heart intact. Along with her dignity.

But he didn't say any of that. Instead, he led the way to the stairs and headed up. At the top, he made a right into the only room on the floor. A space he presumed would be the office. He crossed to the small balcony with the expansive view of the water, and as he stepped onto the landing, he sucked in a deep breath of ocean air. He could write here.

His pulse sped up.

That was the first seed of desire for putting fingers to keyboard that he'd had in months.

Ginger stepped onto the balcony beside him, standing silently, and together they watched the world. It felt as if they did this all the time.

"Your home is beautiful," he told her.

"Thank you."

He couldn't bring himself to apologize for his shitty mood, nor did he believe she expected it. As she always had, she seemed to accept him as he was. "When will it be finished?"

She made a small snorting noise, and crossed to the opposite side of the platform. Putting her hands on the railing, she leaned over and peered down. Her features scrunched up in distaste. "The contractor can't get back out here for two months," she told him, "but I need to be in before Mom's wedding."

"Which is when?"

"Six weeks." She straightened and looked at him.

"Ouch."

"Tell me about it." She leaned back against the railing. "I'll make more calls, see if I can find anyone else to do the work, but at this point, I figure it'll be next year before it's done. I'll find a temporary place to rent until then. It's not ideal"—she shrugged—"but then . . . I should have finished it when it was first built."

She'd mentioned her delay in finishing earlier.

"Why didn't you?" he asked.

Her gaze shifted away. "Fear of making the wrong decisions?"

The words came out as a question, not an answer. "So change it later," he suggested. "It's your house; you can do whatever you want with it. *Whenever* you want."

"I know." She glanced quickly at him. "But it's not just that."

"Then what else?"

When she looked away again, he said her name, and she brought her gaze back to his.

Several breaths later, she uttered a reply. "I didn't want to have to move in here alone." The words were spoken softly, and he heard the vulnerability in them. And he suddenly got it.

This house . . . at this moment . . . was important. It was "the house." He understood that, because he'd just built his own. This house needed to be right. It signified an importance in her life. Her next step.

He thought about the BMW. The fact she'd said she was "moving on with her life."

She'd been waiting for a husband to help make the decisions on this house. He'd done the same thing. Decisions about his own had been made with Lisa—or with Lisa in mind. Having her be a part of it had been vital to him.

"Moving forward doesn't mean what you want is out of reach," he found himself telling her—as if he were an expert on the subject. "It just means that you've moved forward."

And it probably wouldn't hurt him to take a step or two in the same direction.

"But what if there's no going back?" she asked. "This wasn't how it was supposed to happen. What if I move forward and everything else I want gets left behind?"

The slightness of her voice made him want to pull her into his arms.

"Then you find new wants."

She stared at him, seconds ticking away before she spoke again. "And what if I don't like what I find?"

He didn't have an answer for that, because he didn't like what *he'd* found.

His life was not where it was supposed to be, and he couldn't shake his anger about it. He was drinking, smoking, and basically hating anything and everything in his world, and that wasn't a way he'd ever imagined spending his years.

"I'll help you," he said, and her eyes widened slightly.

"With what?"

"The house. I know some people. They owe me a few favors. And besides, I already have a crew heading to town for my parents' home. I'll make another call."

She tilted her head as she watched him. "You'd do that for me?"

"Sure."

"Why?"

He didn't really know. They weren't exactly friends these days. They hadn't seen each other in years. Yet he sensed that like him, she often felt as if she'd been tossed in the middle of the ocean in a sailboat with a broken sail. And a shark had eaten the oars. It was a closeness he remembered having with her from years past. As if they were "one" in some unfathomable way.

"Because I can" was all he said in reply. He didn't have a better answer.

Her brain finally seemed to click into gear, and she nodded. Slowly at first, then her tongue darted out to wet her lips, and her eyes took on a glow. "Do you think it would be possible to get it done before the wedding?"

"Six weeks?" He stared at the house that sat before them, and knew he wanted to make that work for her. He'd have to call in more than one favor. And they'd need a *lot* of people out here. But he'd pull those strings. It would feel good to do so. "We can if you get busy making decisions."

Her head nodded rapidly. "I will. I swear."

A smile broke across her face then, and damned if he didn't have to focus to keep from doing the same.

"Thank you," she gushed. "I owe you. Big-time."

The rush of gratitude that came from her gave him the first real feeling of living in months. He was happy to do this for her, but he also wondered if he wasn't, in a way, doing it for himself.

Did *her* happiness somehow imply that *he* could someday be happy again, too?

He found that he hoped so. Because this anger thing was beginning to wear thin.

CHAPTER SEVEN

I'm telling you, it's a *lot* of men." Ginger bit her lip as she leaned forward and peeked out the kitchen window once again. She'd been doing that on and off for over an hour. "And all hot." She breathed the words into her phone, following them with a very girlish giggle. "And all *right. Next. Door.*"

The sight of the men who'd shown up at the Ridley house that afternoon made her wonder what kind of crew Carter would send out to her house. Because dang. If they looked anything like this, she might have to take the next six weeks off from work just so she could hang around and watch.

"What are they doing now?" Andie said in her ear.

Ginger watched the cutest two, both dark haired, tall, terribly masculine, and very nicely filled out, as they hauled a chunk of the upper cabinets out to the temporary Dumpster that had also shown up that day. "Stripping off their shirts," she fibbed.

"Ohmygod."

She smiled. They might not be literally stripping, but in her mind they certainly were. What a way to cap off an otherwise boring Monday.

"I'm calling a babysitter and catching the next flight down."

Ginger laughed. "Who do you think you're kidding? You've got the man of your dreams already. Right there in your bed every night. Not to mention, you also have his baby."

"Doesn't mean I don't want to catch this show. At least send me a picture."

"Good idea. Hang on."

Ginger took a quick moment, holding her phone out in front of her while at the same time still eyeing every move made by the men next door. There had to be at least eight guys in that one small space. She wondered if some of them would end up at her house.

She zoomed in closer and snapped the picture as yet another dark-haired cutie walked out the front door, but this one looked directly at her. It was Carter.

"Crap." She dropped out of view, squatting in front of the oversized farm sink.

"What happened?" Andie asked. "Did you get the picture?"

"I got caught," she muttered. She banged her forehead against the sink cabinet.

"Oh no."

"By *Carter.*"

"Oh . . ." Andie chuckled in her ear. *"Oops."*

Ginger could picture her friend smiling. They'd already talked about the fact that Carter was home for the next few weeks and that he'd offered to help with the house. And Andie had teased her over the long-ago crush she'd had on him. Ginger had even admitted that they'd watched the sunrise together yesterday morning. Though it had been a friends-catching-up kind of moment, and not anything romantic.

Still, it had been nice.

But he hadn't shown up out there *this* morning.

"Ginger," Andie whispered, as if she were the one hiding below the sink. "What's happening now?"

"I don't know. I'm on the floor." She put her back to the cabinet and settled in, butt on the porcelain tile, legs crossed over each other. No way would she stand back up and look out now.

"At least send me the picture," Andie said.

"Oh, yeah." She'd forgotten about that.

Without hanging up, she pulled up the photos on her phone, chose the one she'd just taken—which had Carter front and center staring straight at her—and texted it over to Andie.

"I got it," Andie said. There was a pause, then Andie hummed under her breath.

"What?"

"He's cute."

Ginger put her phone on speaker and pulled the picture back up. "Ignore Carter. Look at the men in the background. Those are the ones I've been drooling over. They're a little young, but super yummy."

More soft humming could be heard before Andie added, "And you're saying you haven't been drooling over Carter? He grew up nice."

"Carter was always nice. Why do you think I had the hots for him my whole childhood?"

She studied the picture in more detail, and admitted that yeah, he could hold his own with all those other men. In fact, he stood out a little from the rest. There was a strong presence about him.

"Maybe you should go for it with *him*," Andie suggested. "Or is he still married?"

"I have no idea. There isn't a wife here . . ." She wished she'd asked him about his marriage while they'd been at her house, but it hadn't seemed the right time. "And anyway, even if he's not, the man was drinking a beer before the sun came up yesterday morning. And smoking." She made a face. "Not to mention the bad attitude he seems to wear around like a favorite pair of jeans. He's not the Carter he once was."

Not that she'd go for him even if he was the same as he'd been before. He'd never seen her as anything more than a friend when they were kids, and there was no reason to believe that would be any different now. She wouldn't humiliate herself thinking she could get him.

"I *could* go for one of those construction guys, though," she said.

"That you could. Look at the one by the Dumpster with the dimpled chin. Yummmm."

"Right? He was outside when I got in from work. I looked at him . . . he looked at me . . ." Then he'd gone back into the house, but Ginger didn't let that faze her. He'd noticed her. They'd smiled. It had been a moment.

"Hey, wait. No one has their shirts off!" Andie sounded offended in her outburst, and Ginger couldn't help but giggle. Man, she missed her friends living close by. If Andie were still on the island, she'd be sitting in the middle of the kitchen floor with Ginger right now. Roni would be there, too.

But at least she had this.

She and Andie had talked over the weekend, with Ginger providing details of her mother's upcoming nuptials—and garnering a promise that Andie would make it down for the event—but Ginger had chosen *not* to express the jealousy she'd been struggling with concerning the wedding. It was a petty emotion, and she was mostly over it. Plus, she was focused on her house now.

And soon she'd have her house done . . . and maybe someday a man . . .

"So what's he like?" Andie asked. "Other than drinking and smoking."

"Carter?"

The phone was still on speaker, since she was alone in the house. It freed up her hands to finger wave at Mz. Lizzie when she poked her head around the corner of the door. Mz. Lizzie looked the other way.

"I don't know." Ginger eyed the cat suspiciously, and patted the floor. Just once she'd like it if the cat acknowledged her existence. "He seems . . . sad, I guess. And lonely. He doesn't talk a lot, and I haven't seen him smile at all."

"Kids?"

Ginger blew out a breath. "I really don't know more than that, Andie. I know he's here to check on Julie because his mom asked him to, and that he's staying until the Ridleys get home in a few weeks."

"Awww . . . he came because his mom asked him to?"

Ginger ignored the swoony tone Andie had taken. "Julie's been here alone all summer. He should have come home weeks ago." Or years ago, to visit his parents.

"But at least he's there now."

"Sure. At least he's here now." And Ginger wouldn't admit it, but he'd been on her mind all day. She couldn't keep from wondering what had happened to him. He was so different from before. Did it have to do with whatever had happened four months ago?

I'm better now than I've been in four months.

Her heart pounded with the memory, same as it had when he'd said it. Did whatever happened four months ago have anything to do with his wife? Ex-wife?

Or was something totally different the problem?

"I have some news," Andie said, pulling Ginger from her thoughts of Carter.

Ginger quit trying to attract the cat. "Good or bad?"

"Good."

"Don't tell me you're already pregnant again."

Andie snorted. "*No.* This kid has kicked my butt. Another one can wait."

"Okay, then lay it on me."

"I'll be down there next weekend," Andie casually said. "On Saturday. As will Roni."

"Are you kidding me?" Ginger shot to her feet, causing Mz. Lizzie to launch herself down the hallway. "Why?"

As if it mattered. She was thrilled anytime she got to see her friends.

"Kayla worked it out, and Roni's adding one last concert to the tour. It'll be on Turtle Island."

"Seriously?"

"Yes. Even though she played at the convention center earlier in the summer, since the show sold out so quickly, Kayla's been working with Roni's manager to add another stop on the tour. They made it happen yesterday. So it looks like we get a girls' night even before your mother's wedding."

Gratitude filled Ginger's chest. Whether there was a man by her side or not, her life was good. She had the best friends a girl could want.

"Girls' night." She nodded, and darned if tears didn't fill her eyes. She needed a girls' night so badly. "My house won't be ready yet, but let's do it out there anyway. Carter said the electricity and plumbing would go in fast, and everything else we can wing."

"That's just what I was thinking. I need to see this house."

"You do." Ginger nodded again, and turned to face the window. Carter was no longer outside, but there were still several men coming and going. And one *did* have his shirt off now. He was quite sweaty. She smiled at the sight.

"I also need to see Carter in person," Andie added.

"Why?"

"Duh, Ginger. You had it bad for that man. Are you seriously telling me that's truly all gone?"

Ginger stared down at the phone in her hand. "I had a teenage *crush*."

"Yeah, but—"

"But nothing. It was a crush. There's nothing now."

"But I'll bet there could be."

Her friend had lost her mind.

"Just find out if he's married," Andie insisted.

"Why?"

A sigh sounded so loudly through the phone that it seemed to fill the room. "Because you won't know if you can jump his bones until you *know*."

"I have no intention of 'jumping his bones.'"

"Keep an open mind. You never know."

Ginger shook her head. She knew. Not only was Carter not interested in her, but she wasn't interested in him. He clearly had too much baggage. His construction crew, on the other hand . . .

She took one more peek outside—she really had to find an excuse to go over there—then turned from the window and slumped back against the sink. And that's when she realized that she was no longer alone in the room. Carter stood with one foot inside the kitchen, just on this side of the laundry-room door.

Her heart thundered in her chest, and she jerked her gaze to the phone. What had he heard?

"I have to go," she said quickly. She jabbed at the screen, hanging up on Andie before hearing whatever her friend might have said next. Then she stood there, eyes wide as she stared at Carter, pretending she hadn't just been talking about jumping his bones.

"You had a crush on me?" he asked. He seemed as confused as she was mortified.

Without looking in a mirror, she knew she'd turned bright red. It was the curse of her fair skin. "No," she said the word adamantly, but when he continued staring at her, she corrected to "Maybe. A little. But it was a long time ago. Before high school, even."

"I didn't know."

"You weren't supposed to know." Good grief. "It's no big deal. Really. You were cute. I was right next door. Of course I had a crush."

She didn't point out that she'd been right next door, too, but he had *not* had a crush.

But then, she'd been pudgy and even weirder around guys than she was now. And she'd never been naturally girly. No wonder he hadn't been interested.

She crossed her arms, loosely gripping her elbows, and when he continued doing nothing but training those hazel eyes on her, she gave him a bored look to cover her embarrassment. "Did you want something? Or did you just come over to see if the back door was unlocked?"

He looked at her phone for a second—where she still gripped it in her hand. Which was now at chest level. A tiny wrinkle formed on his brow before he finally brought his gaze back to hers. She felt an involuntary flutter inside her chest when their eyes met.

"Sorry," he finally grunted out. He motioned to the back door. "I knocked, but I guess you didn't hear."

He looked at her phone once again, and with his eyes trained in the general area of her chest, her nipples woke up. She felt them tighten behind her T-shirt as if vying for his attention. She ignored this fact and gave him a pointed look. He cleared his throat, and his vision locked on her face. Only her face. Clearly, he'd noticed her reaction.

Great.

"I came to see if you'd be available to meet with my foreman out at the house tomorrow," Carter finally said. "He's heading up the team next door, but will manage the work at your house, as well."

One of the guys from next door would be working on her house?

Without thinking, she turned to look out the window. Which one? The one with the dimple?

"None of those guys are right for you," he said. His voice was gruff and snarly.

"What?" She turned back to him.

85

"I see the look on your face, and I remember what you were like. All romantic and stuff. Get it out of your head. None of them are what you're looking for."

"How do you know what I'm looking for?" Her entire body heated. How much more embarrassment could she take today?

"You're looking just to get laid, then?" he asked.

The temperature of her face went nuclear.

"I didn't think so." He crossed his arms over his chest, and as if the action had called out to Mz. Lizzie, the darned cat came running, trotting right up to his leg. She edged against the dusty denim and rubbed herself all over him like the little harlot that she was.

Ginger narrowed her eyes at the cat, but Carter didn't seem to notice the animal at all.

"Tomorrow?" he asked. "You available or not?"

She mentally ran through her schedule. There were a couple of fishing expeditions lined up, but she wasn't on the books to take either of them. In fact, she'd planned a day of catching up on paperwork before spending time online, perusing kitchen cabinets and countertops. If the house was going to get finished, there were a lot of choices to be made.

"As long as nothing changes at work, I'm available whenever you need me," she said.

Poor choice of words on her part—he clearly didn't *need* her—but he didn't seem to notice.

"Ten o'clock?" he asked. "We'll meet you at the house and do a walk-through. You can tell Gene what you're thinking, and the guys will start working out there next week."

Again, she peeked out the window, and this time she heard him sigh.

The frustrated sound made her smile, but before she could come up with anything witty to say, the back door slammed and he was gone.

~

Ginger wheeled the company truck in front of her house, hurrying so as not to be late. She didn't want to make a worse impression than she already would, and at this point, a bad impression was guaranteed. Her car had a flat when she'd come out to leave the office, two fishing boats had needed last-minute work first thing that morning—sending her in a smaller boat to pick up the load of bait so the charters could still leave on time—and she'd ended up pitching in with the mechanical work upon returning. Once she'd stopped for a much-needed breath, she'd seen that she was dirty from top to bottom.

There'd been no time to run home for a change of clothes, but she *had* managed to pull herself together. Slightly.

She looked at herself as she hopped down from her dad's old F-350, and tugged at the bottom edge of her denim shorts. They were the only thing she'd had clean in her car, and they were indecent. When she'd chopped off the legs last summer, she'd taken about three inches too much, leaving them as over-swimsuit-wear only. Except . . . now they weren't.

Since she'd been left with hot pants on her bottom half, she'd grabbed an oversized Sealine Expeditions T-shirt from the gift shop, hoping to hide the fact that if she bent over too far, the cheeks of her rear would hang out. Then she'd donned her trusty pair of green rubber boots because her tennis shoes smelled like the squid that had spilled when transferring the bait.

With the boots to her knees, and bare thighs above, she looked like a deranged stripper.

Oh, well. She was here to work. Not flirt.

She grabbed a hair band from the dash of the truck and twisted the majority to the top of her head. Her hair had even taken some backsplash from the squid. Then a truck pulled up next to hers, and she noticed that it wasn't only Carter and the foreman inside the vehicle. The man with the chin dimple was there, along with the guy who'd taken pride in going shirtless the afternoon before.

Oh, boy.

She sniffed herself unobtrusively. Yep. She smelled like fish. Per usual.

The man she assumed to be the foreman—due to the quick nod of greeting—climbed from the driver's seat while the other two exited from the back. Carter stepped from the passenger side.

Ginger once again tugged at her shorts, and cast a prayer upward that she'd somehow miraculously smell like flowers. Or look like a girl.

The guy with the dimple took in her legs. "Morning, ma'am."

She blushed. Up close she could see that he was definitely too young for her. Which was too bad.

"Ginger." Carter's tone did *not* have the same soft Southern accent as the hottie who'd just spoken to her. "Meet Gene, your foreman."

Gene—she'd guessed correctly—held out his hand. "Looks like quite a house you've got here." He scanned the two and a half stories with interest. "I can't wait to see what you plan to do with the inside."

"Thank you." She shook his hand, then automatically turned to the other two men. She couldn't help the huge smile that covered her face.

Carter scowled at her.

"This is Gregg and Ian," he said. "They *won't* be working out here."

Ian waved a rolled-up sheaf of papers in one hand. "We caught a gander of the plans and took lunch early to ride out an' take a peek. What a beauty you've got here."

She caught herself giving him her "date" smile. "Plans?"

"I got a copy of the drawings from your original contractor," Carter informed her drily. She didn't even look his way.

Gregg stepped up next, and he, too, held out his hand in greeting. His dimple winked from his chin as he angled his head in a nod, and if he'd been wearing a cowboy hat, Ginger suspected he would have tipped it back. Wherever these boys were from, she wanted to visit.

She put her hand in his and enjoyed the warm grasp. He might be too young, but he was very pretty to look at.

"Nice to meet you in person, Miss Ginger." Gregg's voice was a slow rumble. "We saw you at the house yesterday."

Did that mean he'd seen her ogling them?

Probably. But who cared? She'd ogle again. Every day, most likely. Especially if shirts came off. She wasn't too proud.

Once again, Carter scowled at her. "Can we go in?" he snapped. The man truly needed an attitude adjustment.

"Sure." She started to move in front of them, but considered the steps leading up to the front door and the sad state of her shorts, and held the key out to Carter. "You lead the way."

He gave her a funny look, and she noticed his nose wrinkle slightly as if he'd gotten a whiff of her, but he took the key. Then he and the other three men all headed away from her while she took a moment to pull in a deep breath and reorient herself. It was just men. Hot men, yes. But they were there in a work capacity.

While she stunk and looked a hot mess.

But then she remembered the gleam in Gregg's eyes as he'd taken in her legs, and she supposed all wasn't a total loss. At least she'd captured his attention. If she could manage to look presentable the next time she saw him—

"Were you planning to join us?" Carter yelled out at her. He waited on her porch, while the other men had already gone inside.

She rolled her eyes at the surliness the man was so good at, and hurried to the house. As she passed him, she turned a snarky look his way—and was shocked to see that his gaze was also trained on her legs.

Hmmm.

He'd checked out her butt the other day. Did he like what he saw?

Not that it mattered. She once again picked up the stench of cigarette smoke on him, and promptly put any idea of Carter and his probing eyes far from her mind.

The group of them walked through the house with Carter and her both answering Gene's questions, while Gregg and Ian remained mostly quiet. Occasionally they'd toss out an observation or suggestion, but mostly they spent their time admiring the space.

But there *was* the occasional harmless flirt. It was fun.

Before she knew it, all of them were back out of the house and ready to leave. The other men went on ahead to the truck, but Carter lingered as she locked the front door. Once she'd secured the dead bolt, she dropped the key into his hand. "Thank you again for doing this. It means the world to me."

"No problem."

She gave him a bright smile, hoping to see him ease up on the gruffness, but he shifted his gaze from her to the other men. The usual scowl remained on his face. So she gave up. She'd take his help, and save her good moods for someone who cared. She turned and headed for the steps, but he stopped her with a hand to her arm.

"Don't forget, these guys aren't what you're looking for."

She groaned and turned back. "Really, Carter." Where did he get off? "How do you know what I'm looking for? Maybe I *do* just want to get laid."

That shut him up. But only for a moment. "I thought you wanted something permanent. The type of man to move in here when it's done."

She did, but she refused to admit he was right.

Plus . . . heck, maybe she could use a fun night with one of these guys. For certain she could use a fun night with someone. It had been way too long, and with all the testosterone now running rampant in her vicinity, she might have to pick one out to sample.

"These guys might be willing to move in for the night," Carter warned her, "but they won't even stick around for breakfast."

"Good to know." She eyed him steadily. "I'm not a fan of breakfast."

He stared at her, and she'd swear his bad attitude ramped up even more. "Stay away from them, Red."

She laughed then. Loud and freeing. Because it was so funny to her that the guy with such a clearly messed-up life had the audacity to lecture her on who would and would not be right for her. Gene, Gregg, and Ian turned to see what was so funny, while Carter only glared.

"And wear some damned decent pants the next time," he added under his breath.

This time, it was he who moved to descend the stairs first, and it was *she* who stopped him. With words.

"Why don't you ever smile?" When he looked back, she added, "You used to smile all the time. It was one of the reasons I had that crush."

"You looking to have another?"

"Crush on you?" She snorted. "Not quite. I can find better things to waste my time on. But you *were* my friend once." Her tone softened to show the seriousness of her words. She was worried about him. "Are you okay, Carter? You used to be happy. Optimistic." She paused before asking, "What changed you?"

"Who says I've changed?"

"I say you have. And not for the better. Come on, you hide away in the house, shutting out the world any time you can get away with it, and I doubt you've cracked a smile in years. Your frown has created permanent creases in your face."

"It hasn't been years."

"How long? Four months?"

His jaw went rigid.

"What happened four months ago?" she prodded. "You're the one who brought up that date. Clearly you want to talk about it." Maybe that was a stretch, but *she* wanted to talk about it.

His gaze burned a hole through her. "My mistakenly stating a fact out loud does not mean that I hold any interest in talking about it."

"Are you still married?" She tried another subject.

"You asking because your friend told you to?"

He was referring to the conversation he'd overheard between her and Andie, and her cheeks once again grew hot. "I'm asking because I still care about you. And you're obviously in pain."

"Then you can rest assured that there's nothing for you to worry about. I'm fine."

"Are you?"

Truck doors slammed as the men climbed into the vehicle. She and Carter stayed where they were.

"The fact of the matter is, it's none of your business," Carter told her. He dragged his gaze down her body in an intentionally derogatory move. "Unless you're interested in that crush . . ." His words trailed off.

"Really?" She laughed again. "That's your response to me? Trying to intimidate me with sex. You don't scare me, Carter, so stop being a jerk."

A muscle ticked in his jaw, but he didn't leave. After a few more hard seconds of glaring, he took a step back and blew out a breath. "Stop badgering me, will you? I don't need that shit. My mother does it enough."

"Do you talk to her about your problems?"

"Do I look stupid? Hell, no, I don't talk to my mother about my personal shit."

"You need to talk to somebody." She reached out and touched his forearm when he turned to leave again, and as his muscles jerked under her fingers, she realized that was the first time she'd touched him. The tension in his arm didn't frighten her, though. She kept her hand on him while he remained poised for flight. "I'm here," she said. "That's all I'm trying to say. I'm here if you want to talk."

He remained quiet, and not only did the muscle work in his jaw again, but his hands clenched at his sides. He looked at once angry . . . and relieved. Whatever was going on in his life, he needed an outlet.

Everyone needed someone once in a while.

"Electricity and plumbing will go in first," he said, effectively shutting down the conversation. Then he turned and stomped to the truck.

She followed, stopping at the driver's-side door and waiting until Gene rolled down his window. Then she pulled a card from her back pocket. "My number is on the back." She tossed a quick glance at Gregg and Ian. "Call anytime."

As usual, Carter scowled. Then he climbed in and slammed the door.

CHAPTER EIGHT

The never-ending blink of the cursor annoyed Carter the next morning as he sat at the desk he'd rigged up by his bedroom window, trying to will himself to write. He'd written one sentence.

I will not meet Ginger at sunrise.

Which had nothing whatsoever to do with the book he'd sold, and everything to do with what he'd been battling with the last three mornings.

Ever since watching the sun come up with her by his side, he'd wanted to do it again. So much that he'd been awake, showered, and dressed before sunrise each morning. He'd told himself he'd gotten up to write, but today was the first day he'd actually opened his laptop.

Instead, he'd sat by the window, watching for movement from next door. Monday he'd caught sight of her heading down the back deck steps, but yesterday there had been nothing.

This morning . . . the verdict was still out.

He squinted as a light came on in her bedroom. She was up.

Pressing his face nearer to the window so he could see between the curtains and the window frame, he silently watched. As he did, adrenaline began to pump. He let his fingers slide to his keyboard.

She wore rubber boots and shorts that barely covered her ass.

It wasn't the story he was supposed to be writing, but it was words. He kept going.

And she watched him as if she knew the make and model number of every torture device stashed away in his closet . . .

It stunk as far as good horror writing was concerned, but again, he didn't care. Carter continued letting his fingers work. He turned off his brain—not thinking—and typed. And he kept his gaze glued to Ginger's window.

As expected, the light soon went out, and seconds later the back door opened. He caught his breath. He wanted to go with her. The urge to follow came with a desperation he hadn't felt in a long time. Only, along with the desperation, something else teased at the corners of his mind. Something that frightened him. And kept him where he sat.

It also kept him typing.

The idea of meeting up with Ginger for sunrises gave him *hope*. Hope for what, he wasn't sure. But it was there. Tempting him to reach for it.

And there was a part of him that *wanted* to reach for it. To grab it and hold tight.

Yet, there was so much anger still inside him. Anger that didn't feel finished. And no matter how he looked at it, he couldn't see those two emotions sharing the same space.

The moment Ginger's foot hit the dirt path behind her house, she turned back and looked up at his window. Lifting his fingers from the keyboard, he eased the lid to the laptop closed. The screen had been the only illumination in the room, so he was certain she couldn't see him. Yet it felt as if she were staring directly into his eyes. As if she were repeating yesterday's words.

What happened to you, Carter? You used to be happy. You used to smile.

You need to talk to somebody.

Lisa was what had happened to him.

And though he'd stormed away from Ginger the day before when she'd hammered at him about not smiling, and poked for the details about his marriage, he'd realized as he stood there that he *wanted* to talk to someone. To her, specifically. He'd wanted to open the pain he'd kept closed for so many months, and to tell her—to warn her—of all the miserable ways that life could turn on you.

He'd wanted *her* to be as angry at the crap path his life had taken as he was.

But at the same time, he didn't want to do that to her. She believed life could be good. That finding the "perfect man" would make everything all right. Why should he be the one to burst her bubble?

Hopes and dreams were for the birds. Relationships? The very idea was laughable.

But her house could make her happy. The way he saw it, it was the *only* thing that could. So he was willing to do that for her. To help her with her dream home. And he'd keep the rest of his thoughts to himself.

He continued watching until she turned away and eventually disappeared out of sight. His own house would have made him happy if he hadn't built it with Lisa in mind. For *their* hopes. *Their* dreams.

Or, at least for his.

Who the hell knew what Lisa's hopes and dreams were. He certainly had no idea anymore. Had she ever wanted their marriage to work? Had she ever wanted *him*?

How the fuck could he have been so completely wrong about everything they'd ever had?

A soft knock sounded at his door, and he looked over to find his sister standing there in a pale-blue gown down to her knees, backlit by light spilling out from the open bathroom door. Her belly seemed to be expanding every day. On her small frame, it looked painful.

"What?" The word came out more harshly than he'd intended. He straightened, shifting away from the curtain.

"I'll be late getting in tonight." Her gaze flickered to the window, but she wisely didn't point out that he'd been peeking out like a crazed stalker. "There's a benefit dinner for the gallery after we close," she explained. "It'll go until at least ten."

When he didn't immediately answer, she added softly, "You could come if you want to."

"I don't want to." He flinched at the rude tone, and tried again. "No thanks."

After their talk last week, his and Julie's relationship had eased into a simple—but easy—routine, and he was trying not to bite her head off every time they spoke. He often failed.

Their days consisted of him scowling quietly in the early morning darkness until she got up and opened the blinds all over the damned house, then he'd fix her breakfast—he'd insisted the stove remain in the kitchen until the last possible moment—and then she'd get ready and depart for work.

During the days he helped out with the remodel before making sure Julie ate a decent dinner at night, and he finished each evening with a six-pack. A fact Julie must be passing along to their mother, because she *still* checked in on him every day. And more often than not she asked if he'd been drinking.

But even with the lessened stress in the house, he and Julie still bickered. Often about how she worked too hard or should put her feet up. And he wasn't so obtuse that he didn't realize he was the cause of most of the stress. She *had* tried to nudge him out of his mood, though. He'd give her that. She'd brought up interesting topics of conversation in the evenings. She'd dragged out photo albums, and they'd relived past vacations. They'd even worked together to design the new open-concept floor plan the remodel had grown into.

But all of it had been superficial. He still knew nothing about how she'd gotten into the state she was in, and she knew nothing about what had gone wrong between him and Lisa. And though he didn't seem to be willing to put any personal effort into changing that, it bothered him. He wanted to be closer to his sister. But he didn't know how to do that without opening *himself* up.

Julie rubbed a hand over her stomach and yawned. "If you change your mind . . ."

"When are you going to quit working?"

"What?" She lowered her hand.

"You work too hard," he said. "You're exhausted. When are you planning on quitting?"

"I'm not planning on *quitting*. And I don't work too hard." She shot a look at his closed laptop. "Maybe the problem is that you don't work hard enough. Mom mentioned you haven't been writing. Don't you have a book due soon?"

"Mom needs to keep her mouth shut. And we're talking about you, not me. You're seven months pregnant with a baby who has no father. You can't do everything alone. And clearly you can't work after the baby is born. What are you going to do?"

Yes. He was picking a fight. But honestly, it was all he knew how to do these days.

And he *did* succeed in picking it.

Julie flipped on the overhead light as she rushed into his room, her finger raised and pointing at his face. "Worry about your own life, you jerk. My lack of a man has nothing to do with how long I work before delivering. And I'll most definitely return afterward. I don't need a man to make me happy. I can do this on my own."

Good thing she realized that so young. "So you're just going to deliver alone? Raise my niece alone?"

"Unless you want to be there for me," she taunted. "Want to stick around, big brother?"

He jerked back as if slapped.

"I didn't think so." She smirked. "So leave me alone."

She stomped back out of the room, and for some reason, each step that grew between them seemed like a distance he'd never get back. "I'm just worried about you." He raised his voice to stop her. "I disappeared from your life for too many years. I wasn't there to worry. To keep you from . . ."

He waved a hand toward her protruding stomach when she turned back.

"This shouldn't have happened," he finished, and with the words, recognition seemed to fill Julie's face.

"You blame yourself for me being pregnant?" she asked indignantly.

He didn't *blame* himself, exactly.

"You do know . . . whether you'd been around or not, that wouldn't have changed things? I'm a big girl. I do what I want."

"But I could have been a good influence on you. Kept you from—"

"Having sex?"

He cringed. Whether she was twenty-two or not, he hated the idea of his little sister being old enough to do *that*.

"You know," she mused. "I lost my virginity when I was—"

"Stop!" He held a hand up. "I don't want to hear it. I'm trying to apologize here, and you're fucking it all up."

She stepped back into the room. "This is an apology? For what? And my god, Carter. What kind of an apology is it? You're berating me."

"I'm out of practice," he grumbled.

His words seemed to soften her, and her shoulders slumped. Her face took on a sad, poor-Carter look.

"This isn't about me," he warned, but that didn't stop her. She came closer.

"Isn't it?" she asked. "What happened with you and Lisa? Talk to me, Carter. Clearly that's why you're so angry. Let me help."

"Maybe I'm angry because I'm *here*. I have a life to get back to, you know?"

She swished a hand in the air. "Then go. Feel free. I told you, I'm fine. Don't stay on my account."

"You're not fine. I caught you crying *again* last night." It was a nightly occurrence that ripped him apart each time he heard it. "What's going on with you? You say you and the baby are fine."

"We are fine."

"Then it's about the father? Why isn't he around? Why doesn't he call?"

"What makes you think he doesn't call?" The question was spoken so softly it took a second for the words to register. When they did, they pulled him from his seat.

"He calls?" He crossed the room to her. "When? Who is he?"

"It's not important." She shook her head. "None of that is important. He *has* called, but it doesn't matter. He's out of my life."

"Why?"

She gave him the kind of disinterested look he knew he'd patented over the years. "That's none of your business. How about you tell me what happened with you and Lisa? What split you two up?"

"That's none of your—"

"Okay." She held up both hands. "Tit for tat, I get it. Don't tell me what happened. We all do things we don't want to share with the world. But I do have another question. One I hope you'll actually listen to. Your marriage didn't last, and that sucks. Big-time. I get that. But how long are you going to blame the world and everyone in it?"

The words stopped him. He didn't blame the world, he blamed Lisa.

Ten seconds passed before he spoke again. He counted off each moment of time in his head as he forced himself to pull in a deep breath and let it out again. It was a stress-reducing technique he'd read about a couple of months ago, but so far he hadn't noticed it actually reducing any stress.

It did help him to admit to a truth today, though. He was a jerk.

"I'll try to quit being an ass to you," he grunted out. She was right. He was taking it out on everyone, and that was undeserved.

The corners of her mouth twitched. "That would be nice."

"And maybe you could try . . ." he prompted, thinking if he gave a little, then she could, too. She could try taking it easy since she *was* due to give birth soon.

"Not telling Mom that you're still not writing?" she teased.

Damn. He smiled.

Just like that, his lips curled. And the strangest thing happened with that small lift of his lips. It was as if a chunk of his hurt got lopped off, and he sucked in air all the way to the base of his lungs.

"You're a twerp," he told Julie as she grinned smugly up at him. He reached out and tugged on the ends of her hair. "But yes. Please. *Don't* tell Mom that I'm still not writing."

Julie laughed and left his room, and he returned to his desk. He was glad he'd come home. Whether Julie needed him or not right now, he'd come to realize that he needed her. She'd made him smile.

He glanced out his window once again, saw that the sky was lightening, and he thought about Ginger. *She'd* almost made him smile. The other morning at her house. He'd wanted to. Simply because she'd smiled at him. Similar to how he'd wanted to lift her

T-shirt over her head the day before in her kitchen for the sole sake of seeing what her hardened nipples looked like naked.

He thought about walking into her house and catching her talking about him on the phone. About "jumping his bones."

She'd once had a crush on him, and he'd had no idea. What would he have done if he'd known? Anything? She'd been his friend. And he'd depended on her. That friendship had been the backbone of his life at the time. The same way, he realized, that he could come to depend on her today if he let himself. As it was with his sister, he felt better merely being around Ginger.

But did he want to go there? Open himself up in that way?

It was all too much thinking, he decided. What mattered at the moment was writing. Or the fact that he *should* be writing. He opened his laptop and realized that he'd written quite a bit of his impromptu scene while watching Ginger. He quickly scanned the page, jumping over the words until he landed on a particularly interesting phrase.

> She straddled his legs, the vee of her crotch shadowed in the dim light, and paused before sliding over him.

Carter caught his breath. *Damn.*

> Her green eyes lit with the desire that both of them felt, and burnished copper hair trailed over her shoulders, hiding the light coating of freckles. And then she nodded. Slowly. And his body tensed in preparation for what was to come.
>
> Her heat touched him, sucking the breath out of his body as surely as it swallowed the head of his dick. His chest vibrated from the groan that he held inside. He couldn't let her think he was weak. He *wouldn't* give her that kind of power.
>
> But she was tight and hot, and she pushed down, covering

him to the hilt. And she drained his fucking senses as surely as if she'd opened his head and removed his brain.

And all the time, through every move she made, she looked at him. Watched him with the kind of intensity that not only said that this was what she'd been waiting for all her life, but that she was keenly aware that it was what he'd been waiting on, too. And she finally got the groan he'd been trying so desperately to hold in.

Carter licked his lips. He wrote sex scenes in his books on occasion. That was nothing new. But he was pretty sure the scene in front of him was of him and Ginger. And that *wasn't* his norm.

He kept reading.

Naked from the waist down—save for her green rubber boots—she rode him, her breasts bouncing under the loose cotton shirt, her nipples hard and reaching for him. So he reached back. He pulled both hands from their grip on her hips, and in a single move he had her shirt open, buttons flying. She wore no bra, and his dick surged inside her.

A moan slid from her parted lips, but he wanted more than an unintelligible sound. He wanted her calling his name. Knowing that it was *he* she was with. *He* she would return to.

That *he* was the man who would soon make her come.

He closed his mouth over a pink nipple, and he rose from his sitting position. He needed to be in control. Not her. And he needed to make sure she never looked at another man again.

With almost too much power, he slammed her against the wall.

"Carter!" Her voice rang out in heated passion.

He pumped harder, and she bit into his neck.

Her nails clawed at his back, begging for more. Faster. Now. So he gave her what she wanted.

He filled her, over and over, while her legs clamped tight around his body, her heels digging into his ass, spurring him on. She called his name. He called hers. Sweat slicked their bodies together with each powerful thrust.

And then they were at the precipice, and he didn't give her a chance to catch her breath. He pushed harder, insisting she be right there with him. Shoving her over the edge. He savored her screams and thrilled at the feel of her nails slicing through his skin.

"You're mine," he ground out as the first spurt left him.

She nodded. Made an animalistic growl. Then she lost all ability to speak.

~

Carter beat her to the rock the next morning.

The sun was still fifteen minutes from coming up, but instead of sitting in his room, watching to see if Ginger would head out of the house again, he'd slipped out his own back door and walked over himself. It was either that or reread the sex scene he'd written about her. Again. Which had about driven him out of his mind the day before.

Of course, it would have helped if he hadn't gone back to it time and again, editing and polishing the words. He'd told himself it was a writing exercise. He'd written for the first time in months. It was a positive thing. He was only helping himself by tweaking it.

Only, he'd gone to bed hard, and woken up the same way. For Ginger.

Which was better than waking up angry, he freely admitted. But it had also pulled him from the house this morning. He'd arrived in time to finish a cigarette before she caught him, and now he waited. And he hoped like hell that she showed up.

A bird squawked as it passed by, and he lifted his face to watch it. The morning was damp and slightly cool, and the briskness made him feel alive. It was as if something had awoken inside him.

The day before had been a turning point. He'd smiled in the morning, had dirty nasty thoughts about his friend and neighbor all day long, *and* he'd watched that very neighbor read on her deck late at night, once again pantless.

All in all, it had been a good twenty-four hours.

The remodel was coming along nicely, as well, and he and Gene had spent a couple of hours working through plans for Ginger's house. Carter was anxious for the team to really get started out there. He wanted to see her home come alive.

He *wanted* to see her.

As if his wants could materialize, she was suddenly there. He hadn't realized he'd closed his eyes, but when he opened them, his face still tilted toward the sky, she was by his side, peering down at him, and he wondered if he'd ever told her how pretty she was.

Her hair was twisted to the top of her head, her face scrubbed clean, and a solemnness was painted across her features. It mixed in with the sprinkling of freckles dotting her nose.

She stared at him as if unsure why he was there. If she should stay or go.

And she took his breath away.

She didn't need makeup and dresses. She just needed to be herself.

"I'm divorced," he blurted out. Pressure immediately eased from his chest. Maybe she'd been right. Talking about it could help. "It was final three weeks ago."

She blinked, swallowed, then nodded. "I'm sorry."

"Yeah. Divorce sucks."

Her head angled slightly, as if asking if she could sit down, and he nodded. She lowered to sit beside him, and they both turned to face the ocean. "Do you want to talk about it?" she asked.

He considered it. Truly considered whether he wanted to talk about what had happened. It was a question he'd never allowed before. But, no. Not today. Not yet.

"No," he said.

She nodded once again. "Then we'll just watch the sunrise."

They sat side by side, silent for the next ten minutes as the bright globe inched its way into the sky. The morning wasn't as colorful as some he'd seen, and there were no clouds. The day seemed to simply appear. One moment it was gray, with daylight hovering just beyond the edge of the water, and the next, an explosion of sunlight was everywhere. And as he'd done the day before, he pulled in a deep breath.

"I have countertop samples for you," he told her after he blew out the lungful of air. "They're in my car."

"I'll come over before I go to work and take a look."

The oddest pinch tightened inside him as he thought about her coming over, with Gregg and Ian—and the rest of the guys—being there. They were fascinated with her; he'd heard them talking. And she seemed as taken with them. He'd watched from a distance as she chatted one or another up on her multiple trips home during the days, and he'd wondered if she always came home that much during a workday. Or was she doing it simply to flirt?

Not that it was any of his business. He'd warned her about them. He'd done his part.

Maybe I do just want to get laid.

The words irritated him more today than they had two mornings ago. She deserved more than just getting laid.

"Another bad date last night?" he asked now. He'd seen a car drop her off before she'd gone in the front door fully dressed in a skirt, heels, and a shirt, and come out the back in only the shirt.

"Not a date." She propped her hands behind her on the rock and dropped her head back. "Though not from a lack of trying. One of the local bars has a monthly speed-dating thing. I went with a friend. We both left empty-handed."

"Too bad for them."

She turned her head to look at him, her gaze quietly studying, and he hoped like hell she couldn't see his thoughts. Which revolved fifty percent around the words he'd written the day before. And the other half still wondering about the color of her nipples.

"Do you remember that we used to sit out here and share our dreams?" she asked.

Relief filled him. She had no clue that she was being coveted by her neighbor. "I do. You wanted to be a kindergarten teacher."

The corners of her mouth turned up. "You remember that?"

He nodded. He remembered a lot about her. And about their time spent out here. Like the fact that they used to sketch out the dream homes they'd each planned to build. Their ideas had been very similar. So much so that they'd eventually tossed their separate plans and worked from one sketch. He wondered how many of those same ideas had made it into her house.

Then again, he wondered how many had made it into his own. Was that why so much of hers was similar to his? It was interesting that they'd both hit that point of their lives at the same time.

"You wanted to be an author," she said.

Her words surprised him. "I did." He'd never talked about that a lot. It was one of those dreams that had been more personal than the rest. The kind people would doubt.

She went back to watching the water, seemingly lost in her own thoughts, and he returned to his. Of her. He was intrigued with the color of her hair when the sun touched it. There was blonde in there. He hadn't realized that. Thin streaks of gold, as well as darker reds, mixed in with the copper. Looking at it, he wanted to touch it. Let it slide through his fingers the same way the sun slid over its surface.

"Do you still dream, Carter?"

He shook his head when she glanced at him.

"I do," she said wistfully. "But sometimes I wish I didn't."

Was she talking about her dream of having a family?

"What kept you here?" he asked. His voice croaked out, and he cleared his throat before continuing. "I mean, I know your dad passed away, and that brought you home before you graduated college. But why stay? Why not *be* that kindergarten teacher?" Maybe she *could* have had her dreams. "Did you not want to go back to school?"

"I considered it. In fact, I'd planned on it. But I found that I like running the company. And I'm good at it. *And* it means a lot to me that it was Dad's business." She plucked a piece of grass from the ground and twirled it between two fingers. "I think the kindergarten thing was more my idea of fitting me into the picture I'd painted. You know . . . the husband, four kids, giant house."

He knew. He'd wanted the same, only his picture had been with him sitting in his home office, the ocean outside his window, while he wrote bestsellers.

"You'd make a great teacher. I could totally see you in the middle of a roomful of kids."

She smiled lazily. "Thanks. But the reality is, I probably wouldn't have been great at it. I prefer the freedom to be on the water when I want to be. To not have to look 'presentable' all the time."

He studied her, thinking about her reading on her deck. He had to agree with her there. She was a woman born to not wear pants.

Something surprising happened then. He smiled. And he couldn't *stop* smiling.

Ginger sat up straighter at the change in him, but she didn't say anything. She simply stared.

"You prefer to be outdoors without pants," he teased.

There was a brief pause as confusion passed across her face, before a blush bloomed on her cheeks. He loved how easily she blushed.

"You've seen that?" She sounded horrified. "Me on the deck?"

He let the smile reach his eyes.

She covered her face with her hands. "*Ohmygod.* I'm so embarrassed. It's always dark. I didn't think anyone could see."

"Are you kidding me? That set of legs?" His gaze lowered to her legs. They were displayed nicely in black stretchy pants—the same kind she'd worn that first morning. "Bare?" he continued, and she peeked between her fingers at him. He nodded. "I noticed."

Her blush took on a new shade of red, and his smile grew another inch.

"It's dark when I go out to read," she pointed out. "And my shirt covers everything. I'm *not* indecent." The way she defended herself was adorable.

"No." He chuckled lightly and tugged her hands off her face. "I'll give you that. You're very decent."

"Stop it, Carter. You're embarrassing me."

"Can't help it, Red. You grew up nice." And this was fun. This was what he'd needed. To sit with a friend and simply enjoy the moment. He didn't do that anymore, with a friend or without.

"It's the missing thirty pounds," she said, but her words made no sense.

"The what?"

She stood. And holding her arms out at her sides, she spun in a slow circle. "The thirty pounds," she repeated. "That's why I grew up nice. Most girls go away to college and gain fifteen, I went away and lost thirty."

He took another look, taking his time moving over her body, but not in an appreciative manner so much as contemplative. He didn't remember her being heavier. "That must be what's different," he finally muttered. "I couldn't figure it out."

Her jaw dropped. "Are you kidding me? How could you not tell the difference?"

"I don't know. I never thought about you as overweight."

"You're full of crap."

"No, I'm not." He tried to picture her from before, but all he could pull up was red hair and her smile. Her optimism. "It's not like you were fat. You were just you. Just . . . Ginger."

For a moment she continued to gawk at him as if he were an alien species. Then she flipped the ends of her hair over her shoulder and gave a snooty lift of her nose. "Well, I look amazingly better than I did back then."

This time the path he took over her body was appreciative. "You definitely look amazing."

She didn't respond, just watched him with slightly narrowed eyes. He wished he could read whatever was going through her mind, and he wondered if she had any idea what was going through his. About her body. About her.

About the fact that it had been *months* since he'd had sex.

"How good?" she asked.

"What?"

"How good do I look?" She once again twirled in front of him. "I have trouble getting a man to stick—or even picking one up in a roomful of them, apparently—so something must be wrong with me. Either that, or I'm targeting the wrong 'quality' of man." She stopped twirling, and the seriousness on her face captured his complete attention. "Do you think I'm going after men in the wrong class? You saw my date Saturday night. Was he too good for me?"

He didn't reply.

He didn't know *what* to reply.

"What I'm asking is, how attractive am I? What scale of man should I be seeking out?"

He finally found his voice. "Are you out of your mind?"

"No. I'm one-hundred-percent serious. I don't know what's wrong with me, but if someone would only tell me, I'd work on it. I'll wear different clothes, talk about different subjects. Try a different hairstyle. I just don't want to—"

She bit off her words as if she'd realized her inside thoughts had made it out, and turned quickly away from him.

"You don't want to what?" he asked. He rose from the rock and moved toward her.

"It doesn't matter," she mumbled.

"Answer the question."

She shot him a look, and the way the sun lit her features had him reaching for her. He grabbed her hand. She looked hurt. He knew that kind of pain.

"Forget I said anything else, will you?" she begged. "Just tell me how attractive I am. That's all I want to know. Am I good enough?"

He pulled her back when she tried to turn away again, and reached for her other hand. They stood facing each other, and everything else about the morning around them no longer mattered.

"Answer the question, Ginger Root. You don't want to *what*?"

CHAPTER NINE

Her chest constricted. He'd just played the friend card.

Ginger Root. What a stupid nickname. He'd given it to her when they were eight and she'd tripped on a root while they'd been exploring the island. She'd come away with two bloody knees, and Carter had cleaned and bandaged them for her. She'd hated the name. Only, he'd continued using it throughout the years, usually when she was hurting from an insult or some seeming slight, and in the end, she'd grown to love it. She'd forgotten all about it until now.

Her heart thumped behind her rib cage as her gaze bounced back and forth between his eyes. Could she really admit her biggest fear to him? This wasn't them as teenagers. She couldn't just tell him all her secrets, could she?

"You know I can stand here all day," he threatened.

She smiled slightly. Because yeah, he could. Especially when it came to helping heal her wounds. He'd been that kind of friend.

So yes, she could tell him.

She readjusted her gaze so she didn't have to look at him straight on, and ended up focusing on a couple walking along the edge of the water. They were holding hands, her head resting on his shoulder. They looked like they were in love.

Carter gripped her fingers tighter, and she swallowed around the lump in her throat.

"I don't want to hear that it's *me*," she admitted. The sadness in her own voice wasn't lost on her, and she pulled herself from his grasp. "Do they not like that I own the ferries? The boats?" She gave a tiny shrug. "That I routinely smell like fish instead of flowers?"

When Carter didn't respond, she decided to put it all out there. She glanced briefly at him before darting away. His eyes were too watchful. It was easier to remain focused on something else.

"That's the one thing I don't want to change." Her voice shook. "If it's something about my appearance, I can fix that. But if the problem is *me*. Who I am inside?" She shook her head. "Do I have to change *me* to get the kind of man that I want?"

He watched her differently now. It was a subtle change, but she felt it. More intense.

She slid her gaze back to his, and without intending to, locked on to his eyes. Nerves buzzed with anticipation, and her pulse knocked so hard that it nearly shook her body.

"What kind of man do you want?" he asked.

The answer was simple. "A good guy. One who looks at me and sees someone he wants to be around for fifty years." She bit the inside of her lip and finished softly. "One who loves me just as I am."

He nodded. "You deserve that man."

The sincerity in his voice humbled her. "Thank you."

"With*out* changing," he stressed. "Don't change for anybody, Ginger. You're good as you are."

A mix of gratitude and relief bloomed in her chest, but it just as quickly disappeared. He was talking to the girl she'd been. Her as a teenager. He was remembering their friendship.

He didn't know who she was now any more than she really knew him.

"What if there's no other choice?" she asked softly. Because there might not be.

He shook his head. "There's always another choice."

That's what she'd always believed. Why she kept plugging away at it. Being optimistic that her time would come. But her surety was flagging these days, and the desire to continue putting herself out there was getting harder to come by.

"Maybe I should just quit." It was the first time she'd voiced the thought out loud, and she wasn't sure she meant it.

"Quit dating?" he asked.

She nodded. The very idea broke her heart.

"You ever considered that *you're* the one who doesn't want more from the men you're choosing?"

Was she sending off a don't-ask-me-out signal?

The question bounced around inside her for a moment, but in the end she shook her head. "I *liked* Patrick." At his confusion she added, "Saturday night's date. I got a second date with him, and I wanted a third. Badly."

She'd planned to bring out the lace underwear for the third.

"Then don't quit," he said, seeming to snap out of the intensity he'd had just a moment before. "Keep looking. You'll find someone. And he'll be damned lucky to have you."

"Thanks." She was tired of thinking about it. She offered him a weary smile. It was time to get home and get ready for work. "I appreciate the talk." She looked back at the water and the sun now well above it. "And the sunrise," she added. "It was nice sharing it with you again. I hope you'll come back."

Truth was, she'd hoped all week he'd be out there. Before he'd come home, she'd taken up the habit of driving over to the house for sunrises most mornings. The pier near her house was the most perfect spot she'd ever found to start the day, yet she'd been coming here all week with her fingers crossed that Carter would, too.

His showing up that morning gave her hope. Maybe his hurt would eventually ease.

Before she got fully up the hill, she turned back. "By the way," she called down to him. When he looked up at her, she added, "You look good when you smile. I hope you'll do that more often, too."

She turned to leave, and laughed when she heard "By the way, you look good with no pants on."

~

"I so completely needed this margarita."

Kayla Morgan sucked down another gulp of her oversized, Friday-happy-hour drink while Ginger sat beside her, eyeing both the drink and the woman, and wondering what had Kayla so worked up. She'd barely crossed the threshold of Gin's before catching Kevin's attention and requesting the drink.

Kevin—the newlywed bartender who'd gotten married on Ginger's dinner cruiser almost three weeks before—had nodded understanding, then sent over both Kayla's drink as well as a mug of Ginger's favorite beer. Friday night was beer night, and all of her friends knew it.

Unless she was on a date, of course. Then she ordered wine and sipped. Usually.

But tonight there was no man to worry about, and no need to impress. Therefore, not only did she plan to put away more than one beer, she'd do it in her favorite faded jeans, T-shirt, and flip-flops. Let the weekend begin.

She tipped her beer back, and nodded when the server passed by and silently asked if she wanted a second. Hopefully she'd stop after two—there was no need to embarrass herself in the company of others—but there was no guarantee.

Aside from the middle-of-the-week failed attempt at attracting a man, the week had actually been a good one. She'd met with Gene after work yesterday to discuss final decisions on changes from the original electrical and plumbing plans, and work on both of those had begun today. The men would be out there tomorrow, as well, and it was her belief that before the end of the weekend, if there were a light fixture or toilet in the house, they'd actually be functional.

Of course there wouldn't be either. She hadn't picked them out yet.

But her first focus had been deciding where sinks and major appliances would go. Electrical and plumbing couldn't be finished without those choices being made, and she was glad to have finally crossed that hurdle. Carter had added his thoughts to the discussion, which had helped. He'd also given his two cents about the style of cabinets, floors, and counters he thought would look best, but she hadn't settled on those yet.

"What has you so worked up?" she asked after Kayla had slurped down over half the margarita and finally looked around as if ready to join the rest of the crowd.

Kayla blew out a breath. "Brides."

Seaglass Celebrations' main stream of income came from weddings, and Kayla, being the very efficient obsessive-compulsive that she was, left no detail unturned. That characteristic had a way of leaving her needing the occasional margarita.

"I hope you're not talking about my mother," Ginger said.

Another fourth of the drink disappeared. "No." Kayla wiped the back of her hand across her mouth and held up a finger to get their server's attention. "Your mother is great. Aside from the fact that she had me wedge in a last-minute wedding into our second-most-popular month."

"I worried that might be a problem." October was gorgeous on the island, and once Seaglass got national attention last year, brides had quickly figured that out.

"*Then* she insisted on the senior center for the reception," Kayla added. She ordered a second drink and turned to Ginger. "You wouldn't believe how popular that place suddenly is since they opened the patio."

"It's the view. No sand to contend with, but you still see the ocean. And those trees." Ginger sighed. "Those trees are so romantic."

Live oaks, hanging moss. Ginger had always pictured them in her own wedding.

"It's insane, is what it is." The last few drops of the margarita disappeared. "Any time a new location opens up, anyone with a wedding scheduled within a year goes wild, thinking *that's* the new place to be. And, of course, Mrs. Rylander is in charge of the rentals over there now. My god, that woman can try the nerves of a saint. And we both know I'm no saint."

Mrs. Rylander was one of the feistiest seniors on the island. Roni loved her to death because they'd been next-door neighbors for years, but the woman was definitely an acquired taste.

"But you still love the job?" Ginger asked. Kayla was the only reason Andie had been able to move to Boston without worrying about the business.

She nodded. "The best job I've ever had."

"As long as you get the occasional margarita to help it along . . ." Ginger teased.

"Or two."

The server replaced both their drinks and refreshed their bowl of tortilla chips, pulling a grateful sigh from Kayla, and Ginger buried her smile inside her glass. Since her best friends had moved away, she'd begun meeting up with Kayla on a more regular basis, and without question, Ginger ended up laughing at the woman every time. She was wound so tight.

Owen Elliot, an early-twenties, laid-back sweetheart, passed by with a tray of appetizers held above his head, smiling at girls as he weaved his way between the tables, and Ginger kept an eye on him. But she noticed that Kayla very obviously did not. On his way back, he readjusted his path, bringing them by their table, and paused to greet Kayla. Dimples flashed, and Ginger would swear he didn't even realize *she* was there.

Kayla barely acknowledged his presence before he once again went on his way, eventually disappearing through the door leading into the kitchen. After the encounter, Kayla began repetitively tapping one fingernail against the top of the table, while simultaneously sucking down half her second drink.

"You know he likes you?"

"Don't even," Kayla protested. Which only made Ginger laugh.

"Why don't you ever give him the time of day?"

"Are you kidding me?" Kayla glanced around as if making sure no one else could hear, then tucked one side of her brunette bob behind her ear and leaned in. "I am *not* a Mrs. Robinson."

Ginger laughed again. "No, you're *not*. You're only thirty-one. He's . . . what? Twenty-three? Twenty-four?"

"Twenty-two." Kayla's tone screamed horrification.

"Twenty-two might be fun," Ginger suggested.

"Or it might kill me."

"Please. You could totally keep up with that."

Before Kayla could reply, the door across the room opened, admitting several more men into the bar. Both women stopped talking as two additional early-twenties hotties walked in. Gregg and Ian. The two men seemed to do everything as a pair, and Ginger couldn't help but heat up at the thought of doing *them* as a pair.

Good grief.

She gulped her beer. Southern-boy charm or not, she had no doubt either of them would sleep with her, then be in someone else's bed *before* morning. There would be no staying over, no breakfast, no nothing.

Except probably a rousing good time.

More heat rushed through her. She really did need sex. In a very bad way. But she also needed to feel like she wasn't simply a place to plant a dick.

The door opened again, and Carter walked in.

"Now *that's* a man," Kayla murmured. She still had the straw of her drink between her teeth, but her eyes were glued to Carter. The wind had done a number on his hair, and he'd seemingly forgotten to shave the last couple of days.

Ginger had already noticed that nonshaving feature earlier. As they'd done yesterday, they'd watched the sunrise together this morning. Only, this time, when she'd walked out her back door, he'd been waiting for her. There hadn't been a lot of talk, just easy comfort. They'd walked over together, talked a bit about her house as well as the renovations going on next door, then had silently taken in the sunrise.

They'd discussed the coming day on their way back, and he'd never once brought out one of his nasty cigarettes. Before they'd parted, he'd asked if she had a big date lined up for tonight. She'd asked the same of him. Neither had a date, and neither had bigger plans than dinner and a drink or two.

"That's Julie Ridley's brother," Ginger shared.

Kayla shot her a questioning glance, and Ginger added, "Julie's the new manager of the art gallery."

"Oh. The pregnant girl. Your mother mentioned her brother was in town."

They both kept an eye on Carter as he moved to the bar, and Ginger noticed that they weren't the only ones watching. Carter was a handsome man. At six feet tall, with those sexy eyes and well-fitting jeans, he was easy to look at. It occurred to her that he'd also filled out since he'd shown up on the island. Must be all that cooking he'd been doing for his sister. Julie had put on weight, as well. She didn't look quite as scary-thin anymore.

Gregg and Ian stopped by their table then, blocking Ginger's view of Carter, and Gregg edged in close and shot her a wink. "Buy you a beer, Miss Ginger?"

Dang, but his voice did make her heart skip a beat. Even when used with the pet name.

She took in the beanie covering his head. It left a few dark curls poking out over his forehead. Very cute. Very hot. Then held up her glass. "Seems I'm already taken care of."

"Yeah?" He took the glass from her and downed a long drink, leaving a tiny spot of foam on the corner of his mouth. Ginger stared at it. His tongue darted out to swipe the foam away, and his eyebrows did a sexy little wiggle. "Maybe there's something else I could get you."

Kayla choked on her drink, and Ginger giggled. Then she blushed. Gregg was such a flirt.

And a total man-whore.

"Gregg, Ian," Ginger began. She swallowed, hoping she didn't sound as schoolgirlish as she felt. She motioned to the other side of the table. "Meet Kayla."

"Nice to meet you," Kayla said politely.

Both men turned their attentions to the other woman, and before Ginger knew what happened, the two of them had dragged over chairs and joined them at the small, two-person table. Kayla's chest rose and fell too fast, and she'd picked up even more speed sucking down her drink. She motioned to their server for another.

"So what do you two have planned for tonight?" Ian asked. "We found this great spot—"

"Time's up, gentlemen."

All four of them looked up at the drily spoken words to find Carter loitering behind Gregg—whose arm was now stretched along the back of Ginger's chair. Carter's demeanor wasn't *scary*—exactly— but it did make a statement. It pulled Ian quickly to his feet. Gregg stayed where he was.

"I'm sorry." Ian gulped. "Was this your seat, Mr. Ridley?" Clearly the guy was cowed by the boss man.

Gregg still didn't move, and Carter's attention remained on him.

Ginger leaned in. "We're good, Gregg. Just having a few drinks, then we're going home." When he looked back at her, she added, "Alone."

She saw the disappointment in his eyes, and she felt a little of it herself. She wished she were that type. She wished she were ten years younger.

Then she would take him up on whatever he wanted to suggest.

"You sure?" Gregg spoke the words softly enough that she should have been the only one to hear them. Except, Carter leaned in, mimicking Ginger's previous action.

"The lady said no," he stated.

"Back off," Gregg muttered. But he stood. And turned to Ginger once again. He shot her that Southern-boy smile she'd been on the receiving end of several times during the week. "Maybe next time," he suggested.

Her answer was a goofy smile.

Gregg and Ian moved on, stopping and delivering their same pitch to another table full of girls, and Carter scowled down at her. "Really?" he said. His tone edged on boredom.

She shrugged nonchalantly. "He seems fun."

"You're too old for him."

"See?" Kayla piped in. She looked from Ginger to Carter. "I just told her the same thing. I'm too old for—"

Her words cut off and she did a quick peek around, and Ginger whispered, "O-wen."

Carter lowered to the chair vacated by Gregg. His presence seemed to take up a lot more space around the table than when the other *two* men had sat there, and Ginger scooted her chair over to make room. Then she introduced Carter and began catching him up on the conversation.

"There's this guy who works here . . ." she began.

"Stop it," Kayla demanded, her eyes pleading. "I'm not interested in him."

"No?"

Owen was in the area again, and Ginger smiled knowingly when he once again made a detour that led him by their table. He tipped his head at Kayla as he passed, but said nothing.

Kayla sat, stone-faced.

"That guy?" Carter asked. He reached for a chip from the basket in the middle of their table and watched Owen until he disappeared in the back. "What's wrong with him?"

"He's no older than the two who were just over here, that's what." Kayla's tone said she was more than a little aghast. "And you just told Ginger that Gregg was too young for her."

"Gregg *is* too young for her."

Ginger snorted. "I could hold my own."

Hard eyes turned to her. "He is *not* your type."

"Seriously, Carter," she admonished, "give it a break. I'm a grown woman. I know what kind of guy I want to hook up with and what kind I don't."

"So you're just looking for a hookup now?"

Ginger noticed that Kayla had gone quiet as she watched the two of them talk.

"Find another hobby, will you?" Irritation had her voice lowering. "What are you doing here, anyway? I thought you planned to stay in and cook dinner for Julie." That's what he'd told her earlier. She'd taken that to mean that he'd also laze around afterward, and empty his fridge of whatever beer remained inside.

She hadn't meant to be nosy, but when she'd taken her recycling bin to the road that morning, she'd seen the pile of bottles in Carter's bin. The sheer number had shocked her. Had he really drank that much in the last week?

But there was no other explanation that she could see. Julie certainly wasn't drinking them.

He held up the ticket he'd been given at the bar. "Stove got taken out of the house today, so I'm playing delivery boy."

Across the table, Kayla propped a hand on her fist and gazed adoringly at Carter. The tequila was clearly working.

"Any more thoughts on the kitchen?" Carter asked Ginger.

She stared at him, having no clue what he meant.

"The samples I brought you."

Oh, *her* kitchen. She shook her head. "I can't decide." She tugged her purse from the back of her chair, and retrieved several pieces of granite and stone. She'd carried them around for the last two days, taking them out several times a day, but so far she remained undecided. "I'm leaning toward something that's more beige."

Carter remained silent. She knew this was because he didn't think she needed to go with anything in the brown tones. He thought cooler colors would go better with a beach house.

"You should visit the showroom and see each in person," he suggested.

There was a large store on the mainland that showcased different setups. She'd visited it a number of times over the summer.

"Maybe." She hummed under her breath as she studied the squares, moving them around as if doing so would make the decision for her. "When do I have to make up my mind?"

"Soon, Red."

She sighed. "I know, soon. But . . ." She shot him a pleading look. "Can I have a week?"

He narrowed his eyes on her as if certain she were trying to get out of something, but she wasn't. She just didn't know what she wanted.

"One week," he finally answered. "Then *I'm* making the decision for you."

"No, you're not." She gave him the same squinty-eyed stare he'd just given her. "I'll make my own decisions. I don't need some man to do it for me."

He disarmed her with a wink. "Thatta girl. As long as you *make* the decisions."

The server showed up with Kayla's third drink then, along with another beer. When Ginger reached for it, Carter stared down his nose at her. "Do I need to come back later and pick you two up?"

As if she were the one with the potential problem here.

She once again returned his look, this time going for haughty, but without being able to look down her nose at him, she couldn't pull it off. She took a gulp of beer instead, finishing with as much of a judgmental sneer as she could pull off. "I figured *you'd* be having plenty of your own tonight."

"I can skip it." He looked toward Gregg, who was flirting with yet another tableful of women. "Wouldn't want you drinking too much and doing anything . . . stupid."

She looked at Gregg, too. Then purposefully licked her lips.

Kayla made a little snorting noise, but neither of them paid attention to her. Instead, Ginger gave Carter her best smile, stupidly hoping it would entice him to do the same. She hadn't seen him do anything but scowl since yesterday morning, and she found that she wanted to see his lips curve again. He was beautiful when he smiled.

"Come on, Carter," she cooed when his mouth remained rigid. She lightly poked at his chest, finding it firmer than she'd expected. So she poked it again. Another beer and she'd rub her palms all over that bad boy. "Smile a little." Her voice had lowered, and she bit her lip, hoping she hadn't sounded as sex-crazed as she knew she was.

But still . . . she got nothing from Carter.

Only the same green-brown gaze glowering at her that she'd seen for the last week. She frowned.

"Fine," she scoffed, "but your face might freeze like that."

"How are you getting home?" He ignored her taunting. The man was no fun at all.

"I do know how to call a cab if I need to."

A plastic bag filled with food showed up at the table and Carter stood. "See that you do." He shot once last look at Gregg. "No riding home with strangers."

"But Gregg isn't a stranger."

At Carter's sharp look she wrinkled her nose at him playfully.

"I'm serious, Ginger Root. Don't ask for trouble."

"Okay," she grumbled. "My god, you're tiresome. I won't, I swear. I won't leave with Gregg. You're right, okay? He's fun to look at, but that's all. I'm not interested in what he's offering."

Carter's jaw went tight. "So he's offered?"

Her answer was a lift of her brows, and he shook his head with disgust.

"I feel like I have to keep an eye on you, same as I do my sister."

"Only, I'm not your sister, am I? I'm a woman." She looked him straight in the eyes. "With womanly needs."

He stared at her for a moment, thoughts flickering behind his eyes, and his lips slightly parted. But she'd had too much to drink to have a clue what he might be thinking. Finally, he said nothing to her. He turned to Kayla and nodded. "Nice to meet you."

"Same here," Kayla eked out.

Then he was gone, winding through the crowd. He stopped by Gregg's side, said something, and moved on. Gregg tossed a glance her way before returning his attention to the blonde at his elbow, and Ginger turned back to Kayla.

"Ginger Root?" Kayla asked.

"Old nickname."

"I think it's cute." She glanced in the direction Carter had gone. "And I think *he's* cute. What a sweetheart."

"A sweetheart?" Ginger gaped. "Carter? Honey, you've had too much to drink."

"He's here getting takeout for his pregnant sister," Kayla explained. "And clearly he's watching out for you. He offered to come back and drive us home." She suddenly squinted as if to clear her vision, and stared at the empty glasses scattered over their table. "Do we *need* him to take us home? I've had a lot to drink."

"I can get us home," Ginger assured the other woman. She was on her third beer, but it would last her the rest of the night. "But we're not going anywhere yet. We came to have fun, right?"

"I came for the margaritas."

Ginger chuckled. "That, too. The night is young, though. I say we flirt a little and see where it gets us."

This time Kayla was the one to laugh. "You just flirted all over that man."

The words caught her off guard. "No, I didn't."

"Uh . . . yes, you did."

Ginger hadn't intended to flirt, but she could see where Kayla might have thought that's what she'd been attempting. She *had* rubbed his chest. But had Carter even noticed? If not, it was a little insulting.

"He's just a friend," she pointed out. "We grew up next door to each other."

"And that's all? What about Ginger Root?"

Ginger held in a groan. "That's *all*." What good would it do if it wasn't?

But that same stinking flutter thing that had happened after Andie suggested she jump Carter's bones was back. Fluttering again. She couldn't jump his bones, though. She wouldn't risk that kind of embarrassment.

But she *could* fantasize a little. Because just possibly, she had a little of that same high-school crush going again. Kayla had been right.

He *could* be sweet—when he wasn't smoking or drinking too much. Or just generally being cranky.

And he certainly was nice to look at.

She swung her gaze to the door and saw that he hadn't stepped outside yet. Instead, he stood there, eyes on her. He gave a solemn nod and disappeared into the night. When she turned back to the table, Kayla wore a knowing look.

"What?" Ginger asked defensively.

"Only a friend."

"He is."

"Right." Kayla plucked a chip from the basket. "A friend you wouldn't mind taking care of—how did you put it?—your 'womanly needs'?"

CHAPTER TEN

Womanly needs.

Ginger still couldn't believe she'd said that to Carter. She'd been attempting to aggravate him about Gregg, but had she come off as wanton instead? Desperate?

Kayla had kept on about it well beyond the third margarita and into the fourth, but then they'd captured the attention of a couple of other guys. This time, both men being nearer their age. And finally Kayla had shut up and done a little flirting of her own. The result being that they'd both walked away last night with upcoming dates.

"I found the absolute *best* dress for you this morning." Ginger's mother interrupted the mental replaying of the night before as she and Clint came through the back door. They joined Ginger on the deck, her mom carrying a tray of vegetables and dip, and Clint moving to fire up the grill. They wore matching navy polos and khaki shorts.

"Please tell me it has no ruffles." Ginger reached for a carrot stick.

"Only a few around the neck area." Her mom fluttered her hands around her shoulders. "And the skirt is a little full, but they aren't ruffles."

Ginger stared at her mother. Did the woman not know her at all?

"The best thing about it is the color," her mom added. "You'll love it. The green will highlight your complexion nicely."

"And your eyes," Clint added in.

Ginger lifted a brow. "She talked you into shopping with her?"

He ducked his head as if realizing what he'd given away. He was cute when embarrassed. "She convinced me it would be fun."

"And was it?" Ginger chomped into the carrot while Clint studied his shoes.

"Clinton Connelly," her mother exclaimed at his obvious resistance. She joined him at the grill, one arm sliding around his waist, and leaned into him. "Don't you dare say you didn't have fun with me today. I know for a fact that you did."

Clint lifted steady brown eyes to Ginger and recited "I had fun with her today" as if having been coached to say the words, but behind the monotone, Ginger spotted true happiness.

Her mom huffed at the comment and crossed to settle into the chair beside Ginger. "Don't believe him," she said. "He picked out more for the wedding than I did."

Ginger gawked at Clint. "I've been shopping with her before. Her credit card company and she are on a first-name basis. If what she says is true, then that's quite a statement."

The man came close to blushing, and both women laughed.

It was a lazy Saturday evening, and her mom and Clint had offered to fix dinner. Ginger had offered to hold down her favorite chair. She'd been up since well before daylight, having had a huge charter that morning, and she was beyond exhausted. If it weren't for the fact that she'd picked up another new book at the bookstore after work, she'd turn in early.

Instead, she planned to read until an ungodly hour. The author was another favorite, and was sure to scare, and she didn't have to work tomorrow.

The three of them talked wedding and honeymoon plans over the next forty-five minutes, while Clint impressed with his grilling skills, and they ate fat juicy burgers at the outdoor dinette set.

While cleaning up from the meal, her mother suddenly whirled around.

"Well, if it isn't Carter Ridley," she said with great enthusiasm. Carter stood at the side of the deck, seemingly hesitant at the sight of finding all three of them there, and her mother rushed down the steps to embrace him. "I've been waiting to catch sight of you. Hoping I'd see you without having to break down and invite myself over." She pulled back and took him in, then gave him a smile that was full of love and memories. "But I was just about out of patience."

Carter hugged her back, surprising Ginger with a wide smile of his own. It was a nice moment, and reminded Ginger of the many times both families had enjoyed summer cookouts or afternoons at the beach together.

"It's great to see you, Mrs. Atkinson. Sorry for not being around a lot. I've been . . ."

He paused and Ginger filled in with "Hiding behind the blinds."

"What?" her mom asked, looking up at Ginger.

"Nothing," Ginger muttered. She dropped to her chair and Carter shot her a look, but it wasn't the surly one he'd shared so often since being home. In fact, she wasn't sure what kind of look it was. Inquisitive?

Intrigued?

Wondering about her "womanly needs"? Geez . . . how embarrassing.

"You two always had your secrets," her mom mused, but let the moment pass. She patted Carter's cheek. "Come on up. I want you to meet Clint. Where's Julie?" She asked the question as she led him up the steps.

"She went out with a couple of friends tonight."

"Good for her. She wasn't getting out for a while there. We'll have you both over soon. We'll grill out."

"I'd enjoy that."

Ginger stared. Who was this man? And where was his bad attitude?

Clint had waited on the deck along with Ginger, and when Carter hit the top step, he reached for the older man's hand. "Congratulations. I heard about the engagement. You got a good one."

"Thank you." Clint's voice had a way of booming, but at the same time being gentle. He draped an arm around her mother's shoulders. "And I agree. These Atkinson girls"—Clint took in both women—"they're a special breed."

"That they are."

Once again, Carter gave Ginger a strange look, but she still had no idea what it meant. She was too surprised by his shift in mood to figure it out.

"Want a beer?" Clint asked. He held up the one in his hand.

"Love one."

Ginger's mom looked at her and nudged her head toward the house. When Ginger just stared back, as if not understanding the intent, her mother whispered, "Go get him a beer, Ginger."

Ginger held up her hands in question. What happened to the agreement that she didn't have to lift a finger tonight? But when one side of Carter's mouth lifted at the interaction between her and her mother, she rolled her eyes and crawled from her chair. As she went into the house, she caught herself wondering how bad she looked. Or smelled.

Then she reminded herself that it was only Carter out there. And she wasn't on a date.

"Thanks," he said when she handed him an opened bottle a few moments later. He propped a hip against the railing, and spent several minutes talking with her mom and Clint while Ginger finished clearing the table. On each trip back out of the house, she silently observed Carter. He was definitely different today. Easier. *Happier.*

He was more like the Carter she'd once known.

"Oh!" Her mom squealed as Ginger once again stepped through the back door. She held her left hand out to Carter. "I didn't show you my ring." She flapped her fingers in the air, and the gigantic rock still managed to flash in the almost-set sun. "Isn't it just the grandest thing?"

"It is nice," Carter agreed. He eyed the ring carefully. "Be sure to show Julie."

"I stopped off at the gallery earlier this week," her mom admitted with a grin. "I like to check in on her once in a while." She admired the diamonds for one last second before letting out a wistful sigh and lowering her hand. She peered up at Carter. "She looked good. Said you'd been fattening her up."

"I'm trying. I like to cook, actually. I hadn't done much of it in a while."

"He's fattened up, too," Ginger blurted.

All eyes turned to her, her mother's horrified. "Ginger!" she gasped.

"I didn't mean *fat.*" Carter watched her with a twinkle in his eye, and she explained, "You were too thin when you first came home."

"Really?" he asked. He looked down at himself, his expression turning perplexed. "I hadn't noticed."

"Don't worry. You look good now."

And again, her mouth said what it wasn't supposed to. But he smiled at her once more.

So she smiled back.

"Well," her mother said. "Clint? Can you help me inside?"

"Sure." Clint tossed his empty bottle into the blue recycle bin, glass clinking against glass, and hurried after his intended.

At the door, her mom turned back. "It's really good to see you again, Carter. Don't be a stranger. Julie said you're redoing the kitchen. Does that mean the oven is being pulled out?"

"It went yesterday."

"Then consider our kitchen yours." She glanced at Ginger before adding, "I'll fix you and Julie a casserole tomorrow and send Ginger over with it. But feel free to use our kitchen anytime. I like knowing that Julie is eating better."

"Thank you, Mrs. Atkinson. I appreciate it."

"And for goodness' sake, call me Pam."

She and Clint disappeared into the house, and at the same time the back door closed, the sun dipped below the roofline, and the deck was cast in shadows. Ginger moved to the storage box and found a lighter. As she finished lighting the last of the torches, a second clang of glass rang out behind her as Carter tossed his bottle into the bin.

She looked back. "Want another?"

He shook his head. "I only took that one to be nice."

She considered questioning his words; she pictured the empty bottles from his house once again. But decided to leave it alone. The mood was good tonight, and she didn't want to spoil it. She returned to her chair, and he motioned to the lounger beside her.

"Do you mind?" he asked.

"Make yourself at home. Seems the kitchen is already yours anyway." She winked, and he actually laughed. Not a chuckle, but a laugh.

It took her breath away.

"I wish you'd do that more often," she said. "You're so much more *you* when you smile."

Of course, her words shut him up.

She stretched her legs out in front of her and leaned back against the wooden slats, and they sat silent for a few minutes, each in their own thoughts. Around them the night grew darker. A palmetto bug buzzed by and she swatted at it. She also looked longingly toward the back door. She didn't mean to, but her book was sitting on the counter right inside there. If Carter didn't intend to talk . . .

"Not reading tonight?"

Was the man in her head?

"I will after you leave." She grimaced when she realized how that sounded. "Not that I'm suggesting you go."

"Good." He settled deeper into the chair, mimicking her pose by putting his feet up. "I could stand to do something other than sit behind the blinds tonight."

Her laughter floated through the air. "Sorry about that comment. It was rude of me."

"It's true."

She turned to look at him, but he had his eyes closed. He seemed completely relaxed. It bothered her every time she looked at the house next door and saw that he'd shuttered the outside world. "Did your ex hurt you that badly?" she asked softly.

Since he'd told her that he was divorced, she'd wanted to know more. She wanted to help.

"Yes." His answer was simple. He didn't offer anything additional. So she let it go.

Closing her own eyes, she slouched down in her seat and enjoyed the moment for what it was. Two friends hanging out. Even if she did have a little flutter once again.

"What kind of books do you read?"

She turned her head to look at him when he spoke. He faced her the same way. The light from the fire flickered across his eyes, and though an air of hurt and distance still lingered around him tonight, there was also something more. It struck her that the new thing she was witnessing seemed like acceptance. For what, she wasn't sure. But it was there. He had a calmer, less-defensive demeanor about him.

Had he accepted that his life was different now? Was he ready to move on?

"Horror," she answered. "The scarier the better."

One dark eyebrow shot up while his chin dipped down. "That's what you read out here every night? By firelight? With no pants on?"

She covered her face in embarrassment. "I wear pants *sometimes*." She peeked through her fingers. "And anyway, you should be glad I'm not out here completely naked."

"No." The word was spoken quickly and intentionally, then the corners of his mouth inched up and he totally checked her out. "I *shouldn't*."

"Really, Carter." She made a snorting noise in the back of her throat. "You're flirting with me."

"So? You flirted with me last night."

"I was drunk last night. What's your excuse?"

He paused, his eyes seeming to lose focus for a moment before he answered. "Practice?" The word was a question, but didn't seem to need an answer. "I've been in a slump lately."

Join the club, she thought. Her life often seemed like a slump. But what she said out loud was "I figured along with the smoking and drinking, you were also busy sleeping with all the wrong women."

Wasn't that the stereotype?

"I'm not sleeping with anyone." He spoke quietly. Then the acceptance thing she'd thought she'd witnessed was gone. It was all pain and hurt once again. "You ever feel so badly about yourself that you didn't even want to sleep with the wrong people?" he asked.

"I have." More times than she wanted to admit.

There was something about not being the "ideal" that most men seemed to want. It shamed her at times.

"It sucks," Carter said.

"Yes, it does." She tried to force a smile. To tease away the moment. But she couldn't do it.

"There's nothing wrong with you, you know," he added softly.

Tears burned at the backs of her eyes. How was it that they were suddenly talking about her? "You mean other than the fact that I love the ocean more than dating?" she asked. Then she shrugged. "And yes, I know there's nothing wrong with me."

But that didn't mean she wouldn't have to eventually change.

He reached over and took her hand in his and squeezed. The move made her catch her breath. But then he removed his fingers, and she was left feeling cold.

"So horror stories, huh?" His quick change took her a moment to catch up.

"You got me started on them, don't you remember? I used to devour your Stephen King books. Since then I've read everything I can get my hands on." She curled to her side. She could talk about books for hours. "There's this fairly new author I can't get enough of. Jules Bradley—have you heard of him? I'm in *love* with him." She chuckled as she pictured Julie's bookcase. "Your sister must be, too. She has all his books. She even had his last one before it was released. I have no idea how she pulled that off, but I want her secret."

Carter stared at the sky. "You like Jules Bradley?"

"*Love* Jules Bradley. So much. I heard his next book has been contracted for a movie, which I'll be first in line to see. But wow, his last book . . . have you read him?"

Carter's heart pounded so rapidly as he listened to Ginger talk about how much she loved his latest book that it threatened to cut off all oxygen. He could feel each pump of his blood in the main artery of his neck, as if someone had slit the tiny vessel open and he were bleeding out. He'd wanted to know if Ginger had ever read one of his books, but hearing about it firsthand moved him in a way he hadn't been ready for.

His parents liked his novels. Julie did, too. They were proud of him. And he'd gotten plenty of accolades from readers. But Lisa had never read a single one. She wouldn't lower her standards to such.

He needed to tell Ginger that he was Jules Bradley. To stop her gushing. And honestly, he *wanted* to tell her. But he couldn't bring himself to do it tonight. She'd be embarrassed, and he didn't want to change the atmosphere of the evening.

He'd come over because he'd been sitting in the house by himself, contemplating another night of drowning his sorrows, and he'd realized that he wanted to see Ginger. She hadn't been around that morning.

She'd made it home last night, he knew. Alone. He'd forgone the beer and watched out the window until he'd seen her make it safely inside. But she hadn't been around for sunrise.

So he'd come over, hoping to find her, or entice her to come outside. What he hadn't expected was to discover her there with her mom and Clint. Doing so had sent him back to his childhood. He'd always liked her mom. He'd liked their families hanging out. And he'd suddenly not wanted to be mad and angry, if just for one night.

"You seem lighter tonight," Ginger said, running out of commentary on his books, and mercifully changing the subject. A slight breeze slid a lock of hair across her cheek and he focused on that, because he was embarrassed that she'd picked up on the change in him.

"What does 'lighter' even mean?" he asked.

"I don't know. Not as angry." She gave him a tiny smile. "I worry about you."

He looked down at his hands where they lay clasped in his lap, and thought about the phone call from his mother earlier that day. She'd expressed the same sentiment. Again. "You and my mother, both," he griped.

"I miss your mom," Ginger said breezily as she seemed to curl deeper into the wood of the chair. "Your dad, too. I always loved watching them together. They're so in love."

"Like your parents were?"

"Yeah." She blinked rapidly, and he felt momentarily bad that he'd brought her father up. "They were good role models," she said softly.

He agreed. If anyone ever wanted an example of true love, they'd only had to look at either set of their parents. It was part of why he'd stupidly believed in love for so long.

Hell, it was the exact reason why. And that added to his anger now.

How did it exist for them? Or did it really?

Or had it totally been a figment of his imagination for his entire life?

He knew it wasn't fake, though. His parents were still as in love today as they'd been when they'd first met. Probably more so. And he was anxious to see them again. To see their love. To remind himself that it wasn't all like his life.

"I miss them, too," he said. He looked at Ginger. "And yeah, I feel 'lighter' today." He wasn't sure why, exactly. Maybe the ocean air was getting to him. "Don't tell my mom, though. She'll think she was right."

"About what?"

He paused, only for a second. "She wanted me to come here for *me* as well as Julie."

"Ah. Because of the divorce?"

"Among other things." He pulled a hand over his face and wished he'd taken a second beer. "It's been a rough summer."

"Do you miss your wife?"

He moved his gaze to hers. "I don't."

"But you loved her?"

It was on the tip of his tongue to deny it. He nodded instead.

"What did you love about her?" She asked the question quietly, but it was enough to send his "light" mood into the ether.

His instinct told him to get up. To leave. To ignore her probing. He shouldn't have left the house tonight to begin with. But he kept his gaze glued to hers. "What good would it possibly do to talk about how stupid I was?"

"Love isn't stupid," she objected.

Their gazes dueled as he fought the urge to tell her to face reality. It didn't work for everyone. He shoved to his feet. "Love is idiotic. Thanks for the company."

She didn't reply, and he moved to the edge of the deck. But before going down he looked back at her. She sat quietly in the light of the flames, a slight frown on her face, and his pulse once again thundered. She was his friend. His only one at this point; his months-long bad mood had pushed all the others away. He didn't want to end the evening with this tension.

"I missed you this morning," he admitted. His tone softened, and he tried hard to ease the sternness from his face.

"I left you a note."

"I got it."

After getting up and trying to write again—only to reread her sex scene, this time rewriting it to have her stripping off the faded, curve-hugging jeans she'd had on the night before—he'd come over well before sunrise ready to see her. Only to find a small note taped to her door.

"What's tomorrow look like for you?" she asked.

Relief hit him hard. And unexpectedly. He didn't want to come across as needy, but he *needed* to watch the sun come up with her. "I'm thinking there's a sunrise in my future."

She smiled lazily at him, and he smiled back.

Then she stretched, her arms reaching high above her head and a sleepy little purr slipping out. His breaths grew shallow. It was time to take his returning libido home before he did something he'd regret. He didn't want to hurt her.

"Tell your mom thanks for the beer. And the offer of a casserole."

"Will do." She yawned. "See you in the morning."

He nodded, taking her in one last time, and silently thanking his mother for sending him home. Just possibly he would heal a little before these few weeks were up.

Chapter Eleven

It was already past six o'clock, and she was late.

Ginger hurried into the mudroom Monday afternoon, pulling her shirt over her head before she even made it to the washing machine. She had a date arriving to pick her up in less than an hour, and she was filthy. She'd taken a boatload of tourists deep-sea fishing that morning, had spent the next hour out at the house doing nothing more than watching her home come to life—she had electricity and plumbing installed, and a huge crew of men had shown up to hang drywall today—then she'd finished her day on the ferry.

After departing the ship for the last time, she'd hurried, attempting to edge around a group to get to her car and save a few minutes, only to slip and end up in a mudhole. Not stepped in it, but fell. It had rained last night, and she was well aware that the hole was always there.

And now she was even later.

She shimmied out of her jeans, eyeballed Mz. Lizzie as she pranced into the laundry room with her tail swishing in the air and a yellow bow hanging lopsided around her neck, then dumped her underthings in the machine along with her jeans and shirt.

Meow.

She looked down at the cat. "What?"

Meow.

"Really? You're going to pay attention to me today? What happened, did your mama forget to feed you before she left?" Her mother had gotten off work early, and she and Clint had gone over to the mainland for a business party. They planned to stay overnight, returning on the ferry tomorrow. Which would be convenient if tonight's date happened to turn out spectacularly.

She couldn't see it going *that* well, but just in case, she did plan on bringing out the lace. She was getting a little desperate.

Meow.

"What, silly cat?" Ginger stooped, reaching out a hand to scratch Mz. Lizzie behind the ears, but the cat sidestepped her. Of course she did.

Grabbing the dirty clothes from the weekend, Ginger ignored the animal and tossed the armload in with everything else, added a healthy dose of laundry detergent, and closed the lid. Then she moved to put out food for Mz. Lizzie, but the bowl wasn't empty.

Meow.

"I don't know what you want," Ginger grumbled. She was running too late to play games with a cat.

She grabbed her cell off the dryer, and as if the cat had simply been waiting for her to be done, Mz. Lizzie pranced out of the room, leading Ginger into the kitchen. Where Ginger picked up the scent of something good.

"Did she cook before leaving?" Ginger spoke to herself.

But why? Her mother knew she planned to go out tonight.

Nevertheless, Ginger headed to the source of the smell, which was the oven, and peered in. The heat was still on. Still cooking. And a yummy-looking cheesy casserole bubbled inside.

"What the . . ."

She dug two pot holders out of a drawer, intending to pull the dish from the heat. Only to freeze at the sound of the powder-room door opening and closing. Then footsteps heading her way.

"Mz. Lizzie." She hissed the cat's name in a panic, as if the feline could save the day. Who was in the house? And why?

And where was that darned can of Mace Kayla was always preaching about?

Her questions were answered the instant Carter reached the kitchen door. Ginger's shoulders slumped, and a burst of air expelled from her lungs. "It's you."

Carter stopped in the doorway, and the expression on his face looked as if she'd thrown cold water at him. Or as if he'd seen her naked.

"Ah, crap." Ginger jumped into action, scanning for a dish towel, but there was none. Only the pot holders that were already in her hands. So she slid behind the center island, and covered each breast with a hand-stitched, white-robed angel. Her mother had gotten the pot holders as a Christmas gift last year. Apparently she'd never put them away after the holidays.

Meow.

Ginger gritted her teeth. "I see now, Mz. Lizzie. We have company. Thanks for that warning."

"Uh . . ." Carter looked shell-shocked.

"What are you doing here, Carter?" she asked calmly. Someone had to say *something*.

"Your mother let me in." He pointed to the oven, his arm stiff. "So I could cook."

She nodded. "Okay. Cooking." Why in God's name hadn't her mother warned her? Her mind whirled, trying to figure the best way out of the situation. She could send Carter to her room for clothes.

143

But then he'd have to rummage through her stuff, and she didn't want that.

She could just walk out of there as she was. She wasn't overly concerned about nudity as a general rule. And it *was* only Carter. If it were Andie or Roni she wouldn't give it a second thought.

"Here." Carter thrust an apron at her, his eyes now cast in another direction. His cheeks had turned pink. A feat she wouldn't have expected was possible. It made her even more tempted to sashay right past him in the buff.

But he was trying to be such a gentleman . . .

"Thanks." She took the apron, having to step away from the island to reach it, and slipped the strap over her head. The material was black with white polka dots, there were two large pockets below the belted waist, and the whole thing was edged with a white ruffle. It was cute.

But it made her look a little like a French maid.

Also, the sides of her boobs poked out.

After tying the apron behind her back, she tugged her hair from under the neck strap and picked up the pot holders. She used *them* to cover the outer boob area.

"I'm decent," she announced. Of course, her rear was bare, but he couldn't see that.

Carter carefully turned back.

"For the love . . ." he muttered.

"French maidish, right?" Ginger teased. She figured playing it off would be the only way to keep from turning bright red. She looked down at herself. She hadn't seen this particular apron before, but it totally looked like something her mother would pick out. Very feminine. And kind of naughty.

Carter, clearly attempting to avoid looking at her, went to the built-in oven. He walked stiff-legged and flipped the interior light, actually turning it off, before flipping it back on and stooping to peer through the glass as if his life, as well as that of the casserole, depended on it.

"What are you cooking?" she asked.

"Chicken."

She smiled at his clipped tone. "It smells good."

Time was ticking down on getting ready for her date, but this was actually kind of fun. Carter's embarrassment made any she'd had disappear. And the whole thing struck her as funny.

"Could you please put some clothes on, Ginger?" He still didn't look at her.

"I have clothes on."

He literally growled, which only made her laugh out loud.

"Why are you so embarrassed? I'm covered."

"You're naked."

She moved to his side—being sure to keep her exposed backside away from view—and leaned in, peering into the oven with him. "It looks good," she whispered loudly.

"I swear to God, Ginger. Put on some clothes."

She straightened, but looked down at herself to ensure she truly was covered. There was a bit of cleavage going on, but with the addition of the pot holders at the sides, she was hidden.

"What's the matter, Carter? Never seen anyone in an apron before?" She gave him a toothy grin, and finally, he looked at her. His gaze burned steady, and his jaw was clenched. And then she saw it. Her eyes went wide. "You're turned on?" She glanced down at herself. "By me?"

"You're *naked.*"

"I'm—" She snapped her mouth shut, growing embarrassed herself. "It didn't occur to me this would bother you. You never even noticed me back in high school."

"Sweetheart, we are no longer in high school."

A thrill rushed through her. For two totally different reasons. She went with the safer one. "So you're saying my problem with men isn't my looks?"

A muscle ticked in his jaw. "It is *not* your looks."

"Well, that's"—she cleared her throat—"good to know. Because I have a date tonight," she tacked on, nerves making her voice too perky when he didn't take his eyes off her. "A firefighter I met at the bar Friday night," she rattled. "I'm keeping my fingers crossed with this one." She crossed the fingers of her right hand to show him, but the pot holder slipped and she exposed a curve.

"Damn it, Ginger." He unbuttoned his shirt. "Put this on."

And then *she* got turned on.

The soft cotton of his button-down settled around her shoulders, and she eyed the set of ripped muscles with a fine sprinkling of hair that just happened to be right in front of her. "Wow." She lifted her eyes to his. "You're *definitely* not as scrawny as you first looked."

"You're not helping matters any."

He looked somewhere above her head as she released the hold on the pot holders and slid one arm at a time into the sleeves. The material was warm against her back, and suddenly the only thing she could smell was him. Hot male flesh mixed with sawdust, a bit of sweat, and whatever cologne he'd started the morning with. It was intoxicating, but she fought the urge to bury her nose in the collar and inhale.

When he finally looked back down at her, she realized how close they were standing, and she struggled not to be sucked under by the pulse beating rapidly in his throat. He pulled in a deep breath, expanding his chest toward hers, then blew it out. The puff of air ruffled the hair over her left ear, and her eyelids fluttered. And she was pretty sure that if she were wearing panties, they'd be instantly damp.

"You need to get your ass out of the kitchen, and put on some clothes." His words were too calm, almost cold.

"I have to shower first." Two inches forward and she could put her lips to his neck.

"Get out of the kitchen," Carter ground out. *"Now."*

She gulped, but she didn't waste any more time. She whirled and ran. At the top of the stairs, she smiled. Then she slipped inside her room, closed the door behind her, and pulled Carter's shirt to her nose.

Carter was attracted to her. She had *not* seen that coming.

In the bathroom, she slipped out of the shirt and apron and took the world's quickest shower. After she dried off, she stood in front of the mirror and considered, for one brief moment, walking back downstairs just as she was, and proclaiming that she wanted Carter. At least for tonight.

She got hot all over again.

But that would be silly. She had a hot date on his way to pick her up at that very moment. A guy who, at the very least, stood a *chance* of being long-term. Carter wasn't even in the same ballpark. He had too many issues. Too many hurts. And way too much anger. And she wasn't ready to give up the hunt just yet.

Ten minutes later, she was as polished as time would allow. She wore a cute blue sundress, and slipped into heeled sandals, then gave one last fluff to her hair before grabbing Carter's shirt and heading to the kitchen. With any luck, he'd be gone and she could return the clothing later.

But he stood right where she'd left him, the casserole cooling on top of the stove, his chest still wondrously bare, and his hip propped against the counter. He'd waited for her.

Nerves had her pausing at the kitchen door. She took a fortifying breath and walked in as if she hadn't recently been there wearing little more than the man's shirt and a couple of pot holders.

"Thanks," she murmured as she held the shirt out to him.

This time it was she who didn't look at him. But she heard his every move as he slid his arms into the material.

Her gaze landed on her fingernails, and she bit down on her frustration. Why did she always forget that? Without another word, she yanked open a drawer and dug through the contents. Carter watched her. She came up with a fingernail file as the doorbell rang, but remembered at the same time that she'd forgotten her purse upstairs. And jewelry.

She faced Carter. "Will you get the door for me?"

"You had him pick you up here?" He sounded annoyed. "Do you even know this man?"

"We met the other night, I told you. At Gin's."

The scowl she knew so well was firmly back in place as he finished up the buttons on his shirt. "He could be a serial killer."

"I have Mace," she scoffed. "Plus, the island isn't big. He could find me if he wanted to." She picked at one of her nails. "Will you let him in or not?"

He moved reluctantly in the direction of the foyer, and Ginger hurried back up the stairs. After doing all she could for her nails, she dug out a necklace and pair of earrings, and stepped in front of the full-length mirror in the corner of her room. With three deep breaths, her nerves began to settle.

"You can do this," she urged her reflection. She smoothed her hands down over her hips.

"I don't get it."

She jumped at the words. Carter stood at her open door.

"What are you doing up here?" Her voice climbed an octave. "Did you let him in?"

"He's waiting for you in the foyer." He skimmed his gaze over her body. "Why all the pretense?" he asked. "The dresses, the jewelry . . . You hate that."

"It's called making a good impression." Turning away, she checked her backside and tugged at the material over her hips. "And anyway, I like this dress."

"It's called being fake. Any *anyway*, you make a hell of an impression without even trying."

She stopped long enough to smirk at him. "I am *not* walking down there naked."

Embarrassment colored his features, and his cheeks once again turned pink. "I didn't mean that." He clenched and released his hands, then glared at her. "Just be you. That's what I'm saying. Don't try so hard. *You* are pretty terrific."

He made it sound so easy.

She turned back to her reflection, and tried not to think about how much she wished Carter's words could be true, but her past indicated otherwise. Better to stick with the plan.

Grabbing her purse off the small love seat, she moved across the room. When she reached his side, she looked up at him expectantly, and he took a step back to let her pass. Before she'd gone more than a couple of feet, she turned back. She didn't want to go.

But her date was waiting.

"I don't have a charter in the morning," she told him. Her eyes watched his carefully. "See you at sunrise?"

"Definitely. Let's go out to your house, though. I want to see the view from your deck."

She smiled. "Sitting on the pier out there is even better."

Leaning in to him, she quickly lifted to tiptoe and kissed him on the cheek. It wasn't a move she'd planned, but it felt right. And she liked the feel of his scruffy days' growth of whiskers under her lips.

"Don't forget to lock up when you leave." She winked, then walked away.

As her foot reached the bottom stair, Carter leaned over the railing above. "By the way . . ."

She looked up, waiting to see what he had to say.

He smiled widely, the move so disarming, so sultry, that she lost her breath. "Nice tattoo."

Dang. That fast, and she was turned on again. He must have seen more than she'd realized as she'd dashed from the kitchen.

Because her tattoo rode high up on her hip.

CHAPTER TWELVE

H ow'd the date go?"
Carter stood on the front porch of Ginger's house at dawn the next morning, his hands tucked into his back jean pockets, wishing he didn't enjoy the frown on her face so much.

She eyed him from the bottom of the steps. "I don't want to talk about it."

He winced. "Sorry." It was all he had.

He couldn't very well admit he'd secretly been hoping it didn't go well—he hadn't liked the firefighter who'd come to her door last night. And he certainly wouldn't tell her that he'd spent the previous evening—again—watching for her to return home. There had been no drinking for him—or smoking . . . that had grown old—just in case she didn't show up and he had to go looking for her.

And why? All because he'd seen her naked? Because he'd gotten all hot and bothered when he'd written a sex scene about her?

Or because he'd gotten his nagging question answered when he'd *seen* her naked?

Pink. Her nipples were pink, just like he'd imagined. A very soft, almost-too-faint-to-see touch of color that proudly centered her breasts. A hue that he would have gladly handed over the keys to his custom-built home for just the opportunity to touch.

Fuck. He had to get a grip. Ginger was his friend, and a friend only. Even if he wanted it to be more, what would be the point? She was looking for a husband. A man to give her babies. And that wasn't him. He'd blown the husband and father opportunity with Lisa, and he had zero desire to put himself back out there.

Ginger climbed the steps to him. "Why didn't you wait and come over with me?"

He'd left a note for her that morning. He'd woken up with the desire to actually write *his* book. And he'd wanted to do it here. More than one scene had been in his head when he'd opened his eyes, and once he'd set up a makeshift desk on the top-floor deck, his fingers had flown over the keyboard. He was writing again.

"Couldn't sleep" was all he said.

He knew he should tell her he was an author. That he was, incidentally, one of her favorite authors. But he wasn't ready to talk about it yet. Mostly because until this morning, he'd been wondering if he could still call himself that.

But the two hours he'd spent lost in his head had given him an adrenaline rush he hadn't felt in months. Another morning or two like that, and he'd spill his guts. He wanted to see the look on her face when she found out.

"I was over here yesterday," she told him, glancing behind him to the house. "The walls were going up."

He could see the anticipation in her eyes, and he gave her a teasing wiggle of his brows. "They're up." He nodded toward the closed door. "So the question is . . . see the walls now"—he angled his head toward the water—"or see the sunrise?"

He knew what he wanted.

Ginger bit her lip as she worked through her decision, and as she stood in front of him, all he could picture was her naked body. Again. He'd done that a lot in the last twelve hours.

Normally, the sight of a beautiful bare woman—while arousing—wouldn't send his hormones into a complete rage. But seeing Ginger had done exactly that. Because he'd seen more than her naked body. He'd seen himself waking up.

He'd not only wanted sex, he'd wanted to live again. Even if for only the few minutes it would take to slide his body inside of hers. He wanted to feel something other than misery and anger.

"The sunrise." She'd made her decision. "On the pier."

She reached for his hand and pulled him down the stairs. At the bottom, he wrapped his fingers around hers and took the lead, and two minutes later they were on the pier. Without speaking, they dropped their hands and walked side by side to the end. They sat, feet hanging over the edge, and waited.

Of course, Ginger could only stay quiet for so long. "The way I see it, it's time for you to tell me more about your marriage."

He leveled her with a look. "And why do you think that?"

"Because you saw me naked."

Her green eyes stared, unblinking, back at him. She didn't seem embarrassed so much as exposed. Which she had been. And he wanted her to be again.

For the life of him, he couldn't get that thought out of his head.

"And what does your nakedness have to do with my marriage?"

"Mortification, Carter." She rolled her eyes at him as a teenager might do, and he had to bite down on a smile. "You saw me naked," she explained. "No man has seen me naked in a long time. A fact I thought about a *lot* last night."

"You thought about me while you were on your date?"

She narrowed her eyes. "My date ended early enough that I had time to think after."

"Ten o'clock."

"What?"

He turned away and casually explained, "Your date ended at ten o'clock."

"And how would you know that?"

Because he'd been jealous. He forced a sigh. He preferred her to believe his actions of the previous evening had been born of frustration. "You told a stranger where you lived, Ginger Root. Therefore, I watched to make sure you made it home okay."

"You spied on me?"

He wouldn't tell her that it wasn't the first time. He continued watching the sky.

She poked him in the arm. "You do know that I'm a grown woman? I can take care of myself."

"It doesn't hurt to have backup." He slid her a glance. "So . . . *did* you think about me while you were on your date?"

"I thought about me!" She raised her voice in exasperation. "Me being naked."

He smiled. "I thought about that, too."

"Stop it. You're trying to derail me. The point I'm making is, you saw me naked. Vulnerable. So I deserve a bit of the same. If you don't plan on getting naked, then tell me about your wife."

He looked down at his clothes, and she immediately pointed a finger at him.

"Don't you *dare* get naked."

"Why not?" He pulled out another smile. "You think you might like it as much as I did?"

She blew out a harsh breath, and he couldn't stop the chuckle. Damn, but she was cute. And if he weren't mistaken, she was turned on, as well. At least a little.

Where was this thing between them going? And why was he trying to drive it there?

"Yes." All irritation disappeared from her demeanor with the single word. "I would like it, too." Her honesty moved him. She stuck out her chin. "Now spill."

"Lisa left me for someone else."

Ginger sucked in a sharp breath. "Oh, Carter." Her fingers landed on his arm. "I'm so sorry."

Pressure eased inside of him with the release of the words. He gave her a tight smile and let her touch remain. "No biggie. I wasn't the kind of man she wanted."

Ginger didn't blink. He watched her throat rise with a swallow, then she gave a small nod and her thumb caressed a tiny section of his skin. "I understand how that feels. Not being what someone wants." Her eyes stayed focused on his. "But clearly, it *was* a biggie. It changed you."

It had changed him. And he hadn't even told her the worst of it. Nor did he plan to.

"This is why you feel so bad about yourself that you aren't having sex?" Ginger asked.

He shook his head. "No more, Red. That's all you get. No more talking about the ex."

"But you need to."

"What good would it possibly do?"

"What harm would it do? And it could totally help you."

"Help?" He brought one knee up on the dock, shrugging off her touch. But he faced her dead on. "I don't think so. But yes. *She's* the reason I'm not having sex. Hell, I wasn't having sex *with* her. And now you want me to talk about her? No." He shook his head. "It'll only make it worse. Make me want sex less. And seeing you naked last night . . ." He eyed her carefully as he thought about the surge of heat that had spiraled through him the night before. "Seeing you made me actually *want* it. A hell of a lot. And I liked that feeling." He gave her a hard look. "I'd like to keep it."

She didn't answer. Nor did she seem to breathe.

"So no more sharing about Lisa," he finished and turned back to the horizon. Ginger had been right, this was a beautiful spot for a sunrise. The way they were practically sitting out in the ocean made it feel as if the day were waking up purely for them.

The colors of the sky lightened above the water, indicating that the sun wasn't far behind.

"So you weren't having sex during your marriage?"

Carter's teeth clenched together.

"For how long?"

He scowled at her.

"We're friends, Carter," Ginger said softly. The honesty still burned in her eyes, so Carter closed his. They might be friends, but that didn't mean he had to share his past screwups. "I just want to help," she continued. "Because I want you to be happy again."

Fuck. She had a way of getting to him. He reopened his eyes to find hers right there. Still on his. And he couldn't staunch the words. "I found out about them in May," he said. "But if you count the months before that . . ."

"Months?"

He gave her a quiet stare. It was embarrassing.

"How many months?"

He turned back to the ocean. The sun was there. They'd missed the sunrise. "Before Christmas," he admitted. Shame filled him. Lisa had been home for only one day over the holidays, yet they hadn't bothered. He hadn't seen her for months at that point, and he hadn't cared to take her to bed.

"That's a long time," Ginger said beside him.

"You're telling me." He leaned back, resting his palms on the wood behind him and stared at the sky. "And my god . . ." He blew out a breath. "Could I use some sex."

Then he smiled. Because he realized that telling her about Lisa *had* made him feel better. Lighter, as she'd said Saturday night.

He turned to her. "Especially if you're going to keep running around naked."

She grinned back at him, the look so radiant, it was if his own personal sunrise had just risen. "I promise to check the kitchen for rogue casseroles being cooked from now on," she said. "*Before* I take off my clothes."

"Hey, don't do that on my behalf."

She laughed lightly, but quickly fell into silence, and he watched as she realized they'd missed the sunrise. Her smile dropped, but she didn't seem upset. However, it was as if her entire being was suddenly shrouded with sadness. "It's been over two years for me."

"Damn."

"I know." She twisted her lips. "I told you no man has seen me naked for a long time."

"No wonder you want those dates to work out."

She snorted softly, and he pushed off his hands to sit up straight. An idea began knocking around inside his head. It was probably a bad one. But it wouldn't go away.

"*We* . . . could . . ." He let the words trail off. He didn't look at her.

"We could what?"

He lifted a brow, and without saying another word, he knew he got his point across.

"Carter," she gasped. "We're friends."

He swung his gaze back to hers. "What better person to have sex with? We'd know we'd still be friends afterward." He stared at her mouth. "And I'd be willing to bet we'd have chemistry."

She also looked at his mouth. And she seemed to consider it. A tiny line formed between her brows. She licked her lips. Then, as if coming out of a trance, she blinked and gave him that rolled-eye thing again.

"I am *not* having sex with you," she stated. "You're out of your mind. Anyway, I've got another date Thursday night."

That caught him off guard. "So last night *did* go well?"

"No. Last night was a bomb. He was too immature. But I lined up this one a couple of weeks ago. He doesn't live on the island, only comes over for work every few weeks. We had a really nice talk the day he asked me out."

"Your ability to draw new men so often amazes me." And made him jealous.

"Tell it to my mother," she drawled out. "That's the only thing I inherited from her. Anyway, I have that date"—she shot him a look—"so I'll hold out for that. Maybe I'll get lucky."

He stood and reached a hand down to her. "Let me know if you change your mind."

"I'm not going to change my mind." But her words grew soft as they stood face-to-face.

"Should we kiss just to see?" he asked. Now that he'd had the idea, he wasn't ready to let it go. "Test the chemistry?"

"Carter." The word came out more breathy than she probably realized. "We're friends. Friends can't run around kissing."

"We are friends, and that won't change, kissing or not. And anyway, I'll be leaving soon. It's not like you'd even have to be around me if things got uncomfortable."

Her clear gaze studied him. "You won't come back to visit Julie and the baby?"

The moment changed, and he nodded. Things were different now. Different than just two weeks ago. "I will come back," he said. It was a promise to himself as well as an admission to her. "I won't stay away like I did in the past. But you won't be living beside her anymore; you'll be out here." He squeezed her hand, aware for the first time that he hadn't turned her loose after he'd pulled her to her feet. "So we could avoid each other if we wanted to."

"You make it sound so simple." She sounded as if she was seriously contemplating the idea.

"It could be simple. And I don't think it would ruin our friendship. I really believe that. We're both too smart. Too aware of reality and what we want out of life. You want forever."

"And what do you want?"

"*Not* forever." It was the saddest thing he'd ever said.

"I'm really sorry she hurt you so badly."

He nodded. "Me, too."

They walked a few feet before he cut a glance down at her. "So are you happy now? Feeling better about the vulnerability thing? You got me to talk about Lisa. To tell you all my secrets."

Not *all* his secrets. And she watched him as if aware of that fact.

"I am happy." She tugged on his hand, pulling him closer, and slipped her arm through his. "Thank you for telling me."

It started raining then, just a little, and they stopped walking and tilted their heads to the sky. Silky wetness slid over their faces. It felt to Carter like waking up.

"I didn't know it was supposed to rain this early," he said. Though the forecast called for it later in the day, there were no clouds in the sky yet, just sun and rain. And Carter loved that Ginger didn't seem to mind getting wet. She stood there, her cheeks turned up, with water dripping down over her.

She was beautiful.

"I saw a woman on the ferry the morning I arrived," he told her. "It was drizzling, and she came out with a raincoat on, but the hood wasn't up. She seemed completely unconcerned with the weather. It made me think of you."

Her soft laughter stroked inside of him. "Was that the morning it was so foggy?"

"So bad you couldn't even see the island until we were practically upon it."

Her lips curved more. The pink in them captured his attention, and he knew there was more than one thing about him that had changed over the last two weeks.

"That *was* me," she said. "At least, I was on that ferry. And I didn't have my hood up." She held out her free hand, palm open as if to capture the rain. "Some things never change."

"And some things do." He tugged her. "Kiss me, Red. I have to know."

"Carter."

"You have to wonder a little . . . right?" He gulped with unexpected nerves. "I mean . . . tell me I wasn't the only one feeling something in the kitchen last night."

"You took off your shirt and I combusted," she confessed.

"See?" He could barely pull in a breath. "We could be good together. Blow off some steam." He tried a smile, but it failed. He wanted her. Right now. Underneath him. "Kiss me, Red. Don't make me beg."

"You're already begging."

"And I plan to keep begging until I get what I want."

"Fine."

The word surprised him, and he latched his gaze on to hers. Did she mean . . .

"Lay one on me." Her voice was solid. "Show me what you've got."

Additional nerves hit. So fast he almost changed his mind. But he tugged at her hand once more, and she willingly came closer. Then he cupped her cheek in his palm and brought her mouth up to his.

The first touch made everything inside him clench tight.

Her lips were warm. And damp from the rain. And fuller than he'd realized.

He tilted his head and slid his thumb to the spot just below her bottom lip. She groaned. Then he pressed in harder.

His heart beat so hard it almost vibrated his rib cage, and he would swear that he could feel hers doing the same. And then he parted her lips and touched his tongue to hers, and suddenly nothing about him could be contained.

Ginger's touch lit him on fire, and fear screamed at him to pull back. But he didn't. He captured her face in both his palms, holding her to him, touching her, caressing her. Tasting her. He couldn't get enough. And she was right there with him. Her tongue swiped at his. Her fingers tunneled through his hair. And her lips fought to keep up.

Finally, and with grave reservations, he separated them so they could breathe.

His fingers were still tangled in her hair, and he reveled in the silkiness against his skin.

He wanted more.

"Wow," she whispered.

They stood, faces together, and their bodies trembling.

"You thought that was wow, too, right?" she asked. She sounded as scared as he felt.

Red lights and screaming sirens flashed in his head. A concrete wall slammed at his emotions. All implying the same single word.

Stop!

But another part of him said something else.

"I absolutely thought that was wow." His voice came out hoarse. "Very wow." He traced the pad of his thumb over her cheekbone. Her skin was soft. And the rain made her intoxicating to touch. "This is bad, Red. I'm going to want more."

"No." She shook her head. "No more. It was a test. A single kiss. I have a date Thursday night. I want a happily ever after . . ." Her words trailed off before she finished with "It's going to be a good date. He could be the one."

He wouldn't be the one.

Carter kissed her again.

They moaned at the same time, and again, she was a full participant. The earth moved under their feet.

When they separated, Carter pulled their hands off each other and put a foot of space between them. He gasped for air. "It's yet to be seen if this date is 'the one,'" he said. His voice came out gravelly. "But keep your clothes on for it, will you? He doesn't need to see that."

She stared at him. Then she blinked, nodded, and put another foot of space between them.

"I hope your mother is right, Carter." She said the words softly, giving him the most tender smile he'd ever received. "I hope coming home heals you."

She turned and walked away from him then, and he watched until she'd gotten into her car and driven out of sight. Then he touched his lips. What had he done?

Had that explosion been only because it had been so long for both of them?

The urge to write struck again. He should have an hour or two before anyone else showed up at the house to work, and though he bordered on feeling rude for taking up residence in Ginger's upstairs room, he didn't let that stop him. The words had flowed that morning, and that was what mattered.

He retrieved his laptop from his truck and took the stairs two at a time. Settling in the fold-out chair he'd brought over earlier, he stared through the glass panes of the deck doors and watched the rain now coming down in sheets. It was a glorious day.

And that kiss had rocked his fucking world.

Chapter Thirteen

The slow, steady hum of rain pelting down on the roof kept Ginger in a relaxed state, but not enough to allow sleep to continue. It was time to get up, whether there would be a decent sunrise to view or not.

Of course, she wasn't likely to meet up with Carter for a rainy sunrise.

Which was *fine*. She wasn't sure she was ready to face him again.

She threw the covers back and climbed from her bed. It had been raining since yesterday morning, which had suited her perfectly. She'd been in a rainy-day kind of mood. Because the only thing that had been on her mind the whole day was that kiss. And Carter's suggestion that they have sex.

She'd felt his touch throughout her entire body, and she wasn't ashamed to admit that she wanted more. Her freaking toes had tingled. But try as she might, she'd never been a casual-sex type of girl. She had to at least *believe* it could go somewhere before going to bed with a man. Yet with Carter, she wanted to be different. She wanted to explore that. To enjoy it. Only . . . how?

What she needed was advice. And she knew just the person to give it.

After brushing her teeth, she grabbed a bottle of water from the minifridge she kept in her room, scooped up her phone, and settled onto the cushion of the window seat.

Call me when you get up. I'm considering casual sex.

She hit "Send," and laughed when less than fifteen seconds later her phone rang. Her friends were the best.

Roni's face flashed across her screen. Roni had always been an early riser, so Ginger had hoped she'd be up. And though her friend was now happily married with a kid on the way, she hadn't been shy in the past about having the occasional good time.

Ginger pushed the button to answer. "So how do I make sure it stays casual?" she greeted.

"And good morning to you, too." Roni chuckled. "Who are we talking about, here? Do I know him?"

Ginger didn't answer.

"Oh my god, it's Carter, isn't it?" Roni squealed. "You're going to have sex with Carter! Your boyhood crush. The hottie currently back in town and just next door." Then she sucked in a sharp breath. "Or have you already had sex with him?"

"I have not. And I may not." Ginger wet her lips. "But if I wanted to . . ."

"Does Andie know? Oh . . . do I have a secret? We had a feeling it might lead to this."

"Roni!" Ginger whispered the word as if someone could overhear their conversation. She put a finger to the edge of her curtains and inched it away from the frame. There was a light on in Carter's room. "I'm serious. We kissed. He suggested an affair. And I don't know what to do."

"You kissed?" Roni's excitement was suddenly contained. "How was it?"

"I just need to know—"

"How was it?" Roni demanded.

"Does it matter?"

"Yes. First off, no casual sex if the kiss doesn't blow your socks off. It's just not worth it. But second . . . it was *Carter*. The boy you once would have sold your soul to get a kiss from. How was it?"

"On a scale of one to ten . . ." She gulped. "Fifty."

"Day-ummm."

"I know," Ginger said. "It was *so* good. But Roni, I don't do this. I never have."

"But you've had sex before."

"Of course. But only if—"

"I know. Only if you really had your hopes up about the relationship. Which *means*, with the lame-o dates that you so often find, you're still probably running dry, right? Handling matters yourself?"

She shook her head at Roni's wording. "Two years and counting."

"Oh, honey. It sounds like Carter is exactly what you need."

"Then tell me what to do."

"You got it. First of all, forget the nerves. Toss them out the window. We're just talking sex. Hopefully mind-blowing sex, but still, it's just sex."

"With my friend."

"Right. But that's okay. I had sex with plenty of friends in my day. And we're all still friends today."

This was working. Ginger nodded. It could be done. She wouldn't ruin her life if she decided to go to bed with Carter. She took a drink of her water.

"All you really need to remember is to not overthink it." Roni said.

"No overthinking. Got it. What else?" Ginger chugged another drink.

"Just have a good time, sweetie. Don't play games. Tell him what you like, ask him what he likes. And if it becomes hard to deal with, then call stop. Oh, and ground rules. Talk about it beforehand, set up a few ground rules. Then go for it."

"Okay." Ginger bit her lip. "I can do that." Her heart pounded hard, as if she were at the starting line of the act that very moment.

"And the most important thing . . ."

"What's that?" She peeked out her window again, and saw Carter peeking out his. She lifted her fingers in greeting.

"Make sure he gets you off."

The bottle slipped from her hand, followed by the phone, and she jerked up off the cushion. She swiped at the cell to keep it from landing in the water, and it skidded across the floor, not stopping until it met the wall.

"Ginger?"

She heard Roni yell through the earpiece.

"Hang on," she yelled back.

Leave it to Roni to catch her so completely off guard.

She grabbed the emptying bottle, then tossed a towel over the spilled water and hurried after the phone. Her face blazed as she thought about Carter getting her off. Which *was* the whole point of casual sex. But somehow, seeing Carter through the window as Roni had said that made it all the more real.

She *so* wanted to do this.

But she also *didn't* want to.

"Are you still there?" she asked when she finally got the phone back to her ear. She needn't have asked, because she could hear Roni laughing.

"Oh, sweetheart," Roni said, finally getting control of herself. "You're going to be that man's fantasy, do you know that? If that one sentence caused that much commotion from you, I can't imagine how you'll light up when he touches you."

"Don't I know it." She stood in the middle of her room now, and looked at herself in her mirror. Her cheeks were pink, and her eyes shone as if already in the throes of passion. "It's a fallback plan, anyway. I have a date tomorrow night. I'm hopeful it'll go well, then Carter—and this crazy idea—will be off the table."

"Is he as hot as Carter?"

"How do you know how hot Carter is, anyway? You keep saying that. But you haven't even seen him since you were a teenager."

"Andie sent me the picture."

Of course she did. Her friends had probably been talking about her for days.

"My date isn't bad looking," Ginger answered. Nor was he in the same league as Carter. "And I really think he's interested in long-term. We talked about futures and our lives down the road when we met. It was refreshing to have such an honest conversation with a guy."

And she had to be certain not to overplay it. She didn't want to try so hard with this one.

"Then go on your date. Enjoy yourself, and see where it can go. But Ginger . . ."

"What?"

"Don't close the door to Carter yet, will you? You put so much pressure on these dates, maybe having a good time with him would ease that some."

"That's what he said."

More laughter came through the phone. "I always did like that guy. He's smart."

"And you're a smart aleck. How are you, anyway? Pregnancy going okay?"

"It's great. I'm getting fat."

Ginger crossed to the window and used the towel to wipe up the water. "I doubt it. You're only five months."

"And barely five feet tall. And *now* there's a baby shoved in there. Trust me, I'm fat."

"I'll bet you're cute. But then, you're always cute. I can't wait to see you this weekend. Did Andie tell you we're staying out at my house?"

"She told me you have no plumbing," Roni answered wryly. "If you have any clue about the size of this thing pressing on my bladder, then you'll know that won't work."

"I have plumbing now. Just nothing hooked up yet. But I'm meeting with my contractor today, and I promise, there will be a running toilet in the house before the weekend." She'd already let Gene know that had to be a priority.

Decisions hadn't been made on tile for the bathroom floors and master shower yet, but they *would* be made on toilets and the guest bath and sink today. Having no beds would be the bigger issue, but she had a couple of blow-up mattresses headed her way, and she'd take a few lamps and some of her mother's beach chairs when she went over today. And maybe her minifridge. They would need snacks.

"Then I'm looking forward to it," Roni told her.

They said their good-byes, and Ginger stood and faced her closed curtain. Was Carter still over there? The rain continued to come down, harder now, so there would be no sunrise walk. But she wouldn't mind getting another peek at him.

She opened the curtains. He was there. Smiling at her.

Her phone rang.

"Good morning, Ginger Root."

That freaking flutter went wild at the sound of his sleep-laden voice. "That is such a stupid name," she told him. "But good morning to you, too." If they'd been kids, they would have opened their windows and talked through the rain. Instead, she shoved the wet cushion to the floor and curled back onto the seat. She liked this better. "Guess we're skipping the sunrise?"

"Doubt we'd see much."

"What are you doing over there?" Her attempt to keep the conversation steered away from the subject of them *doing it* had him glancing down before answering.

"I'm on my laptop," he said. "Working on a few things. What's in store for you today?"

"Picking out toilets."

He chuckled, and she caught herself inching closer to the glass. This was the first time they'd talked since he'd kissed her yesterday morning, and it wasn't as uncomfortable as she'd feared.

"What about you?" she asked. "How's the remodel coming?"

"Everything is on target. Need to do a little shopping, pick out a new kitchen table and a few other necessities. But we should be done by middle of next week."

"Just in time for your parents' party." She and her mom had been invited to the anniversary party being held a week from Saturday. "You're heading home after that?"

"Soon after."

They fell silent, but continued to look at each other across the space. She expected him to ask if she'd given any more thought to his suggestion, but he didn't. He just watched.

"I should go." She broke the silence. "I'm taking the morning off to work with Gene, so I should probably shower and get ready."

"And I should probably"—he glanced down again, but didn't finish his sentence.

"Have a good day," she added.

She stood, ready to hang up, but he stopped her. "I wanted to ask you something."

"What's that?"

He was standing now, same as she, and as if he were right there in the room with her, she would swear she could feel the heat from his body wrap around hers. He touched one finger to his window. "Why balloons?"

She stared, not understanding the question at first, then she saw his smile. And blushed as badly as if he *were* standing right there. The tattoo on her hip was a bundle of balloons.

Instead of answering, she shook her head and let the curtains drop closed.

"I'll talk to you later, Carter."

Soft laughter was his only reply.

Chapter Fourteen

A *ding* sounded in the distance as Ginger entered the bookstore during her lunch hour the next day, and Cookie Phillips called out from upstairs, "Be right with you."

Cookie had been manager of the store for the last two years.

"No hurry," Ginger called back. "It's only me."

She breathed in the smell of the books. Lunchtime visits were a normal thing. She loved this store as much as she loved reading, and though plenty of people had tried to get her to go digital, so far she'd refused. There was something about holding a book in her hand.

Plus, she'd borrowed her mom's Kindle one day, and it had gotten lost at sea.

So she stuck with print. They were easier to replace.

She moved between two crammed aisles and ran her fingertip along the tops of the spines, silently thanking her dad for his love of reading. He was the one who'd gotten her started. She used to go out fishing with him most weekends, and he always had a book with him. When Ginger was old enough to read, her dad started bringing her to this very bookstore.

"Whew." Cookie blew out a breath as she hurried down the narrow set of stairs. Her wispy blonde hair danced with her movements. "A kid got a little too rambunctious up there earlier. Took out one of my shelves."

She quit talking as the doorbell sounded again, and both women turned to watch Mrs. Rylander enter the shop. Mrs. Rylander had passed eighty last year, always had a perm of tight white curls, and shared a love of green rubber boots with Ginger. She wasn't sporting the boots today, though, instead wearing royal-blue tennis shoes that matched the T-shirt hanging three inches below her narrow hips.

"I've been looking for you," Mrs. Rylander announced. The thin skin around her mouth pursed as she pointed a finger in Ginger's direction.

Ginger touched her chest. "Me? What in the world for?"

"I need someone on my side, that's what for. That Kayla Morgan and your mom are out to run me out of my new position at the senior center, and I won't have it."

Ah. Her mom's wedding. Mrs. Rylander was the rental contact at the senior center.

"I'm sure that's not their intent, Mrs. Rylander." Ginger slid out from between the two shelves and went over to the other woman. "Why don't you tell me what's going on, and I'll talk to my mom tonight. I'm sure it's simply a misunderstanding."

Wise, but faded, blue eyes squinted in Ginger's direction, then the woman gave a nod.

"I'll get us all some tea and cookies," Cookie offered. "Lunchtime dessert." She disappeared into the back of the store before either Ginger or Mrs. R. could comment, and Ginger edged the older woman to a seat near the register.

"Now, tell me what's going on," Ginger urged.

"I told them sunrise was the best time for the wedding." Mrs. R. crossed her arms over her chest and somehow managed to purse her lips even tighter. "Everyone knows that patio looks out over the ocean. But neither of them will listen to me. Why in hell's bells would someone want to get married on that patio when the sun is setting behind the building?"

She made an excellent point.

"Mom specifically requested sunset?" Ginger hedged around the issue. She knew her mom planned the wedding for early afternoon. They'd all be in the reception area before the sun went down.

"Well, she didn't want sunrise." Mrs. R. turned her head the other way. "Nor did she like any of my other suggestions," she grumbled.

And that, Ginger suspected, was the real issue. "What kind of suggestions?"

Mrs. Rylander adjusted the thin scarf tied at her neck, her fingers remaining at the silk. "The colors," she snipped out. "That Kayla keeps pushing her toward gold and silver, but I keep telling her, gold and silver won't look good with your mama's hair. All that blonde. She needs something stronger." Mrs. Rylander peeked Ginger's way, brushing her eyes over Ginger's red tresses. "A nice bright pink, perhaps."

Ginger held in her cringe. *That* color would not look good with Ginger's hair. And honestly, gold and silver would look good as the backsplash for her mother. There was nothing wrong with the color scheme.

"How about gold and cream?" Ginger tossed out. She'd actually overheard her mother discussing the color change with Kayla the day before. Gold and cream nicely complemented the green Ginger would be wearing, as well as the lace sheath her mother planned to have on. Apparently the change in plans hadn't made its way back to the senior center.

The tightness around Mrs. R.'s lips eased. "Cream is nice," she conceded. She was looking away from Ginger once again. "I married my Henry in cream."

Her Henry had been gone for six years, but never had Ginger seen a woman who'd loved her husband more. "And I'm sure you were beautiful in that color."

Mrs. R. sniffed. "Of course I was."

Cookie showed up loaded down with tea and snacks, but before she could pass out the first cup, the chime of a new customer sounded yet again. Ginger's back was to the door, but she saw Cookie's movements halt. Mrs. Rylander leaned to the side and peeked around Ginger.

And the hair on the back of Ginger's neck stood up.

"Well, hell's bells," Mrs. Rylander murmured. "I'd heard he was back in town."

It was Carter. Ginger didn't have to be told. She could tell by the heat touching her backside.

"He grew up nice," Mrs. R. continued under her breath. "He's as fine as my Henry."

Ginger slowly turned, and as her gaze locked on Carter's, behind her Cookie mumbled something about the tea not being hot enough before slipping from the room. Cookie was nothing if not shy.

The warmth in the hazel depths across the room seemed to indicate that Carter had found what he was looking for. "You're a hard lady to pin down today."

He'd left a note for her that morning, asking her to meet him at the pier for sunrise. The note had also stated that he had something he wanted to talk to her about.

"I had to be at work early," she explained. She hadn't been brave enough to go to the pier. Mostly because she'd feared talking about "something" would lead to more thoughts of them doing "something." And she'd thought about that way too much in the last two days.

"Not working now?" he asked. His gaze briefly shifted to the woman at her side.

"I'm on my lunch break." She grabbed a book off the counter and waved it in the air. "Picking up something to read later tonight."

"Ah." A twinkle lit his eyes. "Not expecting your date to go well, then?"

She blushed. If her date didn't go well . . .

"I expect it to go great," she replied primly.

"What date?" Mrs. Rylander asked.

Ginger ignored her.

Carter eyed Mrs. R. again, as if wishing the older woman away, before switching his attention back to Ginger. "I really did want to talk to you."

"I'm—"

"And it's not about *that*," he stressed.

Mrs. Rylander made a low *hmmm*, before once again speaking up. "About *what*?"

Carter's jaw twitched, and both of them ignored the other woman.

"Don't avoid me, Ginger Root." His voice always turned softer when he used the nickname. And it worked on Ginger every time. "I didn't make that suggestion to—"

"Stop." Ginger cut him off in midsentence. She glanced at Mrs. Rylander again, who gave her an innocent smile, but Ginger could see behind the batting of the woman's eyes. She wasn't the sweet little bystander she was going for. She'd probably already one-handed out a message on her cell phone to the senior center's social-media page.

Ginger moved across the room and grabbed Carter by the elbow. "Outside," she ordered.

"Don't forget to pay for that book," Mrs. R. called out behind her.

Looking down, Ginger realized she still held the paperback she'd grabbed from the stack beside the register. It was Jules Bradley's latest. She set it on the nearest shelf, but Carter picked it back up. He held the door open, and motioned for Ginger to precede him out the door.

Once on the porch, she faced him, and her hands began to shake.

"I didn't mean to make you nervous to be around me," Carter said.

"I'm not nervous."

He directed a look at her hands. She tucked them under her arms and ignored him, shifting her gaze to the quaint gingerbread shingles lining the front of the building, and chewing on her lip.

"Gin—"

"I'm not nervous," she reiterated. "I'm"—she glanced back at him—"embarrassed."

"Embarrassed?"

"You're my friend, Carter. We've always just been friends. Yet . . ." She motioned with her hands, swatting them at him. "You freaking kissed me senseless the other morning. Not to mention, suggested we do *more*. That isn't me. It's not what I'm used to."

A smile covered Carter's face.

"Are you laughing at me now?"

"Not at all." His smile grew wider. "I kissed you senseless?"

She sighed. *"Stop."*

"I can't help it, Red. You kissed me senseless, too." He took a step toward her. "You know it would be good between us."

She took two steps back. "And you said that wasn't what you wanted to talk about."

His heel came off the ground, as if he intended to continue pursuing her, and she turned to leave.

"I'm sorry," he said. "Don't go. I'll behave. I swear. No more talk about kissing, or . . . other things." She peeked back at him, uncertain whether to believe him or not, and he held up the Jules Bradley book in front of him. "*This* is what I wanted to talk to you about."

She remained where she was. "What about it?"

"You asked if I've read his books." He swallowed, and suddenly *he* seemed nervous. "I . . . actually . . . *wrote* them."

His words didn't compute. "What?"

He held the book up to the side of his face and pointed at himself and then the book. "Me. Jules Bradley." His finger motioned back and forth between the two once again. "We're one and the same," Carter finished.

"You're . . ."

And then it sank in. Her jaw went slack. Her childhood buddy was Jules Bradley. He'd done it. He was an author, just like he'd always wanted to be.

And he was *Jules Bradley*.

The blood rushed from her head, and she reached out, grabbing the top of the half-empty clearance shelf that always sat on the porch. Carter came toward her.

"Did you just swoon?" he asked.

"No." But that's exactly what she'd done. And if she wasn't turned on by him before, she sure as heck was now. The crush was definitely back.

No words came to her. What could she possibly say, anyway? All she could do was stare.

Carter gave her a sheepish grin. "Are you mad?"

"Mad?" The word squeaked out through her constricted throat, and she shook her head, the motion seeming to be in slow motion. "Why would I possibly be mad? You did it, Carter. You accomplished your dream. I'm so happy for you."

He looked flustered by her adoration. "I've achieved some stuff."

"You've achieved it all." She wanted to hug him. "Why didn't you tell me before?"

"Because I wasn't writing when I first came home," he explained. "That's part of why my mom has been so worried about me. I sold the new book and the movie deal—"

Ginger covered her mouth with both hands. "So that's true?"

"It's true." He chuckled lightly and reached for her. He laced their fingers together. "But then everything happened with Lisa, and the divorce, and . . ." He lifted a shoulder. "I couldn't write anymore. I hadn't written in months, and the book is due in a few weeks."

"And something has changed now? You're writing again?" If he hadn't told her about this before because he *wasn't* writing . . .

"You," he said. "And your house. The combination has gotten me writing again. Or maybe it's the ocean air. I've missed that. Anyway, that's what I've been doing out at your house early in the mornings. Writing. I sit up in that third-floor office, the doors open to the waves, and the words are finally coming."

"Go over anytime," she told him in a rush. She still couldn't get over who he was. "It can be your office if you want. I don't need it."

He laughed at that, and she forced her look to shift from wide-eyed fangirl to happy friend. He was Jules Bradley, but he was also Carter. He was her friend. Who'd done what he'd set out to do.

Without warning, she pulled him to her. His arms wrapped around her, and he held her tight. Pride swelled inside her. "Thank you for telling me."

"I wanted to when I first came home." He looked down at her. "But then I saw that you read them, and . . ."

"And I gushed like a fangirl."

His arms closed tight once again. "That means the world to me." He spoke into her hair. "To know that you love my books."

"Just keep writing them," she said.

When he finally released her, she took a small step back, and that time she saw something else written across his face. Something that made her think of tonight's date.

"You'll let me know if things don't go well tonight?" he asked. Her cheeks heated at the implication of what might happen if the date wasn't successful. Then Carter leaned in and whispered, "Never mind. I'll watch for you to come home."

And then he kissed her.

His mouth slanted over hers, hot and possessive, and just as it had the first time, it made her toes curl. She wound her fingers into his shirt, capable only of hanging on.

He stroked her with his tongue. His hands roamed over her body. He filled every single one of her senses, and in the span of a few seconds, he seemed to touch her everywhere. It was as if he'd branded her. She shivered when he let her go.

Seconds passed as they watched each other, both waiting for the other to make the next move, both breathing hard. Then he nodded, cupped a hand briefly over his mouth, and slowly backed away. "Don't have too much fun tonight." His voice was scratchy and raw, and held promises that heated her all over again.

He turned to go, rapping a quick knuckle against the glass of the door as he passed it, and causing Cookie and Mrs. Rylander to jump back. "Nice meeting you, ladies," he tossed out.

Carter got into his car, and sped away, and the distant chime of the store's bell sounded once again. Then Cookie and Mrs. R. were standing on the porch next to her.

"What was that?" Cookie asked.

"*That,*" Mrs. Rylander began, her voice all knowing, "was dessert."

"How about going with me to pick out Mom and Dad's new kitchen table?" Carter suggested to his sister. She'd gotten home from work fifteen minutes earlier, and they were sitting on the porch enjoying the end of the day—and Carter was *not* watching for Ginger to exit her house on her way to her date.

"When?" Julie was in one of the two metal gliders her parents had owned forever, her head resting against the back, and both hands atop her burgeoning stomach. Her eyes were closed.

"I was thinking tomorrow."

"You know I work tomorrow." She peeked one eye open to look at him.

He still thought she worked too much. "We could go Saturday."

"Actually"—she yawned behind one hand—"my Saturday person needed the day off, so I have to work then, too."

Carter kept his retort inside. At least she seemed to be doing better these days. She ate more, and she slept more peacefully. In the last two weeks she'd even plumped up and looked like a "normal" pregnant woman. She also didn't seem to be crying as much lately. Which helped him to not lose his mind.

"I'm not big into shopping right now anyway," she told him. "Not after being on my feet all week." She held her feet out in front of her, the long black-and-white dress she wore dropping away from her calves, and he could see her swollen ankles beneath. "You'll have to go without me."

A Volvo pulled up next door, and instead of continuing the conversation, Carter stopped the motions of his glider and turned his attention to the man getting out of the car.

He was tall, blond, and dressed in creased slacks, a button-down, and a blazer. He looked like he belonged on a runway.

"She dates a lot," Julie pointed out.

"That she does."

The man strolled to the front door, but Ginger came out before he reached it. She'd toned her image down tonight. Dark-washed jeans, a dark green top, and sandals. No heels. No dress. And the makeup was minimal.

Carter didn't like it.

"You have the hots for her," Julie said.

He didn't acknowledge the comment.

"That's got to sting. Seeing a different man pick her up so often." She slid from her seat onto his, hunched in close, and began speaking conspiratorially as they both watched the action next door. "Take *her* shopping with you," she suggested.

That was a good idea, actually. Ginger had things she needed to pick out for her house, too.

He'd given her a week last Friday night to settle on the major kitchen decisions or he'd choose them for her. Tomorrow was Friday. It made sense to take her shopping. Or maybe he was simply letting his hormones get the best of him.

Julie jabbed him in the side as Ginger's breezy laughter rang through the night before she slid into the passenger seat of the other man's car. And again, Carter ignored his sister.

Because yes. He definitely had the hots for Ginger. He was jealous as hell right now.

And yes, he wanted her spending time with him instead of some other man.

But that was only because he wanted to bed her. He wasn't about to fool himself that he desired anything more. He might be a bit better than when he'd first shown up, but that didn't mean he was cured. He was still angry. He would still go home in little more than a week. And he had zero intentions of ever considering anything more than a fun, easy time with a woman again.

Uncomplicated. That was the new game plan.

But my god, he did like to kiss that particular woman.

As the Volvo sped off, he relived the feeling of her mouth under his from earlier that day. The touch of her body in his hands.

Julie's phone rang, and Carter pulled his brain back to the present and watched his sister from the corner of his eye. She'd cried less in the last week. Her phone had also rung less.

She looked at it and stopped the ringing. She didn't answer.

But the color washed from her face.

"It's him?" he asked. "The baby's father?"

It was her turn to ignore him, so he held out his hand.

"Hand it over. I'll make sure he never calls again."

She shoved his arm out of the way. "Stop it. This is my mess to clean up."

"I'm your big brother. I get to fix your messes for you."

"Carter . . ." The phone buzzed with a voice mail, and he saw her hand shake.

"Talk to me, Julie." He didn't take her phone from her, but he closed his hand over hers. "It's time. Dammit, you're breaking my heart with all this moping around."

She smiled sadly at his words.

Now that he'd experienced a bit of renewed energy for life—at least for writing . . . and sex—simply by sharing a portion of his burden with Ginger, he understand the importance of talking. Of having someone there to listen.

"You need to talk, Sis, and I'm what you've got. So tell me. What happened?"

"You'll only get mad." She looked away from him. "You'll call me stupid."

She moved to get up, but he pulled her back. Ginger hadn't judged him. And that had helped more than anything. He could do that for Julie. Even if it killed him.

"I won't judge," he said. "I swear."

She shot him a scowl similar to his own. "You're still my big brother."

"I am. And I'll always be." He wrapped an arm around her shoulders and pulled her to his side. "But I can temper that for one night if I have to. Tell me what happened. Why are you here alone? Why will you be raising my sweet little niece alone?"

She shook her head, and he didn't think she would give in, but then tears slowly slipped over her cheeks. Her bottom lip quivered. "Because he's married," she whispered.

Carter closed his eyes. He had to. To keep her from seeing his thoughts.

And he did his best not to let the tension grow in the arm that was around her.

"I feel your anger," she told him.

"Of course you do, but I'm not saying anything." He gave her shoulder a reassuring squeeze. "Tell me the rest."

She turned on the seat so she could look at him, and for the first time, he saw a kernel of hope in her eyes. "Do you really want me to?"

"I do." He nodded. "Talking helps."

"Is that what helped you this week? You talked to someone?"

She'd noticed? "I did."

"To Ginger?"

He chuckled. "Yes, brat. To Ginger."

"You've been sneaking out of the house with her every morning," she accused. "I'm not an idiot. I know that's going on."

"I've not been sneaking. Want me to start waking you to let you know I'm leaving?"

She'd taken to sleeping later the last few days. "No."

"Want me to tell you what we're doing?" He wiggled his brows, and her eyes rounded.

"Really?"

"No." He laughed. "Not really. I'm teasing. We're watching the sunrise together. That's all. And talking."

Her eyes were more blue than green tonight as she studied him in the quiet night. He could hear a car pass on the main street, a block over from the house, but couldn't see it from his seat. "You used to do that with her when you were in high school," she said. "Meet up with her. Almost every morning."

"I did."

"That's really nice. To have a friend like that. Someone to talk to."

He took her hand. "It is."

"I never had a friend like that."

"And I'm sorry about that. I wish I could fix it for you." Because having Ginger in his life had been a big deal, then and now. "I'm your friend tonight, though. I'm your friend forever. Now tell me the rest of it."

She slowly nodded, and apology touched her face. "He was my teacher."

"Julie—"

"You promised."

He had promised. But he now wanted to find the man and beat the shit out of him. He gave a quick nod. "Go on."

"I thought they were getting divorced. He *told* me they were."

"How old is he?"

Humiliation washed over her. "Not that old." Her eyes pleaded with him not to yell.

"How *old*?"

She gulped. "Thirty-eight."

The man who'd gotten his baby sister pregnant was older than *him*?

Instead of expressing his thoughts out loud, Carter forced himself not to look fierce. Then he motioned for her to keep going.

"He might *still* get divorced," she said. "Or so he says. That's up in the air. But when confronted with the decision of whether to file the papers or not, he didn't do it." She sniffled and scrubbed the back of her hand under her nose. "He'd loved her once, and he wanted to try again. He wants it to work."

"Even though you're pregnant?"

She nodded, the move intensely sad. "I'm a nonissue."

"Then why does he keep calling?"

She didn't answer, so he asked another question. "What does his wife think about the baby?"

She lowered her gaze. "He didn't tell her."

"For fuck's sake, Julie. He's an asshole."

"I know. And I messed up. Bad. I know that." She swallowed. "But you can't tell Mom and Dad, Carter. Please. I've learned a lot from this."

"I have no doubt. But just so you know, if he thinks he can simply waltz back into your life if it doesn't work out with his wife, then I'll have to put myself in the middle whether you like it or not."

She smiled wanly. "No need, big brother. I've made that fact clear. He's out. He made his choice. My baby girl is mine alone."

"Then why does he keep calling?"

"We were working out the legal details," she told him. "To give up paternity rights."

"Oh, Julie. I'm so sorry." He hugged her tight. "Life can suck, can't it?"

"Yes." She nodded. "A lot."

He peered down at her. "For me, too. Lisa married someone else. *Before* she divorced me."

Horror filled her eyes. "She's a bigamist?"

"Yep."

"I hope she's sitting in jail."

That had been his first instinct. To report her. Throw away the key. But before he'd even left her apartment, he'd realized he hadn't cared that much.

"I don't actually know what she's doing," he began. "She's out of my life, and that's enough." He wanted to tell Julie the rest of the story. The worst of it. But he wanted to tell Ginger first. She would know what to say. How to help.

Only, *she* was out on a date.

"At least you're giving Mom and Dad a grandchild before writing off the other sex," he added. He dropped his head to the glider and stared at the sky. "I'd hate for them to never have one."

Julie pulled out of his arms. "No, I'm not."

He looked at her in question. Surely she didn't mean—

"I'm not writing off the other sex."

"How could you not? After what this jerk did to you."

"I'm only twenty-two, Carter." She shook her head as if he were missing the whole point. "Why would I chop off a huge part of my life before I can ever live it?"

"I don't know why you *wouldn't*." He sat up straighter on the seat. "I'm not saying never go out with a man again, just—"

"Just have sex?"

Her words made him flinch. "I'm not saying that, either."

"Well, you can't have it both ways."

Before he could come up with a reply, she leaned back into him. And she kissed him on the cheek. "I'm sorry Lisa did that to you. Really, I am. It bites. And I understand why it hurt so much. Why you're scared. But you're still young, too." She suddenly seemed a hell of a lot older than her years. "Don't write off that part of your life, either. You deserve more."

She meant well, he knew. But he didn't have a choice. Handing his heart over to someone—a second time? It wasn't worth the risk.

CHAPTER FIFTEEN

The cab slowed to a stop outside the house, and Ginger took a moment to sit in the dark staring out at the night, before straightening her shoulders and pulling herself together. The driver gave her the total as she opened the door, and that's when the next road bump of the evening hit. She'd forgotten her purse.

She held in a groan. "Do you mind waiting for just a minute? I need to run in and get some money."

"I'll have to keep the meter running."

"I know." A sigh slipped out. This wasn't the first time she'd been caught in a similar situation. She slid from the car and stood. Only to gasp when she turned and immediately bumped into someone. "Crap, Carter. You scared me to death." She shoved away his hand, where it had landed on her elbow. "What are you doing out here?"

"Why are you in a cab?" he bit out. "Where's your date?"

It was midnight, and every house on the street was dark. Carter's included. He should be in bed. Or at least not out here witnessing her humiliation.

"The date's over," she said. She tried to push past him so she could go in for money, but he didn't budge. He had her trapped between the car and the open door. So she gave up. She was too tired for a battle. She peered up at him. "I didn't want him to bring me home, okay? I shouldn't have gone out with him to begin with." She motioned to the cabbie. "Do you have money on you? I'll pay you back."

Carter moved her out of the way and leaned into the open back door. He spoke to the driver, pulled a wallet from his back pocket, and passed over enough money to cover fare plus tip. When he straightened, the car sped away, and he turned to her. He returned the wallet to his jeans, his expression hard and calculating as he studied her. "No need to pay me back. Just tell me what happened."

"Everything," she mumbled, but at the immediate stiffening of his spine, she quickly amended it to "Nothing."

The clench in his jaw didn't release.

"Seriously," she added. "*Nothing*. He was a jerk. I wanted none of it. So I called a cab."

That was a rushed version, but it would suffice. Or so she thought. But instead of accepting her at her word and letting her slink into the house to lick her wounds in private, he folded his arms over his chest and widened his stance. "Do I need to go kill him?"

That made her laugh. Drily.

"You're a good guy, Carter." She gave up on the idea of going in and dropped to the cracked sidewalk where she stood. She wiggled her butt around until she wasn't sitting on any sticks or pebbles, stretched her legs out in front of her, and slumped as if the wind had been sucked from her lungs. "Too good," she added. "I wouldn't let you kill anyone on my behalf."

He lowered to sit beside her, and she tilted sideways until she bumped into his shoulder.

"I'd do it for you."

"I know you would." She patted his arm. "Like I said, you're a good guy. But no jail time for you. You'd lose your prettiness in the big house."

He chuckled at that, and the tension that had been in his shoulders finally eased. His arm went around her, and he rested his cheek against the top of her head. "Tell me about it?" he requested softly.

"Dating sucks." She sniffled. "And I hate it."

His hand stroked her bare arm.

"And really, I just don't get it," she said after a few minutes. She snuggled in closer. "What's so wrong with me?"

"Sweetheart." He tilted her face up to his. There were no streetlights in the area, but the moon was bright tonight. It lit the tenderness on Carter's face. A tenderness directed at her. "*Nothing* is wrong with you."

She wanted to kiss him when he looked at her like that.

He remained quiet and went back to stroking her arm, and she told him about her night. Pricey dinner, nice meal, superior wine. There'd even been a romantic walk on the beach.

"And then I let him kiss me," she said, as if that summed it up.

A muscle flexed in Carter's bicep. "And how was that?"

She peeked up at him again. Did he really want her to tell him about the kiss?

"I'm just saying . . ." He glanced at her mouth. "Was it as good as . . ."

"Carter Ridley!" She pulled out of his arms, turning so she faced him. "This conversation is about me and my pathetic inability to date. We are not talking about *that*."

He nodded like a properly schooled child. "Probably a good idea. Talking about it might lead to . . . *more* of it."

She forced herself not to look at his mouth. Because she wanted to.

"So he kissed you," Carter prompted her to continue. His glance dipped once again, but only briefly. "And it wasn't good?"

"It was fine."

"Fine." He nodded. "Fine can be good." But the Devil danced in his eyes.

"Carter," she ground out.

He blinked innocently. "What?"

"Stop it." She scooted back in, bumping his shoulder with hers. "I'm crushed here. I'm upset."

"I know. And I'm sorry." He fell silent. But three seconds later added, "Bad kisses can do that to a person."

Her snort of laughter caught her off guard.

He picked her hand up and pressed a kiss to the back of it. Then he wrapped his arm around her once again, and as before, tucked her in tight to his side. She liked it there. "Tell me the rest," he directed. "Moonlight walk on the beach, wine, bad kiss . . ."

She smiled easily. This was what she'd wished the date tonight had been. Easy and comfortable. Without having to try. "There's not much more to say. I misjudged him. He wanted to get laid. I didn't."

"I *am* going to kill him."

"No need. I can take care of myself." She pulled her knees to her chest then, and thought about how she kept choosing wrong. She was attracted to jerks, apparently. Except Carter. The memory of Carter kissing her played through her mind. The memory of him touching her.

He was different than other men. But then, he also wasn't emotionally available.

Not that all the men she went out with were, either.

She dropped her chin to her raised knees and replayed man after man in her head. How could she possibly screw up so many times? All the dresses. All the freaking fakeness. She just wanted to be her. She just wanted to be happy.

"I'm sad, Carter. And lonely." She turned her face, resting her cheek on her knees, and watched him. "I was supposed to be married with kids by now. I *really* want to be married with kids."

"Me, too."

At his softly spoken words, she became still.

"I mean . . . I *did*. A long time ago. I thought I would be by now, too."

She nodded in understanding. "It sucks. Not being able to reach out and take something you want so badly. I feel like all I've done for the last few years is put my life on hold. And for what? Something I can't control?" She hugged her legs tighter. "I've wasted so much time. My house should have been completed weeks ago, yet I've dragged my feet on it. I've romanticized my entire life, and for nothing. Not a single thing has turned out as I'd planned it."

"Come on." He stood, and held a hand down for her. "We're getting out of here."

"What?" She let him pull her to her feet. "No. I'm tired. I want to go to bed."

"You're not going to bed. And anyway, if I let you go inside, you'd just take your pants off and go out the back door."

A smile broke over her face.

"No reading tonight," he commanded. "We're going out to your house. I have a surprise for you."

"A surprise?" She shot him a curious look. "Don't tell me you have some other secret identity I don't know about. I still can't believe you're Jules Bradley." And again, she smiled. "That is seriously the coolest thing ever. Did I tell you that?"

One corner of his mouth lifted. "You did *not* tell me that. But you're cute when you go all fangirl on me."

She shoved at him and they began moving toward her mother's place together. "Why do you want to go out to the house?"

"Gene finished a few things today that I think you're going to like. Plus . . ." He captured her hand. "I want to be with you right now. I think you need a friend tonight. And to tell you the truth, I do, too."

His gaze shifted to her mouth once again, and she swallowed the attraction that bubbled to the top. It darn near reached out of her and dragged his mouth to hers.

"We're not going out there to have sex," she told him.

"No, ma'am. I wouldn't dream of it."

"I'm serious."

"Me, too." He kissed her on the nose. "I just want to talk. There's more about Lisa that I could stand to get off my chest."

This was about him, too?

She stared up at him. "Okay." She touched his cheek, pleased that he would talk with her about his ex. "I'll see you in ten."

~

They arrived at the house twenty minutes later. True to her word, Ginger had exited the house a mere ten minutes after she'd gone in. And he wasn't certain she hadn't come out without pants. She'd changed into a flowing white blouse, canvas tennis shoes . . . and not much else.

Of course, the blouse covered her hips, so what was underneath remained to be discovered.

He pulled out the key he'd taken from Gene as they climbed the steps, and opened the door for her, then swept his heavy-duty flashlight into the room. "You really have to pick out fixtures soon."

"I know." She scanned the empty space as they entered, her head sweeping back and forth. "I need to pick out a lot of things. I did bring over some lamps the other day, though. One of them is down here somewhere."

The beam landed on a bare-bulb lamp in the corner of the kitchen, and Ginger turned it on. The room filled with warm light.

"Want to go shopping with me tomorrow?" Carter asked.

When Ginger turned back to him, he continued. "Or if you have to work, we could go Saturday. I need to get a kitchen table, and you need to choose tile, flooring—"

"Countertops, fixtures." She nodded. "I know. My week for deciding is up."

"So . . ." He watched her warily. He was afraid to get his hopes up. "Saturday?"

"Tomorrow. I have plans for Saturday, but I can take tomorrow off." She twirled in a circle, as if being there had erased the disappointment from earlier in the evening. "I'm so excited to focus on getting the house finished. I even picked out the interior colors tonight."

"Tonight?"

She laughed. "Right before we came over here."

She reached behind her and her hand disappeared up under her shirt—and his heart skipped a beat. Then she produced several paint cards. They'd apparently been tucked into a back pocket. Meaning there *were* shorts on under that shirt.

Damn.

"I had these at the house," she told him. "I looked at them before I walked out the door, and I just knew."

He shone his light on the cards in her hands, and she pointed to a pale blue green. It was almost an aqua. "This one for the kitchen. With white cabinets. I love the airiness about it." She dealt out the other cards one at a time. "And this for the rest of the house, these three for the guest baths, and this for my bedroom. What do you think?"

He thought her excitement was contagious. "I think it's going to be magnificent."

She glowed under his praise. *She* was magnificent.

"So what's this big surprise?" she asked. She turned in a circle once again, taking in the shadows cast over the room, and Carter grabbed her shoulders and pointed her toward the dining room.

He nudged her chin up and shone the light on the ceiling, and she gasped.

"My coffered ceiling is done."

"The one in your bedroom, too."

"It's amazing."

She took the flashlight and walked the perimeter of the room, studying the yet-to-be-painted custom trim. Gene's guys really had done a fantastic job.

"He also got two of your bathrooms done."

"Today?" She whirled to him. "I just picked out everything yesterday."

"See what a few decisions can get you?"

"I wish we could go shopping right now."

He chuckled. Because if he didn't, he would kiss her. Then he took back the light and walked her through the remainder of the house. Wainscoting and additional trim work had been installed in the eat-in kitchen, and shelving had been added to a few of the closets.

"This is just what I wanted." They stepped onto the deck off the master bedroom, where she'd seen that her underrailing lights had been put in. She flipped them on. "Thank you, Carter." She pulled him to her for a long hug, and he focused on the dim glow of the lights instead of the soft curves of her body. "Thank you so much for helping me with this." She leaned back and smiled up at him. "My house is becoming mine, and it's all thanks to you."

She hugged him again, and he closed his eyes and wrapped his arms around her.

This hug was different, but neither of them acknowledged it. However, he didn't miss the way their fingers lingered as they pulled away.

She averted her eyes. "Thank you for bringing me over here tonight."

"And thank you for being you."

Her head tilted with a sigh, and she pressed her lips together as if touched by his words. She faced her house from her position at the edge of the deck and simply took it in, then angled her head back to see the smaller deck and office doors above them.

After a minute, her eyes grew wide in surprise.

Turning to him, she pointed at the house. "I'm building *our* dream home," she said urgently. "Do you realize that? Do you remember planning out a house together?"

He'd started nodding before she finished talking. "We had a piece of paper with a sketch on it. We used blue ink, because that reminded us of real blueprints."

"I'd forgotten all about that." Her entire being seemed soft.

"I used to bring the paper over with me in the mornings, and we'd work on it together."

"I wonder where it is now."

He wished he had it. "Probably tossed in the trash years ago."

"Probably." She leaned over the railing to look at the wraparound deck below. "We used to laugh about how someday we'd both end up with the same house. I can't believe I'm actually building it."

"Both of us."

She turned her head to look at him, and he gave a quick motion with his head. "Mine is almost identical to yours. I noticed it the first time I walked through."

Her smile flattened. "You're kidding me."

"I'm not. Only, I don't have this view." He took in the ocean. "I'm looking at the city."

"You have an office on the third floor?"

"My house is only two floors, but the office is sectioned off by itself. There's a deck." He turned to her. "They really are very similar."

"Huh." The expression sighed out of her. "Life is funny sometimes, isn't it?"

"That it is."

They moved back through the house, taking everything in one more time, and ended up in the kitchen, where the small lamp still glowed. He pulled two beers from the minifridge sitting in the corner.

"You stocked my fridge?"

"Gene did. For an end-of-week perk tomorrow afternoon. Not everyone will work on Saturday, and they've been pulling long hours. It'll be empty by tomorrow night." He held one out to her, and as she took it, he watched concern pass across her face.

"I worry about your drinking," she admitted. She rolled the bottle between her palms. "Is it . . . a problem?"

Leave it to her to face things head on. "I'm good," he assured her. "It was a phase."

"A phase?" Her incredulous look reminded him of something his mother might grace him with. "You're thirty years old. Aren't you too old for phases?"

"Probably." He set his beer down, because he wanted her to focus on him when he next spoke. Not the drink. "I've always done everything 'right,'" he explained. "Which got me nowhere. It got me a divorce. So I got angry. And I didn't want to do everything right for once in my life."

"The excessive drinking . . ."

"And the smoking . . ."

Her eyes widened. "That's right. I haven't smelled that on you in a while."

"I tossed them." He gave a small shrug. "They were disgusting."

She laughed softly at his use of her phrasing from their first morning together. Then she grew silent. Finally, she said, "So you're okay?"

"The drinking?" He nodded. "Yeah. It never got out of hand. The rest?" He picked the bottle back up and stared at it for a moment before bringing his gaze back to hers. "I'm getting there. But the thing is, I *want* to be okay. And that's different for me."

She took the bottle opener from the top of the fridge and popped open her beer. After a long swallow, she gave him a single nod. "Then tell me about her."

Which was why he'd brought her over here. To talk about Lisa.

CHAPTER SIXTEEN

He opened his own beer, but he didn't immediately take a drink. Instead, he headed out to the deck, where Ginger had placed three totally girly beach chairs. Two were pink and one purple. They didn't look like her at all. He unfolded two of them and set them side by side, then took his beer and moved to the railing.

It was low tide, and the waves were muted due to being so far out. The night was quiet, and the moon was bright. Ginger came to stand beside him.

"She didn't just leave me for another man." He turned to her. "She married him before we divorced."

Her face showed instant revulsion. "Did you—"

"No." He stopped her before she could ask the obvious. "It wasn't worth it to me. I just wanted out. "

"But . . ." Her mouth hung open slightly. Her forehead creased. "How did this happen?"

Carter spent a few minutes explaining his and his ex-wife's relationship. How they worked. Where they lived. How he'd thought all was fine because he'd grown up with something similar with his parents.

"What I didn't realize," he continued, "was that we weren't on the same page. I was in Rhode Island planning a future, and she was in New York meeting another man. Then there was her business trip to Vegas."

Ginger eyed him shrewdly. "He went with her on that trip?"

"Supposedly they got drunk, had too much fun"—he shook his head, still unbelieving that this was what his life had come to—"and came back married."

"And she didn't own up to her mistake?"

"She preferred him," he said softly. "He was a surgeon."

Understanding settled in her eyes. "Your career wasn't good enough for her?"

"I prefer to spend my time in a room by myself," he pointed out, sarcasm dripped from his words. "Talking to the voices in my head."

Her head began to shake then, and it didn't stop for several long seconds. She just stood there, disbelief in her eyes, disgust marring the curve of her mouth, and her head moving slowly back and forth. She finally spoke. "We both have an interesting way of finding people who want somebody more . . . respectable, don't we?" The words came out very slow and very soft.

"Doesn't seem to be working out for either of us."

"Respectable people can kiss my ass."

That was the first time he'd heard her curse. He lifted his beer. "Cheers to that."

She lifted hers in return.

Each deep in their own thoughts, they moved to the chairs. Her jaw remained tense when she turned to him. "What else?"

"How do you know there's more?"

She reached over and rested her hand on his thigh. "The hurt hasn't left your eyes. Nor has the anger."

The bottle of beer became his focus as the fury he'd grown so comfortable with over the summer surrounded him. He wanted to tell her the rest of it. He needed to get it out. "The house," he began, "it was supposed to fix us."

It occurred to him for the first time that his marriage had probably been beyond fixing well before ground had been broken. He took a long swallow of his beer and finished it off. The desire to fling the bottle as far as he could came over him, so he gripped it tight. Ginger turned her hand over on his thigh, her palm now up, and he grasped it in his.

"When she skipped Julie's graduation this summer, I headed for Manhattan. We'd been apart for months, pretending the issue was work, but I knew. How could I not have known? We'd been failing for years.

"I got to her apartment . . ." He took a deep breath, his chest heaving. The words came out fast now. "I get there. And I'm mad. Furious. But I'm trying to ignore that because I haven't seen my wife in months, right? I should greet her first. Pretend to be happy to see her. And not let on immediately that I'm there purely to yell at her.

"Only, she opens the door." He clenched his jaw and breathed through his nose. "And in one single instant, I knew."

"He was there?"

Carter glared at nothing. The absurdity of his situation wasn't lost on him. "Not him. But his unborn baby was."

Ginger's mouth opened. She covered it with a hand. "She was pregnant?" she whispered. Sheer disbelief was clear in her voice, as well as the inward hunch of her shoulders. He thought she might throw up.

"Five months."

"And you hadn't been with her in that way in . . ."

"*More* than five months."

"Oh, geez." Her hand remained over her mouth. "I'm so sorry, Carter."

"Yeah." He tried to mentally shake it off. He *needed* to get over it. "Life's a bitch."

As if nothing else could possibly be said, they both turned quiet, and he focused on the sounds of the ocean. The moon was full and high; it was a beautiful night. A romantic evening for lovers.

"I hate her," Ginger said beside him. "She didn't have to hurt you like that."

"I hate her, too."

Only, he didn't. Not like he once had. Telling the story had hurt. Telling the story had pissed him off. But his feelings toward his ex-wife had turned more indifferent than angry. It surprised him.

When had that happened?

Ginger stood, the movement jerky, and motioned toward the empty bottle in his hand. "Want another?"

He looked up at her. "I'm good."

"I think I'll have one," she said.

She left the balcony without another word, and Carter suspected she needed a minute to absorb everything he'd just told her. *He* would need a minute. He'd dumped a lot on her. The only thing he hadn't shared was that Lisa should be due any day now. Or maybe she'd already had the baby.

And he didn't care.

In fact, he couldn't care less.

"Let's do it." The words came from behind him, and Carter looked over his shoulder. Ginger stood in the open doorway, the light from the lamp like a halo behind her, and the glow of the moon caressing her face.

"Do what?" he asked.

"It." She nodded quickly. "Let's do *it*. I need to have sex. You do, too. Let's do it."

He blinked. What had he missed? "Just like that?"

"Do you want to talk it to death, or do you want to have sex?"

He stood quickly, the chair tumbling backward in his haste, and was in front of her in two seconds flat. His hands reached out, but he stopped himself before he touched her. He held his breath. "You're sure?"

She was almost panting. She nodded, nerves flaring in her eyes. "If you are?"

It was a question. She'd left it up to him.

Which made it no question at all.

"*Yes.*" He took her hands in his. They were shaking. His mouth met hers, and the shirt came off over her head. He backed her into the kitchen and pinned her against the unpainted wall.

And then her palms pushed gently against his chest. "Wait . . ."

He bit off his groan. "What?" He didn't want to wait. Not now. He wanted to touch.

He wanted to bury himself.

Instead, he peered down at her—white cotton bra, tiny blue jean shorts, flat, toned stomach—and grew painfully hard.

"Roni said we need ground rules for casual sex," she told him.

"You talked about having sex with me with some guy named Ronnie?"

"My friend Roni. You remember her?" She clasped her hands together. "She and Andie used to come down every summer."

He pictured Ginger and her two best friends as they'd been years ago. "I do remember them. You three remained friends all this time?" The idea made him happy. He was glad she had that.

"We did." Her love for her friends showed through. "They're the best. They lived here on the island until recently. Then they got married, are off having kids now. And Roni is playing piano again. Ohmygod, Carter." Her eyes rounded as she got caught up telling him about them. "She is *so* amazing."

"Ginger?"

"What?"

"Shut up, baby." He kissed the corner of her mouth, and pulled a soft moan from the back of her throat. "We'll talk about your friends later. I swear. I want to hear all about them. But, later."

"Right. Because right now we need rules."

"We don't need rules." He put his hands at her waist. "We have fun. That's all."

"Fun. Yes. I can do that. Just sex. Just fun."

"Just sex." He kissed her forehead. "Just fun." He nuzzled her temple. "Can we start now?"

"Oh, yes," she moaned. And then she put her hands on *his* waist. And he groaned as if in pain.

He dropped his forehead to hers. "Protection," he ground out. *Fuck.*

She pushed at his chest. "You brought me out here without protection? Seriously, Carter?"

"You said we weren't doing this!"

What had he done? And what was he going to do about it? He tried to think fast. There was one store on the island that stayed open around the clock.

"I can go to the store," he said quickly. "I'll be fast."

But she laughed before he could pull away. She reached into her back pocket again. And the next instant, she held two condoms between the fingers of her right hand.

"*You* came out here with protection?" he asked.

"What can I say?" She chuckled. "I can't remember to carry a purse when I go out on a date, but for some reason, this wouldn't leave my mind when I went in to change clothes." She waved the two small packets in the air in front of him.

"You said we weren't doing this."

"I did. But I've also been known to be wrong." Her eyes were wide open and guileless. And he was crazy for the girl. "Quit talking and kiss me, Carter Ridley. I'm going up in flames here."

So he quit talking and he kissed her. And more.

~

It was the best sex of her life.

It was also the fastest.

But since it had been over two years, Ginger didn't care. They were still up against the wall, her legs still wrapped around Carter's hips, and his hands still gripping her butt.

"I'm sorry about that," he muttered as his body gave one last shudder. His face was buried in her neck. "It was too . . ."

"*Good*," she breathed.

He grunted, and his hot breath whispered over her skin. "It was too fast, Red. I should have—"

"Done exactly what you did." She pulled back and eyed him through drooping lashes, not regretting for an instant how fast it had been. But quickie or not, she was ready to go again. She wanted to run her tongue over parts unexplored. To let her hands follow. She wanted more orgasms. "Why do you think I brought two condoms?"

He seemed to get it then. She'd wanted fast, same as he. She'd needed release.

And now she needed more.

His fingers clenched into the cheeks of her rear, and she felt him stir inside her.

"I do have to eventually get home," she told him. She was completely ignoring what he'd told her about his past. She'd process that later. "Mom wasn't up when I went in, and I'd hate for her to wake in the morning and worry. But it did seem to me that the powder room down here has a countertop that looked sturdy enough to handle two people."

He chuckled, and then his arms slid up to surround her and he pulled her tight to his chest.

The hair on his pecs teased her nipples as her legs slipped lower to dangle above the ground. Then he turned them both in a circle, similar to what she'd done when they'd arrived. Only she was swinging from his arms, and he wasn't taking in the changes to the room. He was simply enjoying himself.

He was laughing.

"You shock me, Red." He pressed a quick kiss to her lips. "In a good way."

"I shock me sometimes, too."

When Carter separated them, he looked for something to use to dispose of the protection and found an unused napkin from a fast-food joint. While she eyed his naked body, and thought about the fact that he'd just been inside of her. And then she got nervous.

"So it was good?" She asked the question timidly.

"Good?" He jerked his gaze to hers. "You almost maimed me from making me come so fast."

Embarrassment washed over her, and she glanced discreetly at her underwear on the floor. "I prefer cotton underthings," she explained apologetically. "I know it's not sexy. If I'd been thinking about more than condoms—"

"Hey." Carter stepped in front of her, stooping to get in her face when she didn't immediately look at him. "Don't you dare stand there all naked and gorgeous—after being the highlight of my year—and apologize for not wearing lace."

"I do have some," she insisted. "I just don't wear it often." She lowered her gaze to the floor.

"Ginger."

She didn't answer. And she maintained lack of eye contact.

And Carter went silent.

He didn't move. He remained directly in front of her, and she realized that with her downcast eyes, she wasn't simply staring at his feet, but his . . . other stuff.

And he did not seem as if he planned to move away from her anytime soon.

He was waiting for her to look at him, she knew. But she couldn't help it. All her insecurities had hit from out of the blue. She'd been bold and brazen not ten minutes before. Demanding the man take her. Pleasure her.

But now? Now she was naked and vulnerable. Now she had nothing to hide behind. She was just her.

At his continued silence, she finally forced her gaze up to his.

"You're perfect," he said softly. "Absolutely, one-hundred-percent exquisite."

"I am not."

"Then what do you see as the problem? Underwear?" When she shrugged, he looked incredulous. "You did notice that it wasn't your underwear I was interested in?"

She blushed again. "I'm not used to this, Carter."

"I'm not, either. I've been married for eight years. I dated Lisa for the two years before we married. It's been a long time since I've been with another woman."

That helped.

It didn't change anything, but it helped.

"Thank you," she said simply.

"No thanks. We're in this equally, right? Just fun. Just sex. That means that neither of us will owe the other anything, and certainly not thanks for sharing a moment." He lifted her chin when she let it dip once again. "We don't apologize for seeming imperfections, we don't thank the other as if they've done a favor. We take pleasure, and we give pleasure. Equally."

"Those sound like ground rules."

One side of his mouth twitched. "Maybe they are."

He twined their fingers together, and leaned in to place a featherlight kiss on her lips. Which made her want another.

"You good?" he asked as he nuzzled her mouth.

"I am." She bit off her additional thanks. He was right. This was about sex and pleasure. It wasn't about shortcomings or favors.

And she could use some more pleasure.

She peeked down as he nibbled his way to her ear, to see if it appeared he might have had enough recovery time yet. And was pleasantly surprised with what she found.

"So . . ." she began.

When he looked at her, she motioned with her eyes to his midsection, and his resulting throaty chuckle sent shivers down her spine. Her nipples pebbled instantly.

"This might turn out to be the best suggestion I've ever had," he declared.

"I'll be sure to thank tonight's bad date if I ever talk to him again."

He captured her mouth for a hard, intensely mind-blowing kiss, and when he pulled back, he looked almost menacing. "Don't ever talk to him again."

She nodded, completely turned on. "Sounds like a plan." She gulped and licked her lips. "So about that bathroom counter . . ."

"And that one unused condom," he added.

"Take me, Carter. I need you."

Without additional instruction, he scooped her up, and her hands went to work on him. She had parts to explore, and pleasure to be had.

And there were still hours before the sun came up.

CHAPTER SEVENTEEN

Ginger laughed with Carter when he opened the trunk of his rented sedan and they stared into the filled-to-the-rim space. They'd been shopping since early that morning, and it wasn't only the trunk that was bulging with bags. The backseat had also been packed to the roof.

"Good thing we brought my car instead of your tiny hybrid." He did a quick maneuver of toss, shove, and slam, managing to get the final bag tucked away inside, and tossed his hands in the air as if he'd roped a calf and was calling time.

And when he turned to her, his grin was wide. As it had been the entire day.

"You amaze me," he told her. "You drag your feet for months, but when you decide to shop, you're a force to be reckoned with."

"What can I say? When I know what I want, I know what I want."

He grinned at her once more, and clicked his key fob to unlock their doors.

They'd not only picked out counters, cabinets, flooring, and fixtures—and double-checked all decisions against her paint choices—but they'd spent hours shopping for necessities for the house. As well as a few things for his parents' remodel.

She'd ordered a kitchen table before choosing a king-sized bed, a sectional, a love seat, and a large-screen television, as well as dishes, linens, bedding, small appliances, and even cleaning supplies. She'd also chosen outdoor furniture for each deck, a lounge chair to read in, and a welcome sign to hang on her front door.

The furniture would be delivered once the house was finished. Everything else was in Carter's car.

The thing about the day that had surprised her, though, wasn't that she'd *made* the decisions, but that they had been easy to make. Especially with Carter along for the ride. As they'd traversed the many aisles together, contemplating one option over another, he'd resorted to making faces if he'd thought she was leaning toward a bad choice. This caused her to both laugh and often be steered in another direction.

He had good taste when it came to design, so she'd been open to listening. *And* she'd learned a lot. It made her want to see his house, to see what he'd done with *it*.

The entire afternoon was the kind of day she'd dreamed of being her norm. And though it had yet to happen—and it might never happen—the interesting thing was that she was beginning to believe she could be okay if it turned out that marriage and kids weren't meant to be.

She wanted a family and forever. Yes. She wanted love.

But those things didn't define who she was.

"Tell me about Andie and Roni," Carter said as they climbed into the car and he started the engine.

"Andie and Roni . . . they're the best things to ever happen to me."

He backed out of the space.

"They'll both be down tomorrow, did I mention that? Roni's on her first tour since she stepped away from performing a few years ago. I don't know if you remember, but she's a concert pianist." Ginger didn't go into the whys of Roni's temporary departure from her career. "And she's finishing up her tour here. She's also pregnant and has the sweetest stepdaughter. She lives in Dallas with her husband, Lucas, but kept her beach house here. Andie owns Gin's—"

"The bar?"

"Yes. It's named after her Aunt Ginny, the woman she visited here every summer. She also has half ownership in Seaglass Celebrations, the island's premier event-planning company, and she had her first child this summer. She lives in Boston now with her husband, Mark. He's a lawyer in his family's firm."

"You like their husbands, then?"

"Like?" She nodded. "If those two weren't perfect for my friends, I'd be in love with them myself."

He chuckled as he headed out of the parking lot. "You're such a romantic."

She was. She knew that. She liked that about herself. But she wondered if Carter saw what she did when she looked at him. "You are, too, you know?"

He glanced at her. "You think *I'm* a romantic?"

"I do."

He snorted. "Romance is the last thing I believe in these days."

She could understand that, what with the way his ex had treated him. "Yet, at the core of you, it's who you are," she said. "What you wanted." When he glanced her way, his gaze thoughtful, she added, "Marriage, kids . . . the house."

He was more like her than he probably realized.

He went silent, but unlike days past, it didn't seem to be in anger so much as in consideration. He might not agree with her assessment, but she could see that her words intrigued him. After a few moments, he steered the car into a drive-thru ice cream place. "I could use a milkshake," he said. "You've drained me of all energy. Want one?"

"Absolutely."

Once they had their treats in hand and were pulling away from the window, Carter looked over at her. He changed direction and angled into a parking spot. "Her baby was due this month." He made the statement in a matter-of-fact way, and took a drink of his shake as she digested the words.

Ginger immediately understood that he meant his ex-wife. "You don't know if she's had it?"

"No clue." He seemed so much more accepting of his life this morning. Which floored her. They hadn't talked anymore about what had ended his marriage, but she'd been angry on his behalf since their conversation. How did someone do that to a person?

His ex-wife had married another man. She'd gotten pregnant by the other man. Yet she hadn't bothered to divorce Carter first. Ginger would have wanted the woman locked away. For life!

"You're better today," she told him. And she now totally understood the rage that had plagued him for so many months. It was deserved. "You're more like the you I once knew."

He nodded. "I feel more like him."

"Your mother will be happy," she teased. She sipped at her shake. She'd gotten chocolate, while he'd chosen orange cream.

"She's going to wear me out when she gets home. All I'll hear is how she knew what was best for me."

Ginger could picture his mother saying just that. She smiled slightly.

"Well, she was right. Give credit where credit's due . . ." They'd both leaned in toward the other as they talked, but they weren't touching. Just close. The air in the car seemed heated and heavy, and suddenly his ex wasn't on her mind at all. All she could think about was the night before.

Up against the wall of her kitchen.

In her downstairs bathroom . . . before they'd moved to the upstairs shower.

They'd had to air-dry before putting their clothes back on, but it had been worth it. The man was a great lover. And she was ready for round two.

"What should we do now?" she asked. She heard the suggestiveness in her voice, and didn't bother trying to hide it. "More shopping? Catch the ferry back . . ." Or was she being presumptuous? "Or maybe you have other plans for the evening? I didn't mean to imply."

He shot her a promising look. "My plans for the evening involve sticking next to you until you tell me to go away."

"Oh." She licked milkshake off her lip. "Well, then . . ."

He leaned in and kissed her. Then his milkshake was somewhere other than in his hand because he was touching her. One palm cupped her face. The other found her breast. And the taste of orange collided with chocolate. They were sitting in a public parking lot where anyone could see them, but she didn't care.

"I'm wearing my sexy underwear today," she whispered against his mouth.

His acknowledgment that he heard her was a low growl. And his hand tunneling under her shirt.

His fingers found her breast again, this time with only the barrier of lace between his skin and hers, and she pressed herself more fully into his hand. She'd grabbed the lace underthings that morning just to show him that she could do better than plain cotton, but if he kept going the way he was, he wouldn't even get to see them.

She considered the possibility that he might bring her to orgasm without even venturing below her waist. Was that even possible?

She was willing to find out.

"You're killing me," he proclaimed seconds later when her free hand found its own path under his clothes. Only, her fingers had slipped behind the waist of his jeans. She grazed the tip of him.

With both of them breathing hard, they pulled apart. But he remained close. "Any idea how I might get you horizontal this time?"

he asked. "The wall and shower were fun. Great fun . . ." His gaze traveled over her, and she was pretty sure what was left of her milkshake melted from the heat. "But I have more things I want to do to you, Red. Things I need you spread out for."

She nodded. "I have a solution for that." She sounded desperate. She was desperate.

"Yeah?"

"My blow-up mattresses arrived today," she told him. At his questioning look, she added. "I ordered them to use at the house." Her fingers curled around the top edge of his jeans once more. "I saw the boxes being unloaded from the mail truck before we left the ferry."

"A blow-up mattress?" He sounded doubtful.

"It's double thick."

"You think we can keep from busting it?"

Her lace had grown wet. She needed to be naked with him. "I think we have to try."

With a curt nod, he pulled his phone out of his pocket and held it out to her. "Call your mother. Tell her not to expect you home tonight."

A grin settled on her face. "It's already taken care of."

Carter wasted no time once they got back to her place. It took him two trips, but he had everything in the house that they'd need for the foreseeable future. Mattress, pillows, food, a box of condoms, tissues, and towels—in case the shower needed more exploring—and another box of condoms.

She'd laughed at him when he'd picked up the second box at the store, but along with his sex drive, he'd discovered his optimism attempting a return. Extra condoms seemed a good place to start.

"You got that mattress blown up yet?" he asked as he reentered her bedroom. She sat on the floor, her shoes tossed to one side and the bed spread out before her. It remained flat while she studied the instructions. "Out of the way," he said. He reached for the plug and dragged the bed to an outlet.

"You seem in an awfully big hurry."

"Yep."

He *was* in a hurry. He wanted Ginger, and he wanted her now.

Since he'd touched her in the car, nothing else had mattered. She was hot and soft and sexy, and he was hard and needy. Last night hadn't been enough. Tonight wouldn't be, either. But he intended to make the absolute best use of the time that he had.

"I think I'll open the doors." She rose from the floor, and he turned his head to watch her go. She'd mentioned lace, and though he'd been honest the night before when he'd said that hadn't mattered, he hadn't been able to keep from imagining what she'd look like with nothing on but lace panties and her top.

"Take off your jeans," he told her.

She peeked back over her shoulder. "Just my jeans?"

The moon remained bright tonight, and with her standing in front of the glass of the doors, a blue glow seemed to be painted on the other side of her. The sight made his own jeans uncomfortable.

"It's the way I like you best," he explained. "Running around with no pants on. I've had fantasies about that. A lot of fantasies." He nodded, and his throat grew dry. "No pants."

Her fingers went to her waist, and in a second her rear began to wiggle.

Her backside remained in view, and he thanked the Lord for the night and attempted to regain moisture in his mouth.

As the denim slipped lower, her body framed in the French doors, he focused on two things. The tiny strip of white lace now exposed under the hem of her shirt. And his own breathing. He sounded like he'd just run a race.

When her jeans reached her ankles, she kicked them to one side, and once again peeked back at him. "What next?"

"Bra. But not the shirt. The bra only."

He panted as he watched her. Her hands slipped under the thin material that covered her above the waist, and disappeared up to her elbow. Then she was wiggling again. As she worked each arm free before slipping a strap down over it, her rear moved with the motions. Her ass wasn't overly large, but given he couldn't take his eyes off it, it seemed to take up all the space in the room. The curves at the bottom called to him. He wanted his hands there.

"Open the door," he said the second the undergarment hit the floor.

She didn't delay. Both doors opened wide, and wind slipped into the room. She faced him then, her back to the middle support beam, her hands behind her, and her breasts heavy under the filmy top. She gave him a serious "come hither" look, and he rose and went to her.

His hands started at her thighs, his eyes locked on his movements. "You are seriously gorgeous."

Her returning comment was nothing more than a purr, so he explored the lace. With his fingers poised on the outsides of her thighs, his thumbs traced over the leg lines, taking in the soft texture of the material against the even softer touch of her skin. She was a tactile learner's dream. He slid the pad of his thumbs up, their rougher texture outlining the high cut of the panties before dipping down and meeting at the juncture of her legs.

Her chest thrust forward when he pressed against her, and he groaned at the wetness that met him. He wanted to taste her.

"Take them off," he commanded.

He could do it himself, but he wanted to see her own hands exposing herself to him.

They'd been too fast last night. Both taking and giving as if dying of thirst after a months-long sojourn into the desert, but he intended to make up for it this evening. He wanted to touch and taste and explore every last inch of her. And then he wanted to do it again.

Her thumbs slipped inside the front band of the panties, and her eyes hooded above him. She was as turned on as he.

"Push them down," he begged. He ached to see more.

Inch by tiny inch, the lace slid over her hips. And then she was there. He'd dropped to his knees at some point, and the most protected part of her was now within inches of his face. He breathed her in. And this time he said a silent *thank-you* to his ex. This was way better than the life he'd tried to have with her.

His hands once again touched Ginger, his palms sliding from calves to thighs and back again. When he reached her ankles, he helped her to step out of the underwear. And then he simply looked up at her. Her nipples were hard. There was no hiding them without a bra. And her breaths came as short and fast as his.

Then he finally closed the distance and put his lips to her.

She sucked in a breath, and her hands landed in his hair.

"Spread your legs for me."

Her legs edged apart, and he was in heaven. He slipped a finger between her thighs and touched her, drawing the tip along her seam. She was so wet. And so silky. And then he touched her with his mouth. She bucked slightly, and her fingers gripped his hair. But she stayed silent.

He took the silence as a personal challenge—she certainly hadn't been silent the night before—and he resolved to make her scream.

He brought his thumbs back to her, and this time he parted her. She was shadowed with the moon behind her, but not so much that he couldn't take her in. He licked her once more. Then pulled on her lightly with his lips.

She bucked again, and this time a tiny moan squeezed from her throat. So he licked some more. She tasted like heaven.

Her legs parted wider, or maybe he'd done that himself, as he continued to lap at her with his tongue. He used fingers, thumbs, tongue, and teeth. And he didn't let go until he was certain she knew who she belonged to tonight.

At the last second, as she writhed in his hands, he heard a small whisper of "Carter" before her body bowed tight. Her hands clasped the post above her, and a guttural scream started.

It felt as if her orgasm lasted for a full minute as she shook in his hands and pulsed against his mouth. And then her entire body sagged. The breath left her body, and he smiled smugly against her.

He kissed her thighs before rising to his feet.

"I'm wasted." Her head dropped to the door frame behind her, and her arms hung at her sides. "You've ruined me."

"No, baby. I've just gotten you started."

He scooped her up and turned. Then stopped.

They both burst out laughing at the size of the mattress. It was so full, and so rounded on top, that he wouldn't have been surprised to see it explode at that very second. So he yanked the cord from the wall with his toes, grabbed a condom, and went to find a bathroom that had a countertop.

Once he had her lowered before him, he sheathed himself and slid inside her.

They groaned at the same time.

It was too good. He gripped the sides of her hips and pulled back slightly, then slid in deeper. She made a whimpering sound. He liked hearing her. "Pull your shirt off for me."

Immediately, she stripped her shirt over her head. She was beautiful.

There was no light on in the room, but there was plenty of moonlight coming in through the connected bedroom window. He watched her breasts as he continued to pump in and out of her. The way they jiggled was an exquisite kind of torture, but finally he'd had enough. He leaned in on a thrust, and captured a nipple with his lips.

"I've wanted to do this all day long," he murmured around her flesh. He flicked his tongue over her.

"Do what? Suck on my nipple or—" She drew in a sharp breath as he nipped down on her, and she planted her hands on the countertop behind her. Her breasts lifted higher, reaching for him. So he released one hand from a hip to bring her untouched breast to his mouth.

She was all he could have imagined. And more.

And he wanted to do this until he died.

"You don't even have your clothes off," she whimpered.

She put her hands on him, flitting them around as if not sure where to touch, what article of clothing to attempt to remove first. His jeans were open and shoved down just far enough, but that was all.

"I feel like I should be doing something for you, too," she panted.

He captured her hands and held her wrists at the base of her spine. "You are doing something for me." He kissed her hard. "You're being my fantasy."

And then he could hold back no longer. He yanked her hips closer, and she wrapped her legs around his waist. Then he pounded inside her so hard that he feared he might hurt her. Or himself.

"You okay?" he gritted out. But he didn't stop.

She nodded. The move was jerky, and her eyes were glazed.

Seeing her arousal matching his, he brought one hand between them and touched her core. Her moan said that was what she needed, so he leaned in, his body cresting, readying for his own orgasm, and he made sure she took the ride with him.

He didn't slow until they were both drained. What seemed like minutes later, he had enough breath to finally move again, so he eased himself off her and peered down at the wildness of her hair. The fully satisfied glaze on her face. He'd done that for her, and that made him happy.

"You good?" He spoke softly.

She nodded, the move as quiet as his words. "Two times. Thank you."

"Uh-uh," he reminded her. He kissed her fingertips. "We don't thank. And anyway, I didn't do that for you." He pressed a lingering kiss to her lips; she still tasted like chocolate. "I did it for me. I needed you badly. And baby, I'm gonna need more."

Her relaxed chuckle made him smile.

"And anyway, it can be your turn next time." He winked at her.

"My turn?" She eyed him carefully. "To do all the work?" She began to nod slowly. "Okay. But only if I get to give commands like you did to me."

He scooped her up. "Once we figure out that bed . . . baby, you can command me to do whatever you want." He kissed her again. For a very long time. And he prayed for the next few days to go by slowly.

CHAPTER EIGHTEEN

Ginger stood at the open French doors, peering out on to the office deck, aware that Carter had no idea she was there. He'd gotten up two hours earlier and pulled on his jeans, and she'd heard him go out the front door. She'd had a brief moment of worry—Was he leaving in the middle of the night? Had she been the only one to seriously enjoy every last thing they'd done last night?—but then she'd decided that if that were the case, it was too bad for him. She'd had one heck of a good time, and she wouldn't regret it for a second.

But then the outer door had reopened, and as he'd come up the stairs, she'd listened to him bypass her bedroom for the third floor. He'd been up here ever since, and she could only assume he'd been doing exactly what he was now. Writing.

"I brought you a drink," she said, almost regretting interrupting him. She could only imagine what gripping new story he'd dreamed up.

He looked up from his keyboard, his eyes unfocused.

She smiled and held up the selection of water, Diet Coke, and beer, and he finally seemed to see her. His returning grin brought to life the flutter that she attributed only to him.

"Good morning," he murmured. He took the water, and wrapped a hand around her neck. He pulled her down for a quick kiss. Then returned to typing.

She let out a happy sigh. The man was writing again.

With his keystrokes as background noise, she crossed to the other side of the doors and settled on the ground. She popped open the soft drink, leaned her head against the wall, and let the early morning dampness kiss her face. This was *the* best way to start a day.

Closing her eyes, she took in the morning. It wasn't high tide, but the waves were rolling in. She enjoyed the sound of their power as Carter continued to type from the fold-out chair she hadn't even known was at the house. His laptop sat on an old TV tray in front of him. This was what she'd envisioned when she'd built the house. Not Carter, or anyone writing a book in the dark of predawn, per se. But sitting here with someone. Enjoying life together.

"When are your friends getting in?"

She glanced over as Carter took a drink of his water. "Andie will be in before lunch, but she's got a meeting to go over some things about Seaglass," she told him. "Her mother and Kayla run it, and Ginny owns the bed-and-breakfast where they house the majority of their guests. So whenever Andie comes to town, the four of them get business out of the way first."

He took another drink, and Ginger eyed the curve of his neck as his head tilted farther back. The sight reminded her of the way he arched at the peak of passion. She'd licked that neck last night.

Multiple times.

"And Roni?" he asked.

She swallowed her lust. She had a bad case for him.

"Her flight doesn't land until later. I won't see her until the concert, but the three of us are coming over here afterward. Girls' night." She wiggled her brows as if she and her friends intended to have a wild evening. The better guess would be lots of laughter, and in bed early.

She enjoyed the regret in Carter's eyes when he said, "Guess I'm on my own tonight."

"You think you can manage?" The better question was, could she?

"I don't know." He set his water on the ground, and curled a finger toward her. "You're too far away, Red. Come over here to me."

"You were busy." She rose, glancing at the sky as she did. The sun was close.

"Sorry. I woke up with a scene in my head."

"Don't apologize. Just write."

He chuckled, and when she reached his grasp, he snagged her and tumbled her into his lap. And then he gave her a proper good-morning kiss. He tasted of toothpaste. She'd seen a toothbrush beside hers when she'd used the guest bath earlier.

"Good morning." He nuzzled her ear after finally freeing her lips. "I missed you."

She smiled and cuddled in close. "Did the scene come out well?"

"Good enough. I'll fix it later."

His arms went around her, and they both grew quiet as, together, they watched the sun show itself. There was water for miles in every direction, a bright greeting to the day, and she was curled in a warm lap with strong hands at her back. This was a memory she would hold dear.

When she could see blue between the sun and the ocean, she peeked up at Carter. "Will you come to the concert tonight? Not like a date, but as a friend. Julie, too. I'd love for you to see Roni play. She'll blow your mind."

"I've actually seen her before."

She pushed up off his chest. "You've seen Roni in concert?"

His smile was part little boy, part guilt. And totally adorable. "I had a little crush myself."

"You had a crush on my friend . . . while I had a crush on you?"

He grimaced. "Life is funny like that."

"She's married now." She eyed him, pretending suspicion. "And pregnant."

"I didn't say I still had a crush!"

Ginger didn't admit that she was a tiny bit jealous, and Carter tugged her back down for another kiss. He nipped and played, taking his time, and eventually sucking her bottom lip between his. The move reached well beyond her mouth, though, as her breasts ached, once again, for his touch.

She forgot her jealousy and simply enjoyed what he did to her. The man was an excellent kisser.

"I remembered her from her summers here," he told her after depleting all oxygen from her lungs. "And I knew she was a professional pianist, even then. She traveled with her father as a child, right?"

Ginger nodded.

"I eventually bought one of her CDs. I saw her play in New York years ago. She's good."

"Then you'll come?"

"I'm way ahead of you." His hand slid from her back to her rear, tracing its shape with his fingers. "I already have tickets for both me and Julie. You could hook us up, though. Bring us backstage?"

If he would keep touching her, she'd do anything he asked. "It's a deal," she breathed.

His lips sought out the favored spot on her neck, and she considered stripping off her shirt and straddling him right there on the deck. She wondered if the chair would hold if she did.

But then she saw his eyes drift to the laptop. He kept kissing her—slower—but she could see that the story was pulling at his attention.

She should leave him, she knew. Let him write the next bestseller. But the morning was ideal, and she selfishly didn't want to give it up. Workers would be there within the hour, so time was limited. And she wanted to spend that time with Carter. He was so different from a couple of weeks ago.

Carter reached toward the laptop, and with one hand he pecked out a few words.

When he paused, she said, "Could I read it?"

Horror-filled eyes shot back to hers. "Read my book? While I'm still writing it?"

She grimaced. "Is that against the rules?"

"It's against *my* rules. No one reads the book until I'm finished with it."

"Oh." She glanced at the laptop, feeling deflated, and chuckled when he shut the cover to keep her from seeing the screen. "I didn't realize writers could be so particular."

"Definitely particular." He closed his arms around her again, pulling her attention back to him, but this time he turned a contemplative look her way instead of a heated one. Except . . . she also detected a hint of heat beneath the surface, as well. She had no idea what he was thinking.

"What?" she asked.

His eyes flicked toward the computer briefly. This time when he looked at her, the underlying heat was more obvious. "I do have one thing you could read."

"Oh, yeah?"

The fingers at her back slipped under the cotton of the shirt she wore. She'd come out in only the button-down that she'd taken off *him* the night before. "It has nothing to do with the book I'm writing," he warned.

She frowned. "Then what is it?"

"A sex scene."

Golden-green eyes with little sunbursts spreading from the pupils drank her in, and she caught her lip between her teeth. She peeked at the laptop. "And you'd let me read it?"

His hand flattened on her back, marking her skin with a broad patch of heat. He nodded.

"Show it to me," she whispered.

The idea of reading a sex scene Carter had written—while sitting in his lap nearly naked—turned her on. He nodded once again, seeming unable to form words, and quickly tapped out a few keystrokes. Then he turned her so she sat facing the laptop, and clicked one more key.

The screen filled with words.

She wore rubber boots and shorts that barely covered her ass.

Ginger gasped. She looked over her shoulder. "Is this about me?" Her heart beat wildly.

"You leave a lasting impact in those boots, babe."

She gulped and turned back. As she went back to reading, his hands boldly parted her thighs. Her back arched, and her pelvic muscles clenched as if he'd pushed himself inside her. His fingers lazily began to stroke between her legs while her eyes rushed over the words.

She was on top of him, riding him, her breasts bouncing and his mouth seeking. He ripped her shirt from her body, and then she was being slammed into the wall, calling his name.

Her body reacted to the scene, and Carter slipped a finger inside her. She moaned and squirmed against him. He had her drenching wet, and she could feel the hard ridge of him beneath her. She wanted him naked. She wanted him *in* her.

"Keep reading," he urged when her head dropped to his shoulder. He lifted her head so she was once again looking at the screen. "Out loud."

Then he opened the top button of the shirt she wore, and slid his hand inside. He palmed her breast. A second finger slipped inside her down below.

She moaned again.

"Read," he demanded.

"'Her legs clamped tight around his body,'"—her voice shook as she read his words aloud—"'feeling him pulse deep inside her. Her heels dug hard into his ass. The pressure energized him, making it hard to retain control, and his name was wrenched from her throat as he thrust deep once again. The next sound he heard was a whimper.'"

"Carter," she begged. She also whimpered.

He pushed the hard steel of his dick against her bare butt, and she grabbed at his jeans. She wanted to feel him bare against her.

"No," he growled out. His fingers worked faster inside her, and his thumb found her clit.

"Please," she begged again. "I need . . ."

"Keep reading." His other hand squeezed at her breast, alternately pulling on her nipple.

She licked her lips, trying to find the moisture to continue, and couldn't stop the grinding motion of her hips. She needed to come soon. He pumped beneath her once again, and her eyes crossed. But then she forced herself to focus on his words.

"'Sweat slicked their bodies together as he continued, not giving her a second to breathe, and not taking one for himself. He pushed her harder, insisting she join him before he exploded inside her like the animal that he was. And that would be soon. He bit down on her shoulder, and he felt her body begin to soar. He savored her screams when she came, thrilled at the feel of her nails slicing open his skin.'"

"Oh, God, Carter," she whispered.

"'*You're mine.*'" He ground out the next words on the screen, his breath drifting across her ear. He kissed the side of her neck then, sucking her skin between his lips and teeth, and that small action was the thing that finished her off.

She came apart on his lap, her orgasm stronger than any she could remember. He didn't give her time to finish before he stood, her still shaking in his arms, and carried her inside the house. Within seconds he had them back in her bedroom, his pants removed, and a condom in place.

And then he was in her.

He ripped the remainder of her shirt open as he had in the story, parting the material to expose her body to his gaze, and he plunged himself deep. There was nothing gentle about his moves, but she didn't want gentle. Not right now. She wanted to be fucked.

Barely a moment later, her orgasm started again, and she squeezed her eyes tight as he joined her. The sounds coming from him didn't sound human, and that only added to the moment.

She wrapped both arms around his shoulders as he shook against her and held on. And when he was done, a hot breath panted across her cheek, and he touched a soft kiss to her temple.

It was a simple gesture. And it affected her as profoundly as their lovemaking.

It was another one of those moments that would be hard to forget.

~

"You sounded incredible!" Ginger rushed to Roni's side after the concert Saturday night, pulling her friend into her arms and hugging her tight. The top of Roni's head came to Ginger's chin, and her pregnant belly pressed into her lower abdomen. "And you're so darned cute."

She released her hold, but kept Roni's hands in hers. With a sweep of her gaze, Ginger took in the formal black dress, Roni's wild curls, and her seriously cute belly. She glowed.

They stood in a dressing room of the convention center, just the two of them because Ginger had literally run the moment the concert had ended. She hadn't gotten to see Roni yet, and she'd needed to hug her friend.

"How are you?" Ginger asked.

"I'm good." Roni smiled. "Really good. This has been a great tour."

Ginger could see the exhaustion in the tightness around Roni's eyes. "But you're ready to get home? You miss your family?"

Roni chuckled. "Yes. Very."

"And I've no doubt they're ready to see you."

They hugged once more before the door opened and they were joined by others.

Ginger's mother and Clint came in first, followed by Andie, who held baby Teddy, Andie's Aunt Ginny, and Andie's mother, Cassie. Carter and Julie were only a few feet behind everyone, and they stopped just outside the door. Ginger had seen them before the concert started, but their tickets hadn't been with hers so she'd asked them to meet her at the end of the night.

Roni and Andie hugged, and Roni greeted Teddy with the expected baby talk, then she passed around greetings to Ginny and Cassie before landing on Ginger's mother.

"Pam." Roni reached for her. "It's so great to see you again. Huge congrats on the engagement."

"Thank you." Ginger's mother pulled Roni in tight. "And your own congratulations are in order." She pulled back and smiled down at the black-covered bump. "That stepdaughter of yours has to be as overjoyed as you."

"We all are. January can't get here fast enough."

"Speaking of things that can't get here fast enough . . ." Her mother brought Clint into the group. "Meet my fiancé, Clint."

Clint looked dapper in a black suit with his salt-and-pepper hair. He kissed Roni's hand and did a little dip of his head, and Ginger thought every woman in the room swooned. He was such a charmer.

He and Ginger's mom spent a few moments talking with Roni, with Cassie and Ginny adding to the conversation as needed. Cassie took Teddy, and Andie moved to Ginger's side. Flowers appeared—they'd been sent from Lucas and Gracie—and were deposited in the dressing room, then finally, talk slowed. At which point Roni turned a pleasant smile to Carter, who remained just outside the dressing-room door.

She flicked a very quick glance to Ginger—silently questioning if they'd *done it* or not—and Ginger felt her cheeks heat.

Anyone but Ginger and Andie might not have noticed the next look, but Roni totally took Carter in. In a you're-doing-my-friend sort of way. The three of them had been close for years, and it was a given that they watched out for each other. Ginger might just be having a casual relationship with Carter, but she *was* involved with him. And Roni would take him out if he messed up.

"Carter Ridley." Everyone around Roni parted so she could make her way to his and Julie's side. "I remember you from years past."

At that, Carter smiled. It was too wide, and Ginger had no doubt he was remembering his crush. "So good to see you again." He looked at Andie. "And you, too, Andie," he added. "I remember you three hanging out during the summers. You were inseparable. And you drove the boys crazy."

Roni laughed at that. "I doubt it, but that's sweet of you."

"He used to have a crush on you," Ginger informed her.

At the shocked look of both her friends—*and* Carter—Julie spoke up. "He's moved on to Ginger now."

Carter playfully thumped his sister on the back of the head. He smiled to the group. "I'm not sure if any of you remember my annoying baby sister, Julie?"

"I'm not a baby anything." Julie elbowed her brother in the gut.

"I remember you," Roni said. "But you were so young, I don't think we saw a lot of you. Looks like you're not a kid any longer. Congratulations on your baby."

"Thank you." Julie's hands touched her stomach. "And to you, too."

Julie had about six weeks left to go, and she was really beginning to show. And according to Carter, she was having a girl. He'd seemed quite proud that he'd soon have a niece.

Roni and Julie talked for a few minutes about babies and pregnancy, and Ginger tuned the two of them out. She ended up making faces at Teddy, who gooed like the sweetheart that he was from his grandmother's arms. Ginger had only gotten to play with him for a few minutes earlier in the day.

After Andie's meeting, she and Ginger had gone shopping. Teddy had stayed with his grandmother and great-aunt, which had given Ginger and Andie lots of time to catch up. And spend money. Ginger had once again racked up a hefty receipt buying items for the house.

But that left her lacking in the baby-playing department.

"You want your hands on my grandson, don't you?" Cassie asked. Her short red hair was identical in color to her sister's, and the two women stood the same height.

"I do." Ginger reached out. "May I? He's so cute. And I'm desperate for baby kisses."

She took Teddy and proceeded to get lost in teasing the little boy. Baby laughs made her smile. She pressed her nose to his cheek and inhaled. He smelled perfectly adorable.

Carter leaned into her, one arm going around her back, and the fingers of his other hand tickling Teddy's stomach. Teddy cackled with glee, and the two of them smiled at each other as if they'd accomplished something no one else had been able to.

Ginger watched on as Carter continued to play with the baby, and had a moment of sadness for him. He would've been a great dad.

She hated his ex even more at that moment. He deserved the kind of life he'd wanted. He deserved love. But he was closed off from it now, and that broke her heart for him. And if she were completely honest, it broke her heart for her, too. She still had that crush. Only . . . it was threatening to become more. She had to keep it in check.

She joined back in on the games with Carter and Teddy, getting lost in the laughs.

Catching on to the change in the room a few minutes later, they both looked up from the baby at the same time. Everyone had gone silent, all eyes on them. Andie and Roni gave her a strange look.

Carter straightened, clearing his throat, and moved to stand behind Ginger, and Ginger passed Teddy back to his grandmother.

"So we're really staying out at your house?" Roni asked. She flicked one more look at Carter.

"Wait until you see it. It's awesome. And empty." Ginger snickered. "I've got tons of furniture ordered, but it can't be delivered until everything is finished. They did install some of the fixtures today, though, so no more walking around with a flashlight, at least."

"And there *is* a functioning toilet?" Roni questioned.

"Two," Carter jumped in. "As well as a shower. You girls are all set."

Andie and Roni once again eyed Carter.

"If we have time before you leave tomorrow, I'll take you to the unit I rented today." Ginger had bought so much in the last two days that she'd rented a storage unit to hold it all.

"I told her we had plenty of space at the house," her mom informed the group. "She's been out shopping for days. Or that she could take whatever she wants. It's her stuff, too." She put a hand on Ginger's arm. "I hate that you're having to buy everything new."

"I want my own things, Mom." Ginger patted her mom's hand. "For *my* house." She'd saved up for years for this, and she was having fun with it.

"I know, baby. And I'm so proud of you. We'll have to have a housewarming party when it's done. Maybe the day after the wedding? Everyone will still be in town. Will it be ready then? We could do brunch."

"It'll be done," Carter assured her. "I talked to Gene today. Everything has been ordered, and they're on track to finish a few days before the wedding."

"You're such a good boy, Carter." Ginger's mother smiled at Carter the way an elderly woman might smile at someone helping her across the street. Very sweet. And appreciative. "I'm so glad you came home to help Ginger."

Julie guffawed. "Technically, he came home to help me. Not that I needed it."

"Oh, you needed it," Carter told her. "Look at how fat you are now. That's because of me."

Julie made a face at him, and everyone laughed.

"So . . ." Roni began. "About this slumber party we're having." She yawned. "Did I mention that I tend to need more sleep than I once did?"

"Tell me about it," Julie agreed. "It might have something to do with sleeping with a basketball."

There was more laughter all around, and Ginger found herself forcing a smile. She was happy for everyone with babies on the way, or a baby in the room. Truly. No vindictive, evil thoughts at all. But she wanted one, too.

Carter slipped a finger inside the back of her slacks, as if letting her know that he understood, and she leaned slightly back, pressing into his hand.

"Shall we go?" she asked. Roni and Andie readily agreed.

"Can I talk to you first?" Carter spoke near her ear.

"Sure." She turned to her friends. "Give me five minutes." She hugged Cassie and Ginny—and gave baby Teddy more snuggly kisses. "So good to see you all."

The group disbanded, and Carter led Ginger from the room and out the back doors of the convention center. The deck was a story up from the ground, and the building sat directly on the beach. The wind immediately whipped Ginger's hair into her face, and Carter brushed it back.

He kept his hands at the sides of her head, and leaned to touch his mouth to hers. His lips were hot and determined, and his tongue wasted no time slipping between her lips. When they finally separated, they both breathed hard, and she struggled to remember that she would be going home with her two friends and not him.

"What was that about?" She stared up at him, appreciative of his dark suit and freshly shaven jaw. He looked extra yummy tonight.

"I wanted a kiss," he answered. "I needed something to tide me over until tomorrow." He stepped closer, and the fabric of his jacket brushed against the silk of her shirt. Her breasts got in on the action, growing heavy with need. "How early are they leaving?" His words were hot at her ear. He wanted her. She felt a brush of the evidence down below.

"Don't show up out there at sunrise," she warned him. She teasingly bumped him below the belt.

He bumped back. "They'd probably still be sleeping."

"I can't . . ." Geez, he was naughty. She could see the thought in his head. "I am not having sex with you while my friends are asleep in another room," she hissed.

He only laughed. "We could go to the pier."

"*Carter.*"

"They know about us, right? You told Roni."

"I *asked* her questions along the lines of 'what if.' But she doesn't know for sure."

Only, she did. As did Andie. Ginger had seen it in their looks. She couldn't hide anything from her friends.

"Don't you dare," she warned again. The words were a plea as much as anything, because if he showed up at her house before sunrise, she suspected she'd let him do whatever he had on his mind.

"Okay, fine." His sigh was long and fake. Then he winked at her, and a shiver raced down her spine. He could touch her without touching her. "Got plans for tomorrow?" he asked.

"Not for after they leave."

"Take me fishing?"

"Really?" Pleasure filled her. He wanted to go fishing with her?

"Will a boat be available?"

She nodded. "I have a personal one at the marina. We can take it." She paused for only a second. "Should we see if Julie wants to go?"

Surprise crossed his face, and then he kissed her once again. The touch lingered as he slowly pulled back. "Thank you for suggesting that," he spoke against her mouth. "I'm sure she would love it."

Happiness consumed her.

"I need to go. Roni and Andie will be waiting on me." She squeezed his hands and took a step back. "I'll see you tomorrow."

"I'll miss you tonight."

A warm flush covered her, and with a smile on her face, she hurried to her car.

CHAPTER NINETEEN

Ginger licked strawberry juice off her fingertips as she placed the pitcher on the serving tray, where she'd already arranged pretzels, grapes, cheese, and three daiquiri glasses. She worked quickly off the small table she'd grabbed when she'd run home after the concert to change into more comfortable clothing.

While she'd been gone, Andie and Roni had each done the same, with Andie also breast-feeding Teddy one last time for the night and Roni checking in with Lucas. Then they'd all met up at Ginger's house. They'd been there for twenty minutes, and Ginger had already given them a tour, and Andie and Roni now waited on the deck.

Topping off the pitcher of virgin daiquiris with three squirts of whipped cream, Ginger hooked the sliding door handle with her elbow and pushed it open. "Drinks are served."

Roni sat in the purple fold-out chair, a maxi dress covering her growing belly, and her head tilted back. Her eyes were closed, and turquoise-and-brown cowboy boots poked out beneath her dress. She'd always had a thing for cowboy boots.

Andie rose to help with the tray. "These look fabulous."

While Ginger held the snacks, Andie poured the drinks. She passed one to Roni before taking the tray and setting it on Carter's "desk" that Ginger had dragged down from the office. Andie's long auburn curls swung with her movements, and her slightly rounded figure caught Ginger's eye. She hadn't quite lost all her pregnancy weight, but it didn't hurt her looks in the least. Motherhood definitely looked good on her.

"To Ginger." Andie lifted her glass.

"To friendship." Roni followed suit.

"To *you* two," Ginger added. It was nearing eleven o'clock, and though all three of them were exhausted for their own reasons, it was also their night. None of them wanted to call it a day.

"The house is beautiful." Andie told her. "Though I can't imagine how much you'll destroy it trying to decorate it."

Decorating was yet one more way Ginger didn't quite uphold the typical woman's abilities. Anything crafty, really. She could cook. And she could even host a dinner party. She could carry a conversation for hours. But when it came to prettying up a place, she was clueless.

"I picked out the wall colors," she defended. She'd shown them the colors during the walkthrough.

"And that only took you how long?" Roni quipped.

"Touché."

Andie chuckled as she drank.

"Those colors will look terrific, though." Roni softened her earlier teasing. "Just don't pick out any decorations until Andie and I can come back and help you."

"Deal." Choosing window treatments and knickknacks to pretty up the place was best left for someone who actually cared. Ginger was more about the bones than the intricacies.

"Did I mention that Carter recently built a house, too, and that it is apparently quite similar to mine?"

Roni cracked open her eyes to small slits. "How did that happen?"

"It's the funniest thing. We used to plan out our dream house together. Even drew it out."

"I remember that. You guys had this worn-out piece of paper you'd folded and refolded hundreds of times," Andie said. "You showed it to us once. I thought it was adorable . . ." She snickered with the words.

Ginger dipped her fingers into her drink and flicked them at Andie. "I had a crush, remember? It's a wonder I didn't try to name our babies and put them on that sheet, too." She took a sip of her drink before continuing. "The funny thing is, neither of us have that paper anymore. I didn't even remember it until Carter came back. We started meeting up for sunrises like we used to, and that reminded me of sketching out a house together."

"And yet you built the same house?" Roni looked skeptical.

"I guess the memory holds on to a lot more than we realize."

Roni snacked on the cheese as she scrutinized Ginger, before the corners of her mouth suddenly curved and she put a hand to her stomach.

"Baby kicking?" Andie asked. She sat up in her chair.

"Big-time. He's clearly going to be a soccer star."

Ginger and Andie gasped. "He?" They asked the question at the same time.

They were both on their feet and kneeling beside Roni in an instant, their hands going to her stomach. And danged if the little guy didn't kick them, too. Ginger's heart tripped over a beat.

"I'm so happy for you." She hugged Roni. She and Lucas were hoping for a boy.

"I haven't told Lucas yet, so no posting anything on social media." Roni set her drink on the deck and added her other hand to her stomach. Her fingers curved over her belly in a totally maternal way. "Since I was out of town, I couldn't see my regular OB, but I had a checkup with a doctor she recommended. Lucas was sick that he couldn't be there with me, so I told him they hadn't been able to determine the sex. I wanted to surprise him with it in person."

"Did you make it okay on the road without him?" Andie asked. The two of them returned to their chairs.

"I did. He and Gracie visited a couple of times. It was hard being away, but I needed to do this." Roni had been through a rough time before she met Lucas, and had completely quit playing for money. Getting back out there had been huge for her. "I won't tour every year," she added. "I wouldn't want to be away that much. But this one was important."

They talked about tour stops, baby and pregnancy issues, and how family and other friends were doing for the next several minutes, before Andie suggested that they take their chairs to the beach.

"Andie," Roni whined. She held out her feet. "I'm in boots."

"Then take them off." Andie and Ginger were already barefoot. "We're at the beach. We need our toes in the sand."

"You always loved the stinking beach," Roni fussed, but she kicked off her boots and pushed up from the chair.

"I do. But I'm not the one who bought a beach house." Andie turned to Ginger. "Or *built* one." She grabbed the pitcher of drinks while Ginger scooped up the chairs, and together the three of them traipsed single file across the boardwalk. The moon remained high and bright, and they all sighed the instant their toes dug into the damp sand.

With the tide about halfway out, they continued their trek in silent agreement until they reached the edge of the water. Where they splashed their toes in the ocean before unfolding the chairs. Then they plopped themselves down and didn't move.

Roni let out a tired sigh to Ginger's left, while Andie added one from the right. None of them had brought their glasses out with them, so Andie took a swig straight from the pitcher and passed it around. "Sure wish this had some liquor in it," she mumbled.

Roni agreed. "You're a good friend for staying sober with us."

"Are you kidding me?" Ginger said. "It was a no-brainer. I've missed you both like crazy. I'd give up a heck of a lot more than rum for more nights like this."

"Hear, hear," Roni and Andie agreed.

Each of them took a hand of the person next to them, and they sat, letting the ocean wash up to their ankles and the moon shine on their faces. So much peace and joy filled Ginger that she wouldn't have been able to describe her emotions if asked.

"These chairs are ugly, Gin," Andie said a few minutes later. "Did I mention that yet?"

"They're Mom's."

"We're buying you new beach chairs for your housewarming party," Roni added. "Pretty ones that match your pretty house."

Ginger glanced back at the house. "Should we really have a party?"

"Absolutely." Roni said. She was angled as far back in the chair as she could get, and looking about eighty percent asleep. "I might invite Mrs. Rylander. I miss that intruding old woman."

"You'll get to see her at the wedding," Ginger informed her. "Though she'll be attending as a guest, she's the center's contact for reservations now, so she's been sticking her nose into every decision Mom and Kayla make." Ginger took another drink of daiquiri. "I also heard that Chester Brownbomb has been caught flirting with her. It's driving Vanilla Bean crazy."

Chester was Vanilla's man, and all the seniors knew it. It didn't keep him from testing out the waters elsewhere, though.

"I can't imagine Mrs. R. would like his attention too much," Roni mused.

"She called the police on him."

The three of them laughed as they each remembered past run-ins with the seniors on the island. Andie once taught a basket-weaving class at the center, so there had been plenty of adventures.

Another wave rolled in, this one splashing them up to their knees.

"So . . ." Roni began. She yawned behind her hand. "About Carter . . ."

Ginger groaned. "I knew you'd eventually take us there."

"Of course I would take us there. You called me the other day, in a near panic about the possibility of sleeping with the guy. Then he was practically drooling all over you tonight." She rolled her head to look at Ginger. "I take it you slept with him?"

"I did sleep with him."

"Which was my idea, I might add." Andie took ownership before facing Ginger. "I told you to jump his bones when you first sent me that hot picture of him, if I remember correctly."

"And how was it?" Roni asked before Ginger could reply to Andie. "As good as the kiss?"

Ginger couldn't stop the smile that covered her mouth. "Better than the kiss. But I still can't believe I'm having casual sex. I feel so . . . *easy.*"

"Casual does not make you easy," Roni corrected. "Casual makes you satisfied." She eyed Ginger then. "Better than the kiss?"

The question hung in the air, and Ginger found herself blushing.

"Spill," Andie demanded. "I can't see it in the dark, but I know you well enough. You're beet red over there."

When Ginger didn't immediately reply, Roni added, "I'll bet she's not talking because he does dirty, dirty things to her." She glanced at Ginger again. "What dirty, dirty things has he done to you, Gin?"

Andie leaned forward to look at Roni. "Do you think they've done it out here on the beach?"

"I would have."

They continued teasing her, and Ginger found herself alternately laughing and fanning herself. The fanning came from thinking about Carter naked, and all the dirty, dirty things he *did* do to her. The laughing was from the pure enjoyment of being with her friends.

Finally she joined the conversation. "He does have this thing he does with his tongue . . ." she teased, and all three of them fell into a fit of giggles before she could add any additional details. They talked for several more minutes about men, sex, and the overall thrill of having *regular* sex, until the conversation shifted to become more serious.

"So it really is just casual?" Roni asked.

"It really is. He's not looking for commitment."

"Well, it didn't look casual tonight," Andie said.

"What do you mean?" Ginger turned to her. "What did you see?"

They'd kissed out on the deck, but she couldn't imagine that being misconstrued as anything serious. It had been a kiss. And a little pelvic bump. But still.

"Playing with Teddy together, for starters," Andie pointed out.

"And what's wrong with playing with Teddy?"

"Sweetie." Roni leaned toward Ginger. "You two were acting like it was *your* baby."

"We most certainly were not!" Ginger looked from one friend to the other. "It was Teddy. A cute baby. *Her* cute baby. And we both like babies. We were playing with him. That's all."

"You're different with him," Andie said.

"Of course I'm different. I'm sleeping with him."

"I don't mean that. I mean different than you are with other men. Why are you okay with it just being casual? Why aren't you all romantic and planning a wedding in your head like you've done since you were a teenager?"

Because there would be no point. But also, because somewhere inside her, Ginger knew that wanting too much from Carter could destroy her.

She shared Carter's past with her friends then, wanting to be sure they understood what the relationship was between her and Carter. She couldn't afford to have Roni and Andie pushing her to go for more. As her words wound down, they both sat shocked.

Andie was the first to speak. "Married? And pregnant? How does that even happen?"

"They had an unconventional marriage."

"Do you think he's over her?" Roni asked.

Ginger paused before answering. The same question had crossed her mind more than once. He hadn't had Lisa thrown in jail. Was that because he still cared for her? "I don't know. He still holds a lot of anger. He's like me in a lot of ways. He had high hopes."

"His anger could be either at the situation," Roni observed, "or complete heartbreak."

Exactly. And neither one bode well for anything more than casual.

CHAPTER TWENTY

Carter closed his laptop and headed to the bathroom to rinse out his coffee cup. He'd gotten smarter over the last few days, and had added a coffeemaker and mug to their small stash of necessities. Tomorrow would make it a week since he and Ginger had first gotten together, and other than Saturday when her friends had been in town, he and Ginger had spent every night at her house.

They left before the guys got there each morning—Ginger explaining the bed and other paraphernalia as her inability to wait. She was willing to rough it to be in her home early.

It was also the story she'd told her mother.

Of course, Julie knew he hadn't been home most nights, and she no doubt knew why. But she hadn't brought the subject up other than the occasional smug look flung his way when he came in before she left for work. They had a silent truce going on. He didn't hunt up her son-of-a-bitch teacher and kick his ass all the way to hell for getting his sister pregnant and deserting her, and she didn't get in his face about sleeping with his neighbor and friend. It was a system that worked for them.

Additionally, *their* relationship had gotten better over the last week. He would miss her when he went home. And he would definitely visit. Not only to see his niece, but his sister.

He returned to the bedroom and padded to the open deck doors where Ginger remained asleep. They'd dragged the bed outside last night, before he'd proceeded to keep her awake until well into the early hours of the morning.

He should probably leave her alone now. Let her sleep. She didn't have to be at work early, and they still had a good hour and a half before anyone would arrive. They could miss a sunrise together.

But standing there watching her, he knew he wouldn't let her sleep. He wanted his hands back on her, and he couldn't fathom the idea of waiting even one minute longer to do so.

He also couldn't fathom what he would do come next week. Their time was ticking down, but he wasn't ready to call it quits. Yet, he also wasn't willing to stick around any longer. He had a book to finish. And he simply didn't live here.

In two days his parents would return home, their party would be the following day, and he planned to head home on Tuesday—Julie had suggested he go to the OB with her on Monday.

Only, he'd changed since being here, and Ginger had been instrumental in that. The changes had come in forms he hadn't anticipated. He woke every morning now, looking forward to the day. He watched sunrises instead of sitting in the dark. And he didn't hate the world around him.

He was happy. Or, well on his way to it. And he enjoyed every minute spent with Ginger.

He didn't want to give any of that up. Certainly not to return to the depression that had been grasping at him for months. He didn't think he could live like that again. But had he healed enough to maintain his new outlook on his own? And was he really ready to leave Ginger behind?

All were questions he struggled to answer, but what he *could* do at the moment was wake the beautiful woman sleeping naked under the covers in front of him, and make love to her once more before the sun came up.

Losing the jeans he'd tugged on when he'd gotten up to work, he crawled into the bed and aligned himself behind her. She was curled on her side, her body warm and soft, and his hand automatically found his favorite spots. The curve at the top of her hip. The dip of her waist.

He pressed a kiss between her shoulder blades, and felt his body stir in response when she purred and stretched against him. He could do this every day of his life.

Trailing a finger along her spine, he followed it with his lips, pushing the covers away as he went, until he reached the upper curve of her hip. He stopped there, lifting his mouth to trace the small bundle of colorful balloons with his finger. She never had told him why she'd chosen balloons as a tattoo.

She peeked at him, and a tiny smile touched her lips. She was breathtaking in the early morning light. Naked and bare. With hooded, mist-green eyes holding both sleep and desire.

He could be crazy about her if he allowed himself.

"Balloons say to me that anything is possible," she said groggily, without him having to ask. "That there's always hope."

He nodded. He got that. They represented the dream.

"You're the brightest light I've ever met." He spoke with complete sincerity. Then he pressed a kiss to the balloons—wishing he could have some of her light inside himself—and slid back up her body.

He kissed her then, and got lost in the languid stroke of her tongue.

Her hand caressed his face as their mouths fused, and when they pulled apart, he moved to the crest of her shoulder. The skin there was tanned a faint golden color, interspersed with small freckles. He applied soft touches with his lips.

"I love your freckles," he murmured. "I plan to take the time to kiss every one of them."

She lifted a lazy smile his way. "You'll be one busy person."

"I won't mind."

The freckles were sprinkled across the bridge her nose and down her legs. There was even one very cute one right above her left breast. His hand snaked around her waist, and he touched a finger to it. He didn't have to look to know where it was. Then he held her tight and nudged his lower body against hers. He kissed her neck.

She spread her legs just enough to allow him to slide a thigh between hers. And she moaned when he fit the length of his erection tight to her rear.

"I love this," she whispered. Her hand skimmed over his hip.

The morning remained gray and cool, but a six-foot radius of heat inflated around them.

He pressed against her more aggressively. He was ready for more. She nodded as if she understood his need and shifted, arching her back until she ground herself into him. It was heaven. It was torture.

One more shift of her body—and the mattress dipped.

She rolled at an awkward angle, ending up tangled in his legs and staring up at him in shock. A laugh burst out of her. "Stupid mattress. We've ruined it. It keeps leaking air."

He kissed her, his touch hard. He didn't care about the mattress. She responded by capturing his head in her hands and holding him tight. Her lips were dewy like the morning, and he drank long and hard from her. He could not get enough.

"I saw the bed you purchased the other day." He nuzzled underneath her chin when he broke for air. His chest pressed into hers with each breath, rubbing across her nipples. "You won't need this mattress for long." His mouth inched toward her chest. "And I'll be back in November. After Julie has her baby. I could help you break it in."

He hadn't known he was about to make the suggestion, but it was a great idea. It would ensure this week wouldn't be it for them. He could go back to Rhode Island, yet they could still have more.

Only, she stopped squirming at his touch. She looked up at him, her eyes unblinking.

Wariness brought his moves to a halt. Then she slowly shook her head. *No.*

His chest squeezed.

"I don't want 'casual' for the long term. You know that. It's not me. It's not who I want to be."

An emotion quite similar to fear beat at his neck. "Okay."

He couldn't force himself to say anything more. He couldn't force himself to breathe.

"Don't get me wrong." She pushed against the mattress until she sat, leaving him perched on his side. "I'm glad we're doing this. I think we both needed it. And it's been loads of fun. But I've also listened to everything you've said this past week. About how I try too hard with men." She touched her fingers to his lips. "I've thought about it a lot, and you're right. I do. So I'm going to change. I'm going to be nothing more than *me*. Because I still want forever, Carter. I can't give up on that."

He nodded. Of course she did. Which also meant that this week really was it for them.

And that thought brought him a unique kind of pain. One he didn't know how to classify. He didn't want to walk away from her at the end of the weekend. Even though that's exactly what he'd proposed. He also didn't want her to be with anyone else. But he had zero suggestions on how it could be any different.

"I'm a little envious of you," he finally admitted.

Her brow wrinkled. "Why?"

"Because you still believe in happily ever after." And because he wished he did.

Sorrow filled her gaze before the light in her eyes shifted. Her pupils grew larger. "You could, too," she urged softly. "Stay a while longer. You're good here. You're healing. We're . . . good, too. Aren't we? There's no need to rush off." She paused briefly before continuing. "We could—"

He shook his head. He couldn't stay. What would be the point?

He lifted her hand and kissed her fingers, one at a time. Each touch sliced him open inside. She didn't get it. He was too shattered for happily ever after. And too realistic to stay.

"You're letting her win," she told him.

"I'm protecting myself. There's a difference."

He wasn't letting anyone win. Even when he knew that included him. This was the way it had to be. He wouldn't risk the kind of hurt Lisa had inflicted upon him. Never again.

"Climb on top of me," he coaxed. He rolled to his back. "I want to make love to you as the sun comes up. And I want to watch you in the sunlight."

She slid a leg across his thighs, and rolled a condom down over his length. With each stroke, she aroused him further. Then she lifted to her knees and positioned herself above him.

"Let me get you ready," he murmured. He reached for her, but she shook her head.

"I'm always ready with you." She slid down over him, and he sucked in a breath. Chills raced over his chest. She was hot and wet. And tight. A lump formed in his throat at the picture she made sitting astride him. If he were an artist, he'd paint this. Then he'd hang it in his office to gaze upon every day.

She began to move, his hands at her hips. He held her, but he could do barely more than watch. They had a few days left, but for some reason, this felt like it was it. The very last time he'd get to feel her this way.

Or maybe it was simply the most important time.

The sun began to appear, its rays rising up out of the ocean, and a small path of light sliced through the railing, slashing across her chest. She continued to move. Slowly. But her breasts were now high-lighted by the sun. That freckle he loved so much seemed to glow only for him.

Her body did its magic, bringing him close to orgasm with barely more than a few strokes, and he found himself gripping her, forcing himself not to thrust. She was a masterpiece on top of him. One he didn't want to end.

But it did. It had to, as all good things did.

As the full orb of the sun glowed from the bright morning sky, Ginger threw back her head and bit down on her lower lip. Her fin-gers gripped at his waist, and her breasts bounced with each gyration of her body.

And he almost fell in love with his friend.

He closed his eyes and let himself join her. Their release was quiet this morning. But no less intense than any other time they'd been together.

He pumped into her until he was drained. Dry. Then he forced his eyes open. She looked as empty as he, yet she remained on top of him. Sitting tall. Watching. He put a hand to her, running his fingers over her stomach and up to cup the weight of one breast. Then he pictured her round with a baby. She would be beautiful. She would make a great mother.

And though his own mind screamed obscenities at him for think-ing it, he silently issued a wish that she'd find that someday. She deserved it.

She leaned forward and kissed him gently, her breasts swaying against his chest. Then she slid off his body and returned to her side.

She faced the sun, curling into him the way they'd lain when he'd first joined her, and he wrapped an arm around her and held her close.

"You're good for healing a wounded soul, Red."

She gave no response.

～

An hour later, they were showered and dressed, and heading out of the house. Ginger turned to lock the door behind them as Carter watched the first truckload of workers roll in. The vehicle stopped, and Gregg climbed from the passenger seat.

"What's he doing here?" Ginger asked.

A zing of jealousy racked Carter. She hadn't been hanging around the guys at his house as much lately, but he'd still seen her talking with them occasionally. And he'd continued to hear them talk *about* her. "Work is wrapping at my house today," he explained. "He'll be over here until yours is done."

Which irritated the piss out of him, but he'd had no valid excuse for suggesting otherwise. He looked at her, trying to decipher what she was thinking.

"Hey, Miss Ginger," Gregg called out as he hit the porch steps. "Looking good this morning."

Three other men followed him, all smiling at Ginger. It was as if Carter wasn't there.

Ginger grinned back. Carter gritted his teeth.

"You really have to stop calling me that," she told Gregg. "You make me feel old."

"Oh, you're not old." Gregg checked her out in obvious fashion. "You're just right."

Carter's jealousy reached new heights. The kind of heights where he wanted to grip the other man by the throat and toss him from the porch. So he asked himself a question. Was he jealous purely because another guy was flirting with Ginger, or was it because a guy who was *wrong* for her was the one doing the flirting? Maybe his jealousy was simply his way of looking out for her.

She giggled at Gregg, and Carter's balls clenched tight. It was jealousy, pure and simple.

He decided to ignore the entire group of them, who now all stood on the porch, each man vying for his turn at having her attention. No one seemed to be in any hurry to get to work, and Carter couldn't blame them. She was in another pair of her too-short shorts, a T-shirt that did nothing to hide her sweet curves, and she was glowing like a beacon.

From the lovemaking that *he* had provided.

He growled under his breath and stomped to his car. Good thing he'd be leaving soon. He didn't think he could take watching that every day. And he knew that's what would happen. She was ready to move on from him. She'd said as much.

He settled into the car. They'd arrived separately, and he'd intended to leave when she did. But he wouldn't sit there watching her fawn over a bunch of guys who weren't good enough for her.

Giving her a couple of minutes, he pulled out his phone. He'd check his e-mail and the news while he waited. But after loading his e-mail, he paused. There was one from his ex.

What the hell?

He hadn't personally heard from her since *that* day. Everything had been handled through their attorneys. And he didn't want to hear from her now.

He slid his thumb over the message, hovered for a second, then tapped. His heart raced.

**Carter. I'd like to make you an offer on the house. Please give
me a call.**

She wanted to buy the house? *His* house?

Oh, hell no. She'd never even stepped foot in the place!

Fury filled him. How fucking dare she send this e-mail. Or even think he'd entertain an offer on his house. From *her*. No way.

Sonofabitch. Why had he thought for a single minute that life could be good again? There was always someone around the corner waiting to bring him down.

He floored the gas, revving the motor until Ginger looked up. Concern flashed across her face, but he didn't stick around long enough to see if she'd bother coming to his car to ask what the problem was. She had men to entertain.

Without another look in her direction, he put the car into gear and pulled away from the house. She had her car there. She could get herself home.

Or maybe Gregg would take her.

CHAPTER TWENTY-ONE

Nerves pulled at Ginger that evening as she sat by herself at the end of the pier. It wasn't dark yet, but it was well on its way. And she hadn't heard from or seen Carter once since he'd wheeled out of her driveway that morning.

Additionally, the blinds at his house had been closed all day.

She had no real idea what the problem was. Or where he might be. His car had been gone when she'd come out to head over to the house, so she'd hoped to find him here. No such luck. She'd even checked at the rock where they used to meet up in the mornings.

But no. No Carter. No explanation.

No nothing.

Was he mad because the guys had been flirting with her that morning?

That's all she'd been able to guess. She and he had been fine as they'd come out of the house. Yet it didn't make sense that he'd get so jealous. He was leaving. Soon. He didn't want anything more than what they had. And it wasn't as if she'd done anything wrong in the first place. Just harmless flirting. The attention was fun.

But the way he'd revved the motor of his car replayed in her mind. As well as the murderous look on his face. There had to be more to it, but she couldn't begin to guess what it might be.

She reeled the fishing line out of the water, and set the pole to the side. She wasn't in a fishing frame of mind tonight, and had caught nothing in the last hour since she'd been out there. Too much—even more than wondering what was going on with Carter—was on her mind.

For starters, there was their lovemaking from that morning.

It had been intense. And there had been a lot of feelings mixed in with it. At times, both Carter's and her touch had seemed like more than simple sex. Yet . . . he hadn't given the slightest protest when she'd said that his coming back in November to pick up where they'd leave off wouldn't work. She'd told the truth. She wanted a husband, and she intended to resume her search.

But she'd also hoped that Carter might suggest he could be in the running.

She cared about him. How could she not? They'd known each other a long time, and he was . . . her Carter. He was her friend. And he sometimes touched her as if she were more to him. Only, she wasn't.

He was hurt. Possibly still in love with his ex—or at least not over everything that had happened in their marriage—and he didn't see Ginger as anything but fun. She was his sex friend. And that was hard to accept. But she'd known what they were going into this, so she ignored the pain. And she ignored how much she'd miss him once he was gone.

The remainder of the light disappeared from the sky, and she let out a weary sigh. She'd try calling Carter once more, but maybe this was his way of letting her know that this morning had been it. It had sort of felt like the end.

She rose, gathered her fishing supplies, and headed up the pier. And noticed a man walking toward her from the opposite end. He was all shadows, but there was no doubt who it was. Carter had come to her.

She continued moving in his direction, and as she got closer, she saw the anger. She wouldn't have been surprised to see a beer and a cigarette hanging from his hands; he was that different. This was not the man who'd kissed her shoulder that morning and told her he wanted to kiss all the freckles on her body.

This was the man who'd shown up here three weeks ago.

Reaching her, he stopped. His eyes were hollow, and his features hard. It scared her. There was nothing comforting about him at all anymore, and that was a real shame.

He'd already left her.

"She wants the only thing I have left," he announced. His voice was as cold as he.

"She?" Ginger squinted in question. "Who?"

"Lisa."

Oh. Something had happened today. Ginger set her rod and tackle box on the ground while letting thoughts race through her head. She couldn't figure out it. "What does she want?"

"My house. She wants to buy it."

"The house that she *didn't* want?" she asked. Damn that woman for hurting Carter. Again.

"Exactly."

"Why?"

"Beats the hell out of me, but I won't sell it to her. She took everything else." He shook his head, his arms so tight at his sides that they vibrated. "There's no way I'll let her take this, too. It's *my* house. It's all I have left," he gritted out.

Ginger wished he could see that he could have so much more if he wanted it. He could have her.

The thought hit her so clearly, and so honestly, that she knew it was true. He could have her. She could love him forever.

And his complete lack of seeing that broke her heart in two.

She considered for half a second telling him how she felt. Asking him to stay. To see where they could go. She'd tried to suggest it that morning. He didn't have to give up everything they could be because of something another woman had once done.

But Ginger said nothing. She couldn't. He had to decide to move beyond the past himself. And the sad fact was, he wasn't ready to move anywhere but back into his shell of a life.

"I'm going home." His eyes flicked over her. Briefly. But as if he actually saw *her* instead of simply his anger. The lines at the sides of his mouth softened. "I'm taking the ferry tonight."

"You're more than what she's done to you, Carter," she said softly. "You're more than the anger."

"You're wrong." He leaned in then, and kissed her. A light brush of his mouth.

She felt his breath against her lips, and she wished she could fix things for him. She wished she could make him happy.

"Thank you for these last few weeks. For being there for me." He took her hand and pressed another kiss to the back of it. "For this last week. I almost went home a better person than when I arrived, and that was totally you. At least I had a momentary break." He gave a tight smile, but it was void of humor. "For that, I'll always be grateful."

She didn't say anything. He was writing off the rest of his life. For no good reason.

"We're still good, right?" he asked. "I mean . . . we knew what this was going in?"

Her eyes widened slightly. He was giving her "the speech"? Did she look like *she* was the one who didn't have her crap together?

"I'm me," he continued, "you're you. You're going to date. Find the right man."

"I am going to date."

A muscle ticked in his jaw. "Then we're good?"

She was angry for an entirely different reason now. "Yes. We're great, Carter. Try not to drown in utter misery in that big house all by yourself."

He shot her a strange look before tucking his hands into his jean pockets and looking around at the ocean. He pulled a deep breath into his lungs as if wanting one last whiff of salty air, then faced her house and blew it out. She'd left a single light on inside. Her bare kitchen walls could be seen from the pier. It looked as sad and lonely as she felt.

As Carter looked.

"Maybe I'll see you in November." He faced her again.

Her heart splintered. She would do her best *not* to see him in November. Because she didn't think she'd be over him that soon.

"Take care of yourself, Carter."

He gave a nod and turned to walk away.

She turned, as well. Putting her back to him. She refused to watch him go.

CHAPTER TWENTY-TWO

W hite garden lights and soft music greeted Ginger, her mother, and Clint, as they crossed to the Ridley home Saturday night, and stepped onto the front porch. Her mother held an elegantly wrapped package in her hands, and Ginger fought the urge to turn around and leave. It had been only three days since Carter had left, and she wasn't in the mood for this.

He wouldn't be here. She knew that. He'd returned to Rhode Island. He hadn't called.

But that didn't mean she wanted to be in his childhood home. She remained a mixed bag of angry and sad, all rolled into one, and she'd prefer to suffer through that without any witnesses. To maintain some dignity. But it clearly wasn't meant to be.

Her mother had sent Clint out to the house to retrieve her earlier in the day. She hadn't been home since Carter had boarded the ferry. She'd either worked, taken her boat out until late in the evening, or she'd hidden by herself in her big empty house. All alone. Exactly as she imagined Carter doing hundreds of miles north.

Did that make her as pathetic as he? Probably. But she didn't care.

Not yet. She'd snap out of it, eventually, but it wouldn't be tonight. And it wouldn't be because of her mother's sad-faced hugs.

The minute Clint had delivered her home, her mother had reached for her. She knew. Mothers had a way of knowing such things as daughters getting their hearts broken.

But Ginger didn't want to talk about it. Carter wouldn't ruin her. She wouldn't let him.

Her mom lifted her hand to ring the doorbell, but the door swung open before she could push the button.

"Pamela Atkinson!" Mrs. Ridley wore a silk beige jumpsuit, matching heels, and gold accessories. The woman had style out the wazoo. She also towered above her neighbor's shorter frame.

"Happy anniversary." Ginger's mother held out the gift. "And welcome home."

Mrs. Ridley hugged all of them and brought them inside. They were the first to arrive.

"This is gorgeous," her mother exclaimed the instant they walked into the house. She meant the remodel, of course. And yes, it was. Carter had impressed.

The wall between the living room and the kitchen had been removed, the old wallpaper was gone, and the entire space had been updated. Still a traditional style, but in a more contemporary way. The walls were painted a neutral straw color, with custom cream wainscoting running the length of the dining area and down the hall. The floors were a wide-planked, hand-scraped dark stain. And a small pot rack hung in the corner between the sink and stovetop. It showcased a collection of cast-iron skillets.

Ginger remembered as a kid hearing Mr. Ridley swear that those were the only pots worth cooking in. Carter must have remembered, too. It was a shame he wasn't here to enjoy this with them.

"Can you believe Carter and Julie did this for us?" Mrs. Ridley sounded positively giddy as she led them through the space. Mr.

Ridley nodded a hello. He held a snifter of scotch in one hand, and immediately headed to Clint's side.

The kitchen cabinets were a rich honeyed wood, and the granite was a corrugated beige, complementing the walls, and at the sight of them, Ginger had a moment of panic. This was so beautiful. Had she chosen the wrong colors for her house?

But then she remembered Carter's approval. Hers was a house *on* the beach. It fit to make it lighter. Breezier. And she loved all the choices they'd made.

She breathed easily again, and tuned back in to the moment.

"My master closet got redone, as well," Mrs. Ridley continued as she circled the new dining set. She trailed her hand along the farm-style table. "Did he tell you about that? We'll check it out, too. It's a dream, I tell you. Simply a dream. Jimmy can have his gourmet kitchen, but I get my closet. It's so fabulous, I might start sleeping in there."

She laughed, and she and Ginger's mom were soon engaged in a discussion about closets, clothes, engagement rings, wedding plans, and the best places to honeymoon, while Clint and Mr. Ridley enjoyed scotch and talked cuts of meat and how best to reach the perfect temperatures on the grill.

Other people drifted in, filling the room and raising the volume level. Their presence made it easier for Ginger not to be missed as she edged to the side of the space. She wasn't in a partying mood, and she regretted letting her mom talk her into showing up.

She made her way to the bookshelf and couldn't stop herself from taking down one of Carter's books. It was the first one he'd published. She'd started rereading it earlier today.

"He told you, right?" Julie appeared at her side. They stood slightly separated from everyone else, and when Ginger looked at her, Julie nodded toward the book in Ginger's hand.

"That he wrote them?" Ginger nodded. "He told me. It answered my question as to how you had that early copy."

Julie chuckled and Ginger put the book back on the shelf.

"How's he doing?" She could kick herself. Why couldn't she keep her mouth shut?

Julie rested her hands across the top of her belly. "I'm guessing he's back to drinking and smoking, and generally scowling at anyone who dares speak to him." Her answer put a smile on Ginger's face. His sister described him to a tee.

Ginger's smile was sad, though, as was Julie's.

"I'm worried about him," Julie admitted. "He's not answering his phone."

"He told you why he left?"

She nodded. "She wants to buy the house."

"I wish he'd just sell it to her," Ginger mumbled. She'd never seen the house, and she'd hate to consider giving up her own. Yet it felt like a huge stumbling block for Carter. As far as she was concerned, it was time to move past it.

But she supposed that was easier said than done.

"Do you think he's writing?" she asked. She doubted it, but writing would be the best thing for him. She'd seen the joy it brought him. *That's* what he had left. Not some stupid house.

"I have no idea," his sister replied. One hand rubbed over her stomach, and as she looked at Ginger, a tiny pinch formed between her eyes. "Can I ask you something?"

"Sure."

"Did you fall for him?"

Oh. Ginger hadn't been expecting that. "I . . ."

"It's just that I want him to be happy," Julie explained. "He deserves it. He's been good to me over the years, even when I didn't see a lot of him. And now he's hurting. So I was hoping . . ." Her hand trembled as she pushed hair back out of her face. "He changed while he was here. For the better. And I know it was because of you."

Ginger's heart skipped a beat. Hearing that from Julie was powerful, and also a little devastating. She had to blink to keep the tears away. "The truth is, he changed me, too."

For the better.

At that, Ginger decided she needed to go home. This was all too much. "I think I'm going to get going. Apologize to your mom and dad for me?"

"Of course."

She left without saying another word to anyone, and entered her mom's house through the mudroom. She took off her jeans, then did nothing more than stare down at them. She wanted Carter there with her. Teasing her about her preference to read with no pants on. Touching her. She just wanted Carter.

She left her jeans where they were and entered the kitchen, snagging the Jules Bradley book off the table where she'd left it upon her arrival, and slid to the floor. There were too many people next door to go out back and read, so she'd sit against the kitchen wall and huddle in the dark. There was enough ambient light shining in from next door to read by. That would have to do.

But she couldn't bring herself to open the pages. Instead, she let herself cry.

Hot tears rolled over her cheeks, dripping off her chin as she hung her head and wept for the loss of love, and the loss of hope. Not her hope. She would find hers again. But for Carter's. He deserved a life with the promise of expectations.

Soft pats on the floor brought Ginger's head up, only to find Mz. Lizzie standing before her. The cat scrutinized her in the way that only cats can do, giving her a cold, bored stare.

But then she sidled in close.

It was as if Mz. Lizzie knew that Ginger needed to be loved tonight.

Ginger scratched the cat on the back of the neck and let more tears flow. If cat love was all she could get, she'd take it.

CHAPTER TWENTY-THREE

Carter's phone rang for the tenth time that day, and for the tenth time he ignored it. He *still* didn't want to speak to anyone. Not his mother, his sister, his father, his lawyer, nor Lisa.

He might be willing to talk to Ginger, but she hadn't called.

Not that he'd expected her to. She was probably busy dating the wrong guys.

He put his finger to the X key of his laptop and pressed down, filling his screen with Xs. He kept thinking about being back on Turtle Island. He'd missed the anniversary party last night, and he felt bad about it. He'd actually been looking forward to it. And he would miss Julie's OB appointment tomorrow. They planned to do another ultrasound. He would have gotten to see his niece.

And . . . he missed Ginger.

That wasn't supposed to happen. But it did. There was even a little part of him that wished he'd stayed just for her. Had she really been suggesting they could be more? He'd been replaying that last morning with her in his head. Right before they'd made love.

She'd said that he could believe in a happily ever after, too. She'd suggested he stay.

We're . . . good, too. Aren't we? There's no need to rush off. We could—
We could . . . *what?*

He'd interrupted, letting her know that she was wrong. Such a thing didn't exist for him. And he'd accepted that he'd probably never know exactly what she'd been intending to say. Because he'd left, and now he was back here. Stewing.

He typed more Xs, and the doorbell sounded. He ignored it. But when the chime pealed once more, he grudgingly pushed himself out of his desk chair. He was tired of sitting anyway. He'd get rid of whoever was at the door, then go out to find something to eat. He hadn't been in the mood to cook since he'd gotten home, and there was no real food in the house. But then, he hadn't been in the mood to eat, either. Yet suddenly, he found himself ravenous.

Only, the moment he descended the stairs and reached his front door, his appetite disappeared. Lisa stood there. A baby in her arms.

"Your sister told me you were here." She spoke the minute he cracked open the door.

The words renewed his anger. "You talked to Julie?"

"You wouldn't answer your phone."

"Then I hope she told you to go to hell." He moved to close the door in her face, but she braced an arm against it.

"Actually," she began, "she suggested I come here."

Carter stared at his ex-wife. Other than hiding a second marriage and a baby, she'd never been one to lie to his face. Clearly he would need to have a chat with his sister. Seemed she was walking in their mother's footsteps and trying to "fix" him.

"Looks like you made it," he said emotionlessly. "You're here. Now you can leave."

He pushed the door to close it again, unconcerned with how much of an ass he was being. She shouldn't have come. But she played the baby card. She twisted her body so that if he slammed the door, he'd hit the baby first.

At his pause, she slid past him and into his foyer. She was in his house.

"What the hell do you think you're doing?"

"I'm not leaving until we talk."

"Nothing to talk about. You can't have my house." He folded his arms over his chest and stared down his nose at her.

"That's not what I'm here about."

"Then what?"

She sighed and looked around. He saw curiosity flare in her eyes as her gaze landed on the family room. She'd never been in the house, but he'd e-mailed her plenty of pictures as it was being built.

"Can we," she began, "get out of the doorway, maybe? Can we sit?"

"No."

"Okay, fine." She frowned. Then she hoisted the baby to her shoulder, and he noticed that there was spit-up on her collar. He couldn't remember ever seeing Lisa in any way but completely put together. "I'm here to apologize," she told him. "I'm sorry, Carter. About that day at the apartment. I'm sorry that you had to find out that way."

"You're not sorry for marrying someone else?" He finally looked at the baby. It was a girl. "That you had a *baby* with someone else?"

"I'm sorry for all of it. Except . . ." She glanced at the baby. "I'm also not sorry."

"Get out of my house, Lisa. We're done."

Her eyes pleaded with him. "You deserved better from me, okay? I know that."

"I deserved your faithfulness. And your respect. I'm proud of my career. I'm proud of what I've accomplished."

She gave a quick nod. "You should be. It's just . . . it's not the life I envisioned."

"And my wife marrying someone else isn't the life that I envisioned."

She fell silent, and they stared at each other, and he thought back to their college days. He'd cared for her once. A long time ago. Hadn't he?

He'd thought she'd cared for him, too.

"Why?" he asked. He cursed himself for needing answers.

"Actually, I think we did it to each other."

"Seriously?" The fire came back in an instant. "No dice, lawyer. This one is on you."

"Carter, come on. You knew our marriage wasn't good." The baby whined in her arms, and Lisa patted her on the back. Carter ignored the child. "We didn't see each other for months at a time," she said. "We rarely had sex. And we were *okay* with that. For years."

"We were working on our careers."

"But we should have also been working on *us*."

"This house was going to do that for us." He spread his arms wide as if to encompass the entire structure of the home. "It was going to help us. Did you forget that? It's why I built it."

"But I never asked you to build it. *I* didn't need a house."

"I was building it for *us!*"

His raised voice made the baby cry, and Lisa sighed. Her shoulders sagged. "I needed a husband, Carter. One who wanted me and not some fanciful dream. That's what I'm trying to tell you. Not a house. A husband."

"Well, you apparently need a house now." He eyed the crying infant. "Or is that another sort of torture you want to dish out? Buy my house from me just so I can't have it?"

"I want the house," she said calmly. "That's true. But I also don't think you really want it. Not anymore."

Lisa moved past him again, bouncing the baby until she calmed, and Carter ended up following the two of them. They stood in the formal dining room, which was barren of furniture, and Lisa motioned with her head to the picture window. "See that skyline?"

His house sat high enough above the city so that he had great views.

"You love the sand," she said. "Hearing the waves. Breathing in the air. I've heard you say it, and I've seen your passion when you talk about the ocean. I love the city."

He couldn't figure out what she was even doing there, why they were having this argument, but his anger suddenly dissipated. He was so tired of being mad at her. Tired of fighting for . . . nothing. He didn't even know what he'd hoped to gain over the last few months by being mad at the world. And he could see with clarity that he'd gained nothing.

"Let's go into the family room," he said.

They moved through the double-wide opening into the other room, and he offered her a seat. As she settled on the leather sofa, she snuggled the baby in the crook of her elbow, and Carter watched her offer a gentle smile to the child. She loved her daughter. That was clear. And he suddenly couldn't see *them* having a kid together. They were just too different.

The truth was, he'd wanted his plans, his career, more than he'd ever wanted Lisa. How had that never occurred to him?

"You're happy with him?" he asked.

"I am."

"Are you legally married?"

"We are. I came clean the same day you found out."

"And he loved you enough to stay?" Carter wouldn't have stayed. In fact, it had never occurred to him to fight for her. He'd called his lawyer that same day, before he'd ever hailed a cab back to the airport.

"We had a few rough weeks," Lisa confessed. "But yes, he loved me enough to stay."

What a schmuck. "I hate you," he told her.

She gave a sad smile. "I know."

"I could have had you thrown in jail."

"I know that, too." She pulled a folded piece of paper from the baby bag she'd set at her feet. "It's one of the reasons this offer is so generous."

He eyed the paper in her hand. Then her. "I don't need your money."

"Maybe not, but you need something. And I hope you find it. I truly am sorry I had a hand in getting you to this point. I've gone over it many times, Carter, and if we go all the way back to our college days, I'm not sure we were ever right for each other from the beginning. And I think I knew that. I should have declined your offer of marriage."

Her words finished him off. They stared at each other, neither knowing what to say next.

Then she slid the paper onto his coffee table. "I do want to buy this house. I want the life you imagined. I'm sorry to say that. I don't mean to hurt you with it, but I see it now. I understand what you were after. And I want it. Only—"

"Only, you want it with someone else."

"Yes." She looked around the room, taking in the darker wood trim. The atmosphere that was more formal than the house Ginger had built. "And this house suits me. It was designed for me. I want to slow down. Have more kids. It's not all about work for me anymore. I've changed." She looked at the paper. "Think about it. If you decide this isn't the place for you, please give me a call. Or have your lawyer call me. I won't bother you again. But Carter, don't live your life so unhappily because *we* messed up so terribly. You're a great guy.

Go find the right person. One who can appreciate all the things you bring to the table."

He didn't reply, and she walked out of the room, seeing herself out. At almost the instant the latch clicked in the other room, his phone once again began to ring.

Hope sprang from nowhere that it would be Ginger. He wanted to talk to her. He needed to talk to her. But when he pulled the phone from his pocket, he saw that it was his mother. He should have been there for them last night.

He answered the call. "I'm sorry, Mom."

"Carter." He could hear her voice shake. "Are you okay? I've been trying to reach you for days."

"I wasn't in the mood to talk. Lisa wants the house."

"I know. Julie told me."

"You tell Julie she's in trouble with me. She sent Lisa here."

"What? Lisa showed up there?"

"Just walked out the door."

"What happened?"

He forced his jaw to unclench and his shoulders to relax. "We talked."

And he'd needed that talk, he realized. Something had changed in him, and as it had happened when he'd been in Georgia, he felt like he could breathe again. He inhaled air deep into his lungs.

"Are you selling her the house?"

"All I'm doing for the next few weeks is writing." He suddenly couldn't get back to his keyboard fast enough. "I have a book due in three weeks."

And *then* he'd think about Lisa and the house.

"What about Ginger?" his mother asked.

He stared at the phone. "What about her?" Had something happened?

"Julie thought there might have been something going on there. And I'll admit, I could get behind a scenario like that. She's a good girl."

Carter hung his head. "My little sister needs to stay out of my business. Did she bother telling you about the father of her baby?"

Shame instantly filled him. That had been a low blow.

"Actually, she did. We had a long talk about it today. She messed up, and she knows it."

"He hasn't called her again, has he?" Carter would hunt the man down if he had.

"No. He hasn't called. Legal documents arrived Friday. He's out of her life for good."

His heart thudded with relief. Thank goodness for small victories.

"Now about you and Ginger."

"There's nothing with me and Ginger, Mom. She's a great person. And a good friend. But we were just having fun. Julie has it wrong."

"Are you sure? She was over here last night, and . . ."

He held his breath. "And?"

"She was sad, Carter. She seemed hurt. She left the party early, and I couldn't help but wonder if it had something to do with you. I thought maybe she was missing you."

He'd certainly been missing her. "Probably not."

He settled in the spot Lisa had vacated, and pictured her baby in her arms. He really had wanted that life. And he really hadn't had a clue that he'd been going about it all wrong.

"Can I ask you something?" he said.

"Always."

"How did you and Dad do it? All this time? You still love him, right?"

"Of course I still love your father. More than ever."

"But how? Why does it work for you, and not for everyone else?"

269

"Oh, baby. I'm so sorry your marriage didn't work out. But things happen. People grow apart."

"She thinks we weren't right for each other to begin with." Her words had shocked him.

There was a pause before his mother answered. "She could be right."

"Do you think so? We shouldn't have been together in the first place?" He needed answers for it to all make sense.

"You need your mama," she said without preamble. "I'll book a flight."

He chuckled. He did love his mother. "I do not need my mama. I'm fine. And don't you dare come up here. I'm just trying to figure things out. I really wanted it to work between us."

"I know you did. But that doesn't mean that if you found the right person today, you couldn't still make a marriage work. It could be better than you even imagined."

"But how would I trust that it was the right person?"

"You'll just know, Son. It'll feel right."

Except he'd thought it felt right with Lisa.

Hadn't he?

Ginger's voice asking him why he'd fallen in love with Lisa was suddenly in his head. And he still had no answer. Their marriage had simply been the next logical step in their relationship. It was what people did.

He could think about this for months and get nowhere.

"I need to go, Mom. I have a book to finish."

"Can I assume you'll be ignoring your phone again, then?"

He smiled. His mother knew him well. "Absolutely. But this time only because I'm working. Text me if Julie goes into labor, will you?"

"You'll be here?"

"I'll catch the next flight down."

"You're a good boy, Carter."

"Thank you, Mom. I love you. Tell Dad I love him, too. I'm sorry I wasn't there last night."

"That's okay. You've had a rough year. But we'll let you make it up to us," she teased.

"How about a bathroom remodel next time? It'll go with that spa-sized closet I gave you."

She laughed. "No bathroom needed. Just you. I can't wait to see you again."

"I'll come down for the baby, and I'll even stick around for a while."

Except, he hoped Ginger was already moved out before he went back. He didn't think he could sit there and watch her read on the deck without going over.

And he certainly couldn't stand around and watch for her to come home with another man.

CHAPTER TWENTY-FOUR

With shaking hands, Ginger slid the key to her house into the lock on the front door. Her excitement was palpable, and her nerves on edge. Her house was finished.

She was there by herself, but that's as she'd wanted it. Her mother had offered to come with her. The two of them had spent a lot of time together over the last three weeks. Ginger had returned to living with her mom until the house was complete, and they'd worked most evenings finalizing wedding details. Her mother would make a stunning bride in three short days.

But today was Ginger's day. She was entering her completed house for the first time. And she was a changed woman. She was Ginger Atkinson. Ferry-boat owner, fishing-boat captain, and all-around fantastic person. And she was proud of it.

Carter had done that for her. For which she would forever be grateful.

She stepped across the threshold, and emotion swelled inside her. This was her home.

Remaining where she stood, she let her gaze sweep over all she could see. The coffered ceilings, the airy paint colors, the kitchen counters and cabinets. The light fixtures above her head, and wood flooring beneath her feet. She could see the deck from the front door, and past that, her boardwalk and the beach. This was where she would make a home. Forever.

With or without a man.

She wiped at the tears trekking over her cheeks, and forced her feet to move, pressing a hand to her mouth. It was simply stunning. Everywhere she looked. Gene and his men had done exceptional work.

When she reached the kitchen and stepped to the other side of the peninsula, she dropped her car keys to the granite, and lowered herself to the floor. There was no table in the way to block the view out the bay windows, and the day was bright and happy.

So she sat with her legs crossed over each other, and she let memories of her dad consume her.

"I did it, Dad," she whispered. With all her heart, she wished he was there with her. She missed him every day.

She also knew that if he were there, *she* wouldn't be. Not here. She'd be off somewhere being a kindergarten teacher, probably wearing stodgy dresses every day, and married to some boring principal who was losing his hair. And she'd likely rarely get out on a boat.

She wouldn't have this piece of land. Or this house. She certainly wouldn't have this view.

And she wouldn't be the woman she was today. She owed her dad.

But she also owed Carter. Desperately, she wished Carter were there with her, too. He'd had a huge hand in getting the house finished. But mostly, she just wished he was there with her. She missed him. Her heart ached for him.

He hadn't called since he'd left. Three weeks, and not one word, which hadn't surprised her. She had, however, broken down and asked

Julie about him again. He was writing. Which had given Ginger a great deal of relief.

He'd also talked to Lisa, which had *not* necessarily made Ginger feel better.

He'd needed to do it, though. She understood that, so she was thankful he'd taken that step. It was a chapter in his life not yet closed. He needed to move past it. And Ginger hoped talking to his ex-wife had helped him to do that.

But she wished she could find out how it had gone. How he was now. Either Julie didn't know, or she hadn't wanted to divulge, because she'd shared nothing.

A car pulled up outside, and Ginger took one more swipe at her face. No one who knew her well would be surprised that she was standing inside an empty house crying happy tears, but that didn't mean she wanted to be so blatant about the fact.

She rose, and headed for the door. She wasn't officially moved in, but she'd hung the welcome sign the minute she'd arrived, so whoever had just driven up would be her first official guest. She had to go greet them.

Both front car doors opened, and her tears resumed. Her first guests were her two best friends in the world.

Andie and Roni squealed from the driveway, and then they were running. Well, Andie was running. Roni kind of hustled with her belly cupped in her arms.

"You're here!" Ginger squealed back, bouncing up and down on the porch before getting swept up in a group hug. She hadn't expected to see them until the wedding.

"We wanted to come early and surprise you," Andie told her.

"Your mom called and said your house would be ready today. So we packed our bags."

Ginger grinned from ear to ear. "You came early just for me?"

"For no one else," Roni assured her. "We even came alone. The men are bringing the kids later, so it's just the three of us for two whole days. But don't worry. They'll be here early Friday morning to help."

"To help what?"

"We're moving you in." Andie beamed at her. "Decorations and all. You have a housewarming party on Sunday, have you forgotten? We can't have guests in here without the place looking like a million bucks."

"You're going to shop for me?" Ginger laughed.

"We're going to shop *with* you," Roni replied. "And then we're going to sit back and direct the men as they unload the furniture and hang pictures."

"You guys are the best."

"That we are." Andie hugged her again. "But then you're going to repay us with babysitting duty."

Ginger readily agreed and led them inside, and together the three of them oohed and aahed over each feature of the house. Eventually, they made their way to the third floor. She, Andie, and Roni entered the office, and Ginger's tears once again returned. Only, this time they weren't due to happiness.

Roni slipped an arm around her. "Should I hop a plane and go kick his ass?"

Ginger hiccupped on a sob. "You're six months pregnant, so I think, no."

"I could do it. I've got a mean roundhouse kick."

"I'll bet you do." Ginger smiled and leaned into Roni while Andie snuggled in on the other side. They stood in front of the closed deck doors, watching the glistening water on the other side.

"He still hasn't called?" Andie asked.

Ginger shook her head. "I shouldn't have broken the rules. It was supposed to be just sex. Just fun. I clearly can't handle that."

"Only because it was Carter," Roni soothed. "You've always wanted that man."

"Well, I got him. For a few days, anyway."

"Call him," Andie urged. This wasn't the first time she'd suggested it. "Tell him how you feel."

"It's not just about how I feel. He isn't ready for anything more. And I don't know if he ever will be. I won't settle for less." She pulled out of her friends' grasp and opened the doors wide. The sound of the waves filled the room. Then she imagined the keys of Carter's laptop clicking one last time.

She closed her eyes and listened.

Then she sucked in a breath, blew it out, and accepted reality.

"I'm moving on," she told them. "A new chapter in my life. Starting today. We don't talk about Carter again."

Chapter Twenty-Five

Three days later, Ginger stood beside her mother on a bright October afternoon, Spanish moss swaying above them, and all of Pam and Clint's friends and loved ones looking on. The minister stated the vows for the couple to recite, and Ginger watched on with pride and love.

There wasn't a single place in the world she would rather be at that moment.

Her mother was beautiful. And Clint was exactly what she needed.

"I now pronounce you husband and wife."

Clint turned to his bride, and Ginger witnessed the most beautiful sight. The man was completely over the moon for her mom. Love and tenderness burned from the depths of his eyes, and Ginger knew that her mother would forever be taken care of.

Clint cupped Pam's face in his hands, and as he touched his lips to hers, a warm breeze passed through the trees. It slid a comforting touch over Ginger, and she lifted her eyes to the sky. Her father had just blessed this marriage.

The gathered crowd cheered, and Ginger's mother reached for Ginger's hand. They hugged, and danged if tears didn't threaten to ruin Ginger's mascara.

"Don't cry yet," her mother whispered. "We haven't taken the pictures."

"Leave the girl alone, Pam. Makeup can be fixed." Clint winked at Ginger, then he pulled her in for a tight squeeze. "You're beautiful. I love the changes to your dress."

She smiled. She'd convinced her mother that the gown needed a few alterations, and after having all ruffles removed, she'd chopped off the bottom two feet of fluff and separated the dress into two pieces. Her mother might like the girly stuff, but at the sight of Ginger in the more pared-down, formfitting dress, she'd admitted that this was much better. *This* fit Ginger.

Once finished with the official photographs, Ginger did a quick outfit change and headed into the rec room where soft lights glowed and music was pumping. Her mom and Clint had decided against a formal dinner, instead opting for a more casual atmosphere, so some people were eating finger foods, some dancing, and some simply checking others out.

Like Chester Brownbomb and Mrs. Rylander. Apparently calling the cops on the man once hadn't been enough, as he hadn't taken his eyes off the woman all night.

Of course, Mrs. R. seemingly had no clue. She'd decked herself out in a flower-print dress that was a little too large and had probably been in style fifty years ago, had a hot-pink bow stuck in her hair, and had made herself Kayla's shadow for the evening. Chester was then shadowing Mrs. R., and Vanilla Bean was giving them both the evil eye.

There was nothing like hanging out at the senior center.

Two hours, three beers, and pretty much no food later, Ginger was ready to go home. She'd danced with Clint, Clint's brothers, Clint's nephews, several local men she already knew, Chester Brownbomb, and at least six other men she'd met tonight.

She'd tried, really she had. Fun was happening all around her, and to anyone watching, she probably looked to be swept up by it, as well. But she couldn't shake Carter from her mind. She wasn't even supposed to be thinking about him, yet she sure would love it if he were there with her right now. She wanted to call him. She needed to know that he was okay.

"Dance with me?"

She turned slowly, Carter on the brain and a frown on her face, to find Patrick, the real-estate agent slash flute maker, smiling at her side. She'd seen him at the wedding earlier, but hadn't caught sight of him on the dance floor in a while.

"Hi, Patrick," she greeted warmly, doing her best to shove Carter from her mind. However, she did nothing to hide the exhaustion in her voice. "How are you?"

"I'm doing good." He eyed her carefully. "Are you okay?"

"Just taking a breather."

"So no dance for me then?" he teased. He had the cutest eyes. Blue, but there was a maturity in them that said he wasn't all play. And she remembered thinking at dinner that first night that he looked a little like Carter.

He still did.

"I saved one for you," she told him. She put her hand in his.

And she did not let herself cry at the fact that she'd rather be dancing with a different man.

A new song began from the DJ, a slow one, and Patrick gave a gallant little bow before sweeping her into his arms. His moves made her laugh.

"Anyone tell you that you're the hottest thing in the room tonight?" he asked as he twirled her around the parquet dance floor.

Ginger took a moment before answering, peeking around at the other women in obvious fashion, taking in each of their gray or white heads. Then she reset her gaze on Patrick's. "Given that ninety percent of tonight's population is over the age of sixty, I'm not exactly sure that's a compliment."

He chuckled. "Total compliment. Anyone who shows up at her mother's reception in jeans . . ." He flicked a glance over her and nodded decisively. *"Hot."*

"The jeans *have* attracted attention tonight," she confessed. She'd swapped them for the skirt. "More than I expected."

"Well, I have to admit, I was surprised. After the look your mother gave you on our first date when you showed up in jeans, I wouldn't have expected to see it again."

Ginger groaned. "You saw that, did you?"

"I saw that. The question I had was, did she think you weren't dressed up enough for *me,* or for the restaurant?"

"Probably both, but her focus was on you that night."

He gripped her hand tighter. "Then let me set the record straight. She was wrong. "

Ginger dipped her head with a smile. "I appreciate that. And let me go on record to apologize for our second date. I've learned a few things since then. I was trying too hard." She released his hand and brushed her fingers in the air in front of her. *"This* is me. Not the woman who got into your car that night."

"This is a much better you."

"Thank you."

He retook her hand.

"I might even occasionally smell like fish," she added with a mutter, which only made him laugh.

They danced through the rest of the song, laughing and talking all the while, and when the song ended, he looked down at her before letting her go. His voice turned serious. "Would this 'you' be what a man would get if he were to ask you out again?"

Her shoulders drooped. A month ago, and those words would have made her night.

But she wasn't ready yet.

"I'm kind of," she began, having to glance down before finishing. Her breath came out ragged as she pushed out, "*Not* over someone. Yet."

She bit her lip. She was *supposed* to be over him by now.

"I get it," Patrick said. He squeezed her hand in understanding. "But maybe I could try again next month?"

Gratitude ballooned in her, and she gave him a sad smile. She wanted to hug him for both the understanding and the willingness to wait. "No promises, but yes. Please try again next month."

"You can count on it." He brushed his lips across her cheek, then he released her and stepped back. "Be good to yourself, Ginger."

"That I can promise. It's my number-one priority these days."

Patrick left her where she stood, and suddenly Roni and Andie were at her sides.

"You okay?" Roni asked.

Ginger shook her head.

And the next thing she knew, her friends had helped her into her car, and driven her home. Which she greatly appreciated. She was done for the night.

She just wanted to be alone. With a good book, if she couldn't have the real thing.

CHAPTER TWENTY-SIX

Carter stood outside the house that wasn't his, eyeing the key in his palm and seriously contemplating breaking and entering. He really shouldn't just open the door and go in. It was the middle of the night. It was illegal.

And she might not be alone.

Especially considering the texts he'd gotten from his sister earlier in the evening.

> She's the life of the party.
> She's dancing with a hot man.
> You're going to lose her, you idiot.

What Julie hadn't known—what she still didn't know—was that he'd already been in the car, heading Ginger's way, when her texts had come in. And he prayed now that he wasn't too late.

Julie had also texted him several times over the last few weeks just to "update him on their neighbor." He'd told her to stop it. He and

Ginger were nothing. Yet every time he'd pulled himself out of the book long enough to check his phone, he'd missed Ginger even more.

Early yesterday morning he'd finished the book. And not long afterward, he'd gotten into his car and headed south. He'd driven over sixteen hours, had awakened a coastal fisherman and paid him a hefty sum for a lift to the island, and now that he was here, he didn't want to wait one minute longer. He wanted to see Ginger. *Before* the sun came up.

But could he just open her door and go in?

He turned back to face the driveway. Only his car and Ginger's sat there. So if she'd brought home a guy from the wedding, she'd driven him there herself.

Or maybe she'd gone to his place.

Panic began, his pulse beating rapidly. He couldn't be too late. Not after all this time. Ginger was the one.

It had taken him way too long to see it, but she was it for him. He had to win her over.

He put the key in the lock and turned. The house was dark and silent, and he hoped to hell she wasn't equipped with her can of Mace, but he'd take it if he had to. He just had to get to her.

Slowly moving through the darkness, his hands full with the items he'd brought for her, he headed for the stairs. Hopefully she'd still be asleep. And hopefully he wouldn't give her a heart attack by showing up like this.

But when he got to her room, her bed was empty. His heart sank.

Then he saw her through the French doors.

It was a warm night, and she'd apparently taken advantage of it. The underrailing lights were on, and she was reclined in a wooden chair, her bare legs stretched out before her. But she wasn't sleeping. She was reading.

He crossed the room, dropping his gifts off on the bed, then moved on to the doors. The instant he pushed open the door, she was out of her seat. She whirled toward him, one arm pulled back as if ready to release, and Carter raised his hands in front of his face.

"It's just me," he exclaimed.

"What the crap?" she screamed. "Carter! You scared me to death."

He slowly lowered his hands, peeking out above his fingertips, and letting his gaze eat her up. "I'm sorry," he pleaded. "Please don't spray me with Mace."

She had on a tight green top that stopped at her waist, and tiny white cotton panties riding high on her thighs. And that was all. Bare legs shone in the moonlight, and if he wasn't already in love with her before, he would have fallen right then.

"It's not Mace, you moron." She lowered her hand, her chest heaving with her breaths. "It's a freaking horror story. One of *yours*! And I did not need to be scared to death while reading it! Good grief." She was still yelling, and he noticed that her hands were shaking.

"I'm sorry." He tried the lame apology again. Maybe this hadn't been the right approach.

"Ring a doorbell or something," she growled out. Then her eyes narrowed to thin slits. "How did you get into my house?"

"I . . . uh . . ." His sister was right. He was an idiot. "I still have my key. I made a copy before so I could come in when I wanted to write."

The look on her face was not welcoming. "I should call the cops and have you arrested."

"I really hope that you don't."

"Give me the blanket off my bed." She jerked her arm out stiff, holding her hand outstretched in front of her. "And I'll *think* about not calling them."

He hated to cover her up, but he'd already crossed too many lines unannounced. So he returned to her bedroom and grabbed the gray throw tossed across the end of the giant king-sized mattress, and he couldn't help but picture her in there. With him.

He swallowed and turned back. He couldn't think about sex right now.

"What are you doing here?" she asked as she wrapped the blanket around her shoulders and crossed it at her waist. Her legs disappeared from view. "Is Julie in labor? Is something wrong?"

He shook his head. "Julie's fine. How was the wedding?" he asked.

"It was great. My mother is happy. The wedding was beautiful."

"And you had a good time at the reception?" He hated the jealousy burning inside him, but he couldn't help it. He had to know. "I heard you danced with several men."

She lifted a hand, palm up, as if to ask, *What the fuck?* "Are you keeping tabs on me?"

"No," he answered quickly. "Julie. She . . . felt I needed to know."

Ginger crossed her arms under her breasts and scowled at him. "Well, I don't know why she'd think that. And yes. I did dance with several men. I had a terrific time."

"And you were in jeans, I understand."

She let out a dry laugh. "Yeah, I was in jeans. I was the freaking life of the party."

"I wish I'd seen it."

She didn't reply. He wasn't sure if he preferred her sarcasm or silence.

"So did you line up some dates?" he asked. He really was pathetic.

"Are you kidding me?" Some of the anger seemed to leave her, and her posture softened. Slightly. "No, Carter. I didn't line up dates. What are you doing here?"

The time had come. Either his marathon drive paid off, or . . .

"I had to see you, and I couldn't wait another minute to do it." He opened his heart, and prayed that she could see what she meant to him. "You've always been a constant in my life, since practically the day I was born. I hadn't realized how much that meant to me until I came back last month. You were still here. We still had our mornings.

285

And that . . ." He paused, wishing he were doing a better job explaining himself. "It's the most special thing I've ever known."

"Sunrises with me are the most special thing you've ever known?"

"*You* are the most special thing I've ever known," he said. "Your friendship. Us. Knowing you and I could just . . . be. You were my friend for all those years, but you were also more. I was just too stupid to notice."

She blinked, and he saw that her jaw had grown tight. Her eyes gave nothing away.

"Please say something."

"It's the middle of the night, and you've snuck into my house to tell me that you value our friendship. What am I supposed to say?"

"How about if I also tell you that I love you?" Cold terror dried his mouth. "And that I sold Lisa the house. I called my lawyer before I left. Told him to make it happen. And I found this." He pulled a paper out of his back pocket and handed it over to her.

He'd found it about two hours before he'd gotten into his car to come here. He'd pulled it from an unpacked box, and he'd just known. Everything had become clear.

Ginger unfolded the paper, and he leaned toward her, wanting to look at it with her. She smoothed a finger over the faded blue lines of their blueprint.

"I didn't know I had it," he said softly. "It's our house. This house."

"My house," she corrected.

Her words scared him. "Your house." He took her hand in his, and when she made eye contact, he ignored the fear inside him and plowed ahead. "I love you. I know you may not feel the same way, but I had to come tell you. I had to see if there was a chance."

"Are you really over Lisa? You were so hurt. You went home so fast."

"Sweetheart, being over Lisa was never the question. The hurt came from what I'd thought I'd lost—my plans. The life I envisioned.

It was never about losing *her*." He dropped Ginger's hand to hold his arms out to his side. "I wanted this. I wanted what you want. And in the blink of an eye, she took that from me."

"And now you think you love me?" Her look grew more skeptical. "Maybe you just see me as another way to get what you once wanted."

"No." His desperation grew. "I can see where it might look like that, but you're wrong. It's not about the house. It's about you. You have your daddy's soul and your mama's beauty. You make *me* a better person. I love who we are together. That's why I left so fast when I got Lisa's e-mail. You and I were getting too close, and I think subconsciously, I knew how badly you could hurt me. I wasn't ready to risk that."

"But you think you are now?"

"I know I am now."

She lowered her gaze, and he could see tears on her eyelashes. The day was just beginning to lighten, making her more visible to him, and she looked sadder in that moment than he'd ever seen her.

"Please tell me there's a chance," he whispered brokenly. "I know we were just having a good time before. But I thought you might have wanted more. That last morning, I felt something. I thought you did, too. I'm sorry I disappeared. That I haven't called. But I had to deal with my own crap. To find myself again, like I've watched you find yourself. But I do love you, Ginger. More than I ever knew was possible."

She was staring at him again. Wearing a look that said he'd played his last card. And lost.

"Okay." He stepped away from her. "I'll go. For now. Give you time to think about all this. I brought you something, though. I need to get it."

He returned to her bedroom for only a few seconds, and when he came back, he passed over the first item. A three-ring binder. "I finished the book," he told her.

Her eyes rounded.

"You get the first copy."

She took the book, and after glancing at it, carefully set the binder on her chair. Her interest lay more on the other item in his hand. It was a bundle of balloons of all colors, tied together by their strings. He'd driven with them for the last half of the trip, and two of them were drooping already.

She licked her lips. "What's with the balloons?" She sounded as scared as he felt.

"I want to be your dream, Gin." He held them out to her. "I want to be your hope that happiness can always be found in the world. This is my promise that I'll be that for you. Always. If you'll allow me to."

She took them, and when she said nothing, he nodded and turned to go. He had no words left.

"Don't go." Her voice reached him before he stepped through the open door.

He closed his eyes. Nerves threatened to cut off his air.

And he slowly turned back.

Chapter Twenty-Seven

I love you, too."

A rush of air came from Carter at Ginger's words, and she moved to stand in front of him. Silently, she watched him, enjoying the shocked look on his face. She might love him, but this wasn't over yet. She still had questions. And she needed promises more concrete than balloons.

Though she *would* give him credit for the balloons. He understood her.

"You have to be sure." She said the words softly. "These are big gestures." She looked at the book lying on the chair. "I get that. And I appreciate them. But this is a big deal. I don't want to get my hopes up for you, Carter. Not if you're not positive that I'm the one for you. I'm in a good place now. I don't need a man. And I certainly don't need to be crushed by one."

"I would never hurt you." He touched his fingers to her arm. "Not in that way. Though Lord knows I can be stupid. I might accidentally cause pain, but when I do, baby, just tell me. I'll fix it. And yes, I'm sure. I'm positive. You're perfect for me. And if you'll have me, I plan to marry you."

Could it really be this simple?

"Just like that?" she asked. Fear and hope warred together and had her hands shaking once again. "We're childhood friends, I grow up and you see me naked, we have a little *casual* sex, you go back home the instant your ex-wife waves, and suddenly . . . you want to marry me?"

He smiled, and the heat from it torched her a little.

But she had to ignore that heat until this was sorted out.

"I absolutely want to marry you," he confirmed. "But good call on the nakedness. I think it was the angel potholders that did it for me. I plan to buy you a replica pair as a wedding gift."

She rolled her eyes at him, and at this point she had to fight off her smile. She was caving; she could feel it. But that might be okay.

"I haven't said I'll marry you," she pointed out.

"I am aware of that fact. You haven't said anything, really. Other than that you love me."

His eyes burned steady on hers, and she saw the fear still in them. He'd laid his heart on the line for her. And that's what she'd needed. She still wasn't positive, but if he'd just shown up and said that he wanted to pick up where they'd left off, maybe take it a layer or two deeper, that wouldn't have been enough. She'd changed too much over the last few weeks. She wanted all or nothing.

And the truth was, she wanted it all. With Carter.

"You scare me," she told him. "You could hurt me a lot."

"I understand that. I'm scared, too. But I also think I could make you happy a lot. And I swear I'll do my best to make that happen."

Ginger didn't take her eyes off him. She wanted to believe in this. All of it. But it was so sudden. But then, hadn't she waited thirty years for this? She'd known him her whole life. Loved him as a friend forever.

Why couldn't it so easily be more now?

"Sit with me until sunrise?" she asked. She needed to calm down and think. And the two of them at sunrise was always the best time for her to think.

"That's why I drove all night," he answered solemnly.

And that almost won her over. Together they turned, the balloons still in her hand, and they settled into one chair, her on his lap.

She loved him. And she'd told him. And that had felt unbelievable.

There was no way she would let him get away from her now. But he'd made her wait three weeks for this. She would make him wait at least three minutes.

The sun was closer than she'd realized. She'd sat up all night, rereading his latest book. She looked at the binder he'd brought her, and she felt his love encircle her. He'd given her his book.

She reached for it, and opened it across her lap.

To Ginger Root
My friend. My soul mate. My love.
Let me be your balloons forever.

"That is the corniest dedication ever." Her voice wobbled, and tears once again spilled from her eyes.

"You wound me, babe."

She looked up at him. "I mean, really. What are people going to think? Let you be my balloons forever? Ginger Root? They'll think I'm insane."

"Well, you *don't* wear pants."

"*Carter.*" She elbowed him in the chest. Then he smiled at her and pressed a slow, hot kiss to her mouth. He left her breathless.

"They'll think I'm the luckiest man alive," he told her after they parted.

"And I get to be the first one to read it," she whispered. She sighed in great satisfaction, but then made a face at him. "You do know that it'll only take me a couple of days to finish it."

"*Readers.*" Carter rolled his eyes as she liked to do. "They can be so demanding."

"Good thing I got your office finished. So you can get busy on the next one."

The smile froze on his face. Then he looked up.

"I had Gene add in a special writing corner for you. I noticed that if the sun is up, you sometimes turn your back to the ocean when you write, yet you still seem to want to hear the waves. Now you have a spot in the room where you can do that."

"Baby." He pressed a kiss to her hair. "I love you so much."

"I love you, too. But can we really do this, Carter? Can we love each other? After all this time?"

"We already do. That's a given. It's the 'more' I'm after now. I want forever. With *you.*"

She tucked herself in tight against his chest, her balloons waving in the morning breeze, and the sun silently slipping from behind the ocean. It rose up, shining bright on their faces, and she tilted her eyes to meet his. "And I want forever with you."

EPILOGUE

A lmost five months later, after Julie had delivered a healthy baby girl, and Roni had delivered a bouncing baby boy, Ginger stood at the end of the short aisle, her arm hooked through Clint's, and couldn't take her eyes off her tuxedoed fiancé standing under the arch of live oaks.

Roni's stepdaughter, Gracie, stepped to the side after dropping rose petals along the path and beamed a proud smile back at Ginger, and Clint asked, "You ready for this?"

Ginger took in the small assembled crowd and the ocean beyond. The morning was still gray, but that would soon change. "I've never been more ready for anything in my life."

She saw Kayla nod discreetly—Mrs. Rylander, who stood at her side, nodded, as well—and then the wedding march began to play. Roni and Andie waited for her at the end of the aisle, with Carter and Julie on the other side. Ginger and Carter hadn't wanted a large ceremony; there had been only one requirement. It would take place at sunrise.

Ginger started moving, all eyes on her, and she felt her dad's whisper touch her cheeks. She stopped walking, tears suddenly spilling over her lashes, and she shook her head at Carter's panicked expression. She touched her father's wedding ring, which she wore on her right thumb as her "something old," and Carter nodded in understanding. She'd wanted to marry here on the senior-center patio, where she'd last felt her dad's presence, in hopes that he would be there with her today.

Before she could start moving again, Kayla appeared, a handkerchief in hand, and blotted at Ginger's cheeks. Andie and Roni smiled from the front, and baby Teddy gurgled from his grandmother's lap.

As Kayla cleaned her up, Ginger caught her mother's eye. Pride shone bright.

Ginger blew her mom a kiss, nodded at Clint, then made her way to her future husband.

After the vows were spoken, and as the preacher pronounced them husband and wife, the sun slid into the bright morning sky, bringing with it a bounty of color. As Ginger looked at Carter, she'd never seen more love shining her way. She'd just married the man of her dreams.

And she was his dream, as well.

"I love you," he said. He kissed her then, and as he pulled away, all three babies in attendance began to cry. Carter chuckled under his breath. "I vote we add to that sound as soon as possible. They're going to need friends to play with."

"A baby?" They'd talked about having kids, but hadn't decided on when.

"If we're having four, we'd better get started."

Her mouth curved with a huge smile, and she nodded her agreement. That was the dream, after all. Big house, four kids . . . amazing husband. Little had she known, the life she'd always wanted had been the life she'd soon find.

ABOUT THE AUTHOR

Photo © 2012 Amelia Moore

As a child, award-winning author Kim Law cultivated a love for choc-olate, anything purple, and creative writing. She penned her debut work, "The Gigantic Talking Raisin," in the sixth grade and got hooked on the delights of creating stories. Before settling into the writing life, however, she earned a college degree in mathematics and worked for years as a computer programmer. Now she's living out her lifelong dream of writing romance novels. She's won the Romance Writers of America's Golden Heart Award, been a finalist for the pres-tigious RWA RITA Award, and served in varied positions for her local RWA chapter. A native of Kentucky, Kim lives with her husband and an assortment of animals in Middle Tennessee.